The Happiest Days

Cressida Connolly

FOURTH ESTATE • *London*

This paperback edition first published in 2000
First published in Great Britain in 1999 by
Fourth Estate Limited
6 Salem Road
London W2 4BU
www.4thestate.co.uk

Copyright © Cressida Connolly 1999

'Change Partners' (on page 171): Words and music by Irving Berlin
© 1938 Irving Berlin Music Corp., USA
Warner/Chappell Music Ltd., London W6 8BS
Reproduced by permission of I.M.P. Ltd.

10 9 8 7 6 5 4 3 2 1

The right of Cressida Connolly to be identified as the author of this
work has been asserted by her in accordance with the Copyright,
Designs and Patents Act 1988.

A catalogue record for this book is available from the
British Library.

ISBN 1-85702-715-9

Typeset by Rowland Phototypesetting Limited,
Bury St Edmunds, Suffolk
Printed in Great Britain by
Cox & Wyman Limited, Reading

Contents

How I Lost
My Vocation

I suppose you could say I wasn't a very sociable sort of child. I didn't have many friends, and I lived very much inside my own head, in my imagination. I wanted to be a priest when I grew up, because a life of contemplation appealed to me. I wasn't the sort of child who ran with a gang, shooting pebble catapults at starlings or practising wheelies in the road outside our house. In winter I liked to stay indoors reading or just lying on my bed, thinking about things. I never wanted to go and kick a ball around the freezing recreation ground with the other boys. I preferred my own company: solitary things. Looking back, you could say I was a bit weird. A bit of a creep, even.

Catholic Granny was mum's mum; but my mother wasn't a proper Catholic. She was something called Lapsed, only spoken of in a whisper; it was nearly as bad as being a Protestant. My father was a lapsed Protestant, but that was too awful to speak of at all. It broke Catholic Granny's heart, her beloved daughter turning her back on the True Faith. She prayed for her every morning and she recruited me, on the sly, to do the same. At least my aunt Rose practised, still. I was a good boy, she said. A special boy. The Lord had Special plans for me, said Catholic Granny, and I knew it was true. I had a picture of Jesus in my bedroom and when

I looked at Him I knew he was looking back at me. He was calling me to His ministry.

It was my father who called his mother-in-law Catholic Granny. It was sort of a joke. His own mother was called Granny Hughes, and she was different altogether. She had long thick eyelashes like spiders' legs and there was always a funny brownish line around her mouth which my mother told me was drawn on with a special pencil, just for lips; and I was not to make remarks about it. Granny Hughes was podgy and she smoked cigarettes all the time. She was the only person I'd ever met who talked on the telephone for fun – not to make arrangements, like everyone else I knew. She'd laugh and chat for ages, and when she'd finished there would be an ashtray full of stubs stained with bright lipstick, like the traces of tomato ketchup on an empty plate.

Granny Hughes always wore a gold bracelet with a locket of brown hair inside. You could see the hair, because the locket had glass sides. The hair had belonged to her other son, dad's brother, who had died when he was twenty-one. My mother said this was a terrible tragedy for Granny Hughes, and that we should all be sorry for her; but she didn't seem miserable at all. I didn't like her very much and she certainly never took any notice of me. When I prayed for the Conversion of Granny Hughes I felt extremely pious, but sometimes – especially when she had recently been to visit – I left her out of my prayers altogether.

Every summer until I was eleven my parents rented the same house in Devon for our holidays. I loved it there, by the sea. As you came over the headland to the beach you could tell whether the tide would be in or out, even before you could see the water. You could tell that it was low tide from the warm smell of seaweed and crab shell and the faint tang of tar. At high tide there was only the smell of the water itself; like fresh air, only heavier inside your nose. I liked it best when the tide was out. The worm casts which wiggled underfoot in the damp sand were like live spaghetti between my toes. And I spent ages looking in the rock pools. There were tiny shrimps, not pink or brown like when you ate them, but see-through; and slippery weed like wet fur, the startling green of apple peel.

I wasn't supposed to go down to the beach on my own, but my mother and father never got up until late into the morning; sometimes not until lunchtime. They didn't notice whether I was in the house or not. At home they were usually in a bad mood in the mornings, but here they were different. Instead of complaining of headaches, my mother would be giggly and her face would have a pinkness about it. When my father teased her, she laughed instead of snapping at him like she did at home. They stayed up late at night: that's why they slept late. After supper, when I had gone up to my room, I'd hear them put on the gramophone. They played Ray Charles records and drank cocktails together. There was an old book in the rented house, *The Savoy Book of Cocktails*. It had a green and gold cover with a geometric picture of a man drinking out of a shallow glass – it was designed in cross-section and the cocktail forked like lightning as it went down inside the stylised man.

My parents loved this book. At home they drank gin and whisky, but when we were on holiday they made it their business to try as many of the recipes as they could. They bought maraschino cherries and tequila and Grand Marnier and every night they mixed drinks. I'd be able to tell which ones they'd been trying out by the debris the following morning. My mother didn't believe in washing up at night. She said it was bourgeois. I loved the little red and pink paper parasols which my father bought to go in the drinks. In the mornings before they were awake I'd go into the kitchen and pocket any

3

parasols they hadn't used the night before, and dip my finger in the glasses to see what the drinks had tasted like.

So they listened to Ray Charles and sat next to each other on the tatty sofa with the French windows open and the light from the room casting shadows on the sandy grass outside. Sometimes they danced. Sometimes they shouted, and occasionally when they fought one of them would break a piece of crockery or glass. It was just something they did from time to time. I knew to wear my gym shoes when I came downstairs in the morning. One summer, when I was very small, I'd trodden on some broken glass. I'd tried not to disturb my parents – they didn't like to be woken up – but it bled and bled until I was frightened and went to get my mother. She had to get dressed and take me to the cottage hospital. I had to have seven stitches. I've still got the scar.

The summer I have in my mind – the summer when I was ten – Aunt Rose came to stay. There was something wrong with Catholic Granny. My mother had to keep going back up to Bristol, where we lived, to take Granny to the hospital for her treatment, and Aunt Rose would look after us while Mum wasn't there. That was the idea. Mum and Rose would take it in turns to be with their mother; would take it in turns to cook for me and Dad, and have a break and some sea air. And when Granny stayed overnight in the hospital, they could both be at the seaside together for a day.

Aunt Rose was different from my mother. She was kind like her, but she was kind in a practical way, by doing things – she never hugged you like mum did. She got up early in the mornings and made cooked breakfasts: bacon and tom-atoes and eggs fried on both sides. Actually I was so used to finding my own food in the mornings – bread or a banana, whatever was there – that her hot breakfasts seemed a bit sickly. I quite liked the eggs, though.

4

I usually went out before my parents were up. The path sloped down through a field of grass and then rose through trees before winding steeply down to the sea. A fork to the left led to the coastguards' cottages and the church. There were always crickets buzzing in the long grass at the edge of the field, and the whizzing sound of skylarks overhead, like the swish of bicycle wheels. I knew every step of the way. Between the meadow and the woods the track was enclosed by bracken and stumpy hawthorns. The bracken was taller than my head. Catholic Granny had taught me that snakes lived in places where bracken grew, and that the way to protect yourself from them was to whistle as you walked along. A snake could hear a human whistle at a great distance and would slither away. If Adam and Eve had whistled in the Garden things might have been very different, she said darkly. She had a great terror of vipers and always whistled whenever she was out of doors, except in the street. I kept completely silent as I walked through the bracken: I longed to see a snake, but I never did.

On my walks I generally went down to the beach and looked for shells, or bits of driftwood. But sometimes I took the other track and visited the church. It was a Protestant church: it didn't have any statues of Our Lady, nor Stations of The Cross. There was no confessional; no candles for sale. But Granny said that all the Protestant churches were ours really, especially the old churches. A wicked king had stolen them, but they were Catholic by right. Any member of the True Faith could avail himself of them, if he so chose.

It was cool and dark inside the church and there was a pleasant musty dampness which made it feel especially holy. It was always empty. I'd sit in the front pew and sniff my knees: the salt air and sunlight made the skin smell different than it did at home, almost like caramel. My legs were brown from the sun, but they would be marked by little white scratches from the prickly bracken. I'd lick my fingers and rub the spit across the scratches till they disappeared, like lines of chalk. Then I'd play priest. I would go right up to the altar and say bits of the Mass, before entering the low pulpit to embark on my sermon. I was very strict. My sermons always began with stern admonishment: my imaginary congregation were habitual sinners, who constantly erred and strayed like lost sheep. I included bits of Bible stories and prayers: the rich man and the eye of the needle; pray for us sinners now and at the hour of our death.

God was angry, but he was merciful. And so was I, His earthly representative. If my congregation would repent and face the Lord, they would be redeemed. If they humbly begged Our Lady for her intercession, she would grant their prayers. But only if they knelt before God with a truly penitent heart! Sometimes I got quite carried away with the force of my message, and shouted at the empty pews. Anyone who knew me would have been amazed, because I was generally such a quiet and biddable boy. I was surprised myself. After my sermons I felt all trembly, as if I'd been too long in the sun without a hat. When I wasn't in the church it made me blush to remember this forceful side of my nature – it was almost like being someone else.

With Aunt Rose about it wasn't so easy to go off on my own. My mother was very easygoing. She slept a lot and lolled in the sun during the afternoons, listening to the light programme on the wireless, or reading – she didn't really care what I did, so long as I was safe and happy. Sometimes she played games with me, but only at her own instigation. She was an inspired playmate, when she was in the mood: she'd dig fantastic moated sandcastles and make galleons out of driftwood; or build impossibly tall houses of playing cards. Aunt Rose didn't exactly play, but she was organised and attentive – the opposite of my mother, really. She liked having an outline for the day. Over breakfast she'd always ask me the same question, as if it were me who were in charge of things: So, what's the plan? And I'd always answer that I didn't know, which was the cue for her to suggest a series of activities: a walk to the beach, a swim, a trip into the village for provisions. On Sundays, she'd drive to the local harbour town to attend Mass, and I would go with her. We always had an ice-cream cornet afterwards. My father said that Aunt Rose was a creature of habit, because she lived on her own. When I grew up and became a priest, I knew I'd be a creature of habit too.

My mother was soft and pretty, but Aunt Rose wasn't. Catholic Granny said that Rose was elegant. She was tall, with long haunches and wide shoulders. Her neck was long, and the way she wore her brown hair – in a loose bun, with wisps escaping – made it seem even longer. She wasn't a cuddly sort of woman: she was more like Granny, her mother – lean, efficient. You couldn't sit on Catholic Granny's knee. Not that she ever told me not to, but I just knew it wouldn't have been right. You couldn't sit on plump Granny Hughes's lap either; but that was because she didn't like children, whereas Catholic Granny did. Catholic Granny and Aunt Rose were calm and straightforward, and they were reliable as well. They always did what they said they'd do; they never forgot a promise. They didn't seem to have the same wide register of emotion as my parents: they were always the same, day or night. I knew that I was made of the same material as them, although I admired the dazzle of my mother and father.

While my mother was looking after Granny, Rose took me for picnics on the cliffs. My father stayed at the house, on his own. We'd walk through the bracken to the woods, then up the path to the church and along the cliff path until we found a spot we liked. We didn't talk much when we were together, but I liked being with Aunt Rose and I think she enjoyed our expeditions as well. We were company for each other, but we didn't stop each other from thinking our own thoughts. Even when we sat down in the bushy grass to eat our lunch we wouldn't say much. We just sat side by side, facing the same way so that we could both see the sea. Aunt Rose liked looking at birds, and from the cliffs you could see gulls and cormorants and oyster catchers. I liked thinking.

I thought quite a lot about Judas Iscariot. I thought that, in a way, Jesus had actually needed someone to betray him; otherwise he couldn't have been crucified and died for us. If He hadn't been betrayed, He might just have died of oldness: the whole story would have been different. If Our Lord had got old and a bit gone in the head, like Grandpa Hughes had before he died, then He wouldn't have been able to shed his blood for our sins. So Judas was essential, really.

To take your own life was the very gravest of mortal sins. It seemed as though that was the worst thing Judas had done: not selling Jesus, but hanging himself from a tree out of shame. Yet Jesus had forgiven him. But no one else forgave him any more and he was condemned. I felt sorry for him. After all, he'd made it possible for Our Lord to do what he had to do, and die on the cross so that man would be forgiven by God for ever after. When I was a high-up priest – or if I became a Monsignor – I would talk to the Pope about Judas. I would tell His Holiness that, since Jesus had forgiven Judas, we ought to do the same.

Of course I didn't only think about religion. I thought about the Airfix models I collected too, and about scones and cream and red jam and how glow-worms glowed. I thought about my mother and father and I wondered what was wrong with Catholic Granny. Whenever my mother came back after two or three days with Granny she would be especially bright and high-spirited. She'd laugh a lot and do things she never normally did, like clean out the kitchen cupboards. There was something a bit wild about her. When I asked her about Granny she'd start talking about other things. Even Aunt Rose – generally to be relied upon for her directness – was fuzzy about her mother's health. It was as if they didn't know what the matter was. I overheard them mention radio therapy: did that mean that Granny had to listen to the wireless to get better? I didn't want Catholic Granny to be too ill, because I usually spent every weekend with her when my parents were busy, during term-time. I even had a separate toothbrush at her house. We did jigsaw puzzles together and ate Garibaldi biscuits, which Granny called squashed flies.

When my mother was with Granny, Aunt Rose and my father didn't play the gramophone or drink cocktails together. Instead my father drank whisky on its own and read the newspaper for the second time and Aunt Rose cooked and then, after dinner, she did the washing-up. They didn't stay up late – they never seemed to have much to say to each other. I would go up to my room, as usual, and lie on my bed listening to the sounds in the house below me. It would still be light outside and I could hear the swallows swooping through the pale sky, and the floorboards creaking as they cooled.

One night was different. The evening had passed quietly, as it generally did when my mother wasn't there, and I'd gone to bed early. She was coming back the next day and I was looking forward to seeing her: if I went to sleep it would make the waiting time pass quicker. But something – a noise outside – woke me up. I looked at the little red clock beside my bed and saw that it was after four in the morning. The sun wasn't up yet, but the darkness was thinning. I thought I could hear voices in the garden, so I got up and went to my window and looked out.

On the lawn below, my father was playing croquet with Aunt Rose. The grass was bleached from the sun; from above it looked nearly white. In the half-dawn it was almost as if it was the ground and not the sky that was the source of brightness. My father's shirt was undone and he was holding a glass in one hand and leaning on his mallet, watching Aunt Rose. She was standing a few feet away from him with her legs apart, tentatively swinging her mallet back and forth between her calves; getting ready to aim the yellow ball through the hoop. I could hear their low voices, but I couldn't make out the words they said.

And then, all of a sudden, my father was standing behind her and his arms were around her shoulders and his head was buried in the hair at the back of her neck. I had been watching Aunt Rose take aim and didn't notice him step across to her and fold her in his arms. Because that is what he did. I'd heard someone in a war film say that, once: 'Oh, Jack, fold me in your arms.' I'd thought they'd got their words in a muddle, but when I looked down at my father and Rose I saw what it meant. My father never hugged people. It must have been a mistake: sometimes adult people said and did things they didn't mean. But he didn't stop embracing her. They just stood there for such a long time, so close it was as if they were two colours smudging into each other. They swayed a little, almost as if they could hear music.

I got back into bed but I didn't go back to sleep. I lay and watched the light from the window turn from grey to gold until it gradually settled into the whiteness of day. Then I got up and pulled on my shorts and T-shirt and crept out of the house to the beach.

Later that morning my mother came back and it was Aunt Rose's turn to go and stay with Granny for a couple of days. My father seemed just the same as normal – everything did. We were nearing the end of our time in Devon and my father came to the beach and we all three played catch on the shingle, until someone's Labrador dog got our ball and bounced into the waves with it and wouldn't bring it back. We went out in the car and had lobster sandwiches in a tea shop. They were made with sliced white bread and Heinz salad cream and my parents kept saying it was much the best way to eat lobster, and laughing.

When Aunt Rose joined us for the last weekend of the holiday, I watched her keenly. I don't know quite what I was looking out for. In a way, it was more to try and see what it was about her that had made my father hold her like that, than to see if she'd changed towards him. Anyway she hadn't. She was just as she always was. I didn't really mind that he'd hugged her while they played a game of croquet at four o'clock in the morning. I was used to the peculiarity of adults. It was just odd, curious. Aunt Rose was so ordinary, so familiar, that I couldn't see what it was about her that had made him feel so passionate.

We were due to leave on Sunday, so on Saturday afternoon I strolled off to have a last walk on my own. Mum and dad were having a lie-down – what they called a siesta – and Rose had wandered off somewhere. I walked with bare feet, knowing the danger I was in, relishing it. If I trod on an adder with no shoes on, I could get a serious bite. The track to the field, exposed to the sun, was painfully hot against the soles of my feet; but when it reached the woods the path was suddenly cool. The difference between sun and shade was so great that it hardly seemed possible that it could be the same path. The smells of wild honeysuckle and elderflower mingled on the warm air. Their scent made me feel excited and happy, as if I had something to look forward to.

I decided to take the left fork and go up to the church. I would save the beach for last. The inside of the church was so dark and cool after the August heat that it took me a minute to get used to it and be able to see properly. I didn't feel like giving a sermon today, so I wandered up to the front and looked at a tomb on the right of the altar. The tomb had a statue of a man and a lady on its lid; you could see their buckled shoes perfectly, but their stone faces were chipped and flattened with age. They didn't seem tall enough to have been real people. I wasn't really thinking what I was doing: I was just wondering about how short the stone people were. I climbed up on top of them and lay face down on the lady's front. I was nearly as tall as her, and I was only ten. Either they weren't very realistic statues, or people in history had been smaller – I'd ask my father about it, later. It was very uncomfortable, lying on the stone lady. She was much harder than her carved bosom and full skirt made her look. And much, much colder.

I would have got down then, but the church door opened and I heard someone come in and take a few steps before sitting down in a pew; somewhere near the back, from the sound of it. I couldn't actually see, from where I was lying. I didn't know what to do. No one had ever come into the church before. I could feel my heart beating against my ribs and the stone chest of the dead lady. I might get told off – they might be able to tell I was a Catholic and inform me I wasn't allowed in here, whatever Granny had said. I might be trespassing, and I knew – everyone knew – that trespassers will be prosecuted. The person who'd come into the church might even call the police. I didn't know what to do, so I just lay still. Then I heard her. It was a woman, and she was crying. At first she just whimpered a bit, but then she started a low-pitched sobbing.

The first thought I had, then, was that someone who was crying wouldn't tell me off. But when the relief of that had sunk in, I realised that if she was crying she must be very unhappy. It didn't feel right to just lie there and listen, especially not in a church. It occurred to me that maybe God had sent me, that day, to cheer this poor lady up. I didn't know what to do, but I couldn't just do nothing. So I got down from the tomb and tiptoed down the aisle. In my bare feet I made no sound on the stone floor.

The lady had her head in her hands, like an old person praying. I'd got to about three feet from her when I saw that it was Rose. I just stood there, looking at her bent head while she wailed. Then I went and put my hand on her shoulder.

She didn't jump and she didn't look up either. She carried on crying and I carried on standing there. Gradually she quietened down and I kept my hand on her shoulder while she did. Then she put her hand for a moment on mine and said:

'Oh, Francis. You're a good boy, Francis.'

She didn't sound at all surprised that I was there, just very tired and sad. In the end I said:

'Are you all right, Aunt Rose?'

'I'll be all right. I need to blow my nose, that's all.'

She still had her head in her hands. I had the feeling she didn't want me to see her face; that seeing her face would have meant asking things and explaining things that were better left unsaid. So I told her I was going, now; and she nodded.

I left her sniffling in the dark church and ran back up to where the path forked down to the sea. I didn't want to think about why she was so upset. I was half afraid it might have had something to do with my father and the way he'd held her that morning in the half-light. But what worried me even more was that she might have been crying about Granny. Maybe Granny wasn't ever going to get better. Maybe I'd never be able to stay with her again. I'd have to be with my mother and father all the time and it wouldn't be cosy any more, always with my parents. I did love mum and dad, but they didn't really understand about not being an adult, how different I was to them. Thinking this made me feel almost giddy, as if I'd been spinning round and round too fast and could fall over, now I'd stopped.

I went down on to the beach. The tide was still going out, so I walked across the slope of shingle on to the slippery rocks at the water's edge. I crouched down and looked into one of the rock pools. I could see anemones beneath the surface of the water; pink and wavy, like a tiny baby's fingers. The anemones above the water were tight shut, clinging to the rock; black like pieces of shiny wet liquorice, or bleached pale as spat-out chewing gum. Everything looked so clean. Reflections of the clouds scudded across the surface of the pool; when I put my hand into the water they disappeared. I wished that I could stay there for ever, just looking at things.

But we went home the next day.

None of this is what made me decide I didn't want to be a priest, after all. That didn't happen until more than a year later, after we got home from the next – the last – summer in the house in Devon. But I suppose I started to have doubts that autumn, when Catholic Granny was ill.

I was taken to visit Granny twice a week and I stayed at her house three or four times before she went into hospital full-time. There was a funny, stale smell in her house now. She moved much more slowly than she had before, and she was nearly bald. You could clearly see her scalp, its surprising shine. She said that it was the treatment she'd been having that had made her hair fall out, but she didn't mind because it was so grey anyway; she was going to go out and buy herself a lovely auburn wig as soon as she felt a bit better. She'd glance at herself in the hall mirror and say:

'I look like a newly hatched parrot. Quite hideous.'

Catholic Granny never complained about having a pain or going to hospital for her treatments. But, when she was told she had to go and stay in hospital – it was in October – she did clutch my hand in her bony one and ask me to pray that the Lord would deliver her. She looked at me so keenly that I knew it was urgent.

I went to the church and lit a candle for Granny, paid for out of my pocket money. I prayed and prayed to Our Holy Mother because I knew that the Queen of Heaven was full of mercy and never ignored our prayers. But I didn't pray that Granny would be delivered, I prayed that she'd be saved. I wanted her to get better. I didn't want her to go and join the angels, and her husband who I'd never met, and Grandpa Hughes. I felt a bit guilty about my prayers, because I knew that Granny was looking forward to Heaven. But I needed her here, on earth, with me. I asked Mary to tell God that I would give my life to His Service if He would save Catholic Granny. I'd never touch my willy again; I wouldn't expect the new bicycle I'd been wanting for Christmas.

Each time I went to the hospital with my mother my granny would ask me to pray for her; and each week I repeated my promises to God. My bargaining. I added new, more extravagant ones: I'd never eat chocolate again. I'd give my Airfix models away to poor children. I'd stop watching television. I'd always do my homework and never tell fibs to the teachers about losing my book.

One Wednesday at the end of November, when mum and I went to visit, I was sure my prayers had been answered.

Granny was still wafer-thin, but she had a kind of glitter about her; a spark which was obviously the spark of life. Her eyes were bright and she talked very fast. She kept pulling the blanket right up to her chest and she said, for the first time in weeks, that she was hungry. My mother went off to try and find some biscuits and I stayed beside her, listening to what she said. Her mouth seemed very dry, so it was hard to make out some of the things she was talking about. I gave her some sips of water. She kept saying that she was worried about her television licence. She was sure the payment on it was overdue. I told her I'd make sure that mum looked into it, but she wanted Aunt Rose to investigate. She got quite agitated about this: it had to be Rose, she insisted, because Rose knew where she kept her important papers.

When my mother got back with some custard creams, Granny said she wasn't hungry after all. She said I could eat them for her. She always liked feeding me up; she wasn't a hugging sort of person, so she used food instead to indicate her favour. When we left the ward that evening, I felt better than I had for ages. Granny was on the mend, I was sure of it; she might even be home in time for Christmas. But the call came from the hospital early the next day to say that she'd died in the small hours of the morning.

At first I just couldn't believe that she wasn't there. Then, for a long time, I felt so sad that I couldn't really concentrate on anything. By the time spring came, after she'd been dead for several months, I began to feel angry. I felt angry with her for leaving me on my own and I felt even angrier with God for not answering my prayers. You can't feel angry and let down by something you don't believe in. I knew that God existed, but I began to wonder whether he wasn't more like the Old Testament God – full of wrath and vengefulness; causing plagues of locusts and things – than the kindly bearded Father Christmas God in the New Testament. Maybe God wasn't actually all that nice. Or maybe he wasn't not nice; perhaps he just had too much to do. I thought about how many people there were in the world. How could God possibly answer all those prayers?

I still didn't stop wanting to be a priest; not yet. That happened when we were back in the house in Devon, the following summer. Two things happened to make me change my mind about my vocation. The first was that I met an old lady on the beach. She wasn't as old as either of the grannies were, or would have been; but she had wiry grey hair and lots of wrinkles on her face. The way she was so interested in things made me realise she was probably younger than she looked at first.

It was in the afternoon, while my parents were having their rest. They always seemed to be tired. I'd gone down to the shore by myself and I was a bit disappointed to find the woman there. I'd hoped to be alone at the cove, because being alone was better for pretending adventures. She had the bottoms of her trousers rolled up and I would have said she was paddling, except that she was looking down at her feet all the time, and she seemed to be concentrating. It was almost as though she was working and not enjoying herself at all. I went over to the rocks on the far right of the little beach. The tide seemed to be coming in, but there were still enough exposed rocks to scramble about on. Out of the corner of my eye I saw that the old woman was sidling towards me.

I'd seen her coming, but when she spoke it still made me jump.

'Brachiopod,' she said, handing me a stone. She had a deep voice.

I took the pebble and looked at it. It was like a mussel

shell, only it was heavy and one side was bigger than the other. I didn't know what to say, so I didn't say anything.

'The most widespread of fossils. You may keep it, if you wish.'

'Thanks. Thank you.'

'Of course, one would rather find a trilobite, but one would have to look in the cliff wall for those.'

We both stood still in our bare feet.

'Are you interested in fossils?' she asked. It was the first time she'd really looked at me.

'I don't really know. I like looking in the rock pools, though.'

'I see. Less a palaeontologist than a marine biologist then.'

'I'm not sure actually.'

'Palaeontology is the study of the geological past,' she said crisply. 'Marine biology is the study of the organisms which live in the sea. It seems to me that you are of the latter persuasion.'

'Well, I do like things here. Crabs and anemones and things. You know.'

'Yes. A marine biologist it is then.'

'I s'pose so.'

Again we stood without speaking. I said that I was going to climb over the rocks and see what I could find in the pools which always formed on their far side. She said that was a good idea. We clambered over and crouched down to inspect the largest of the pools. She didn't smile at all and she didn't talk much, but I could tell she liked what we were doing. The only things she said were the names of things: serrated wrack; grey sea slug; snakelocks anemone.

I'd never met anyone who spoke like this before. I thought it was great. It meant you just said what you knew about, instead of fumbling around through the words in your head trying to explain what you felt or thought or believed. Just saying the names of things was like reading a label: it was so clear, so certain. We stayed on the beach for ages, the old woman and me. After we'd looked in the rock pools we walked up to the foot of the cliff and she began to poke about in the rough shingle which had collected there, until she found a stone with a pretty pattern in it.

'Fossilised coral. Devonian.'

'Because it comes from Devon?'

She smiled at that.

'Not, actually. Devonian is the fourth period of the Palaeo-zoic era.'

'Oh.'

I didn't understand some of the things she said – words I'd never heard before – but it would have been rude to admit that, since she was behaving as if I was an expert on everything. When I looked at my watch I saw that it was nearly half past seven; my mother would be worried if I stayed away from the house this long.

'I've got to go now,' I said.

'Very well,' she answered. She didn't catch my eye – she was looking out at the sea.

'Goodbye, then.'

'Yes.'

I hoped I'd see her again, but it didn't feel right to tell her so, so I just ran off up the wooden steps. I turned to wave at her when I got to the top, but she didn't look round.

I never did see her again, but I did think about her; and sometimes I recited the names of things like she had, only I did it silently, in my head. On the last day of the holiday my mother told me that my father wouldn't be coming home to our house when we got back to Bristol. He was going to stay with some friends nearby and I'd still see him whenever

I wanted, but from now on I'd just be living with her. It wasn't anything to do with me – it wasn't my fault – but she and daddy kept fighting all the time and they both thought it would be better to try and live apart for a while.

I knew it wasn't true. I knew it wouldn't be just for a while. They'd never be together any more and I'd be alone with my mother and she'd cry all the time and forget to buy milk for breakfast and not keep her promises; just like she already did, only worse. I didn't feel angry with her, or my father, but I did feel angry. Now I didn't have Catholic Granny to go to, I'd be stuck with just mum the whole time apart from the odd visit to Aunt Rose; and I'd have to look after her and my father wouldn't be there to cover it up when she said embarrassing things in public.

It didn't happen overnight, but after that it gradually dawned on me that I'd never be a priest after all. When I looked at the picture of Jesus in my bedroom at home I thought he looked sad, as if he didn't have enough power; like a magician who'd lost his bag of tricks. I still believed in his Goodness, but I didn't think I would devote my life to his Ministry now. The world was too unreliable; people said things that weren't true and did things which I couldn't understand. I knew I'd always love God, just like I loved my mother and father – but maybe God was like them: not actually unkind, but just not perfect. It was disappointing, but I knew I'd be all right.

I had decided on a new career and I was sure that I'd be happy in it when I grew up. Sometimes at night, after I'd switched off the bedside light, I'd say the words quietly to myself in the dark, under the covers. Saying the two names was nearly like hugging them. Marine biologist, I'd whisper to myself, before I shut my eyes to sleep. Marine biologist.

Canada

The argument started in the car on the way to the zoo. Sarah had, as usual, timed their departure with military precision. She had filled the boot with enough nappies, wet-wipes, cartons of Ribena and other assorted paraphernalia to survive a siege which – as Chris pointed out – was an unlikely eventuality to befall them in their thirty-mile journey. They left promptly at ten thirty, to coincide with the baby's morning sleep. Six-year-old Tom and three-year-old Hannah had each been given an apple for the journey – big ones, to ensure optimum silence.

For the first ten minutes no one spoke, and Sarah tried to breathe deep and low into her diaphragm as she'd been taught in parent-craft relaxation classes. Going anywhere with the children – and especially with Chris and the children – made her tense. She looked out at the passing fields and tried to enjoy herself.

'What's the name of that writer, you know, the American crime writer who died?' asked Chris, as they reached the main road.

'Which one?' said Sarah.

'The hard-boiled one. Died recently.'

'I can't think of one who's died lately. Not Raymond Chandler?'

'No.'

'Dashiell Hammett? Mickey Spillane?' Sarah was reaching the outer limits of her knowledge.

'No. Not them.'

'Actually, I think Mickey Spillane's still alive.'

'Well, it's not him anyway.' Chris was becoming impatient. 'One of this guy's books was made into a film.'

'That could be anybody. Are you sure you don't mean Raymond Chandler?'

'No! I've already told you it's not him.'

'Not the man who wrote *The Maltese Falcon*?'

'I don't know – who did write *The Maltese Falcon*?'

Sarah looked out of the window and sighed. 'I don't know.'

In the back of the car, activated by the sound of her parents' voices, Hannah began to chant songs from her favourite film, *The Sound of Music*. 'Doe, a deer, a female deer; pray a drop of golden sun . . .' droned Hannah.

'Not pray, stupid. Ray,' said Tom.

'No, pray. It is pray,' insisted Hannah.

'Mum! She doesn't even know the words,' Tom appealed.

'Don't be unkind, darling,' said Sarah. 'She's doing her best.'

Chris shot a conspiratorial glance in his wife's direction; a look which Sarah, faintly irritated by the American writer conversation, pretended not to see. Generally they enjoyed the way their children paraphrased songs, even encouraging the errors, which gave a pleasingly individual stamp to the clichéd tunes. Their children's malapropisms made them feel special. But Tom had had enough of singing silly words and wanted to do things properly now, like they did at school.

'Why do you ask, anyhow?' said Sarah.

'Ask what?' Chris was overtaking.

'About this dead author thing.'

'Oh, that. It was because I heard Michael Palin on the radio this morning.'

'What's that got to do with it?'

'Because he's written a book himself, something to do with Ernest Hemingway.' Chris spoke with exaggerated patience, like someone explaining directions to a foreigner. 'And him mentioning Hemingway made me think about other American writers, and then I remembered this dead guy.'

'Except you didn't. You didn't remember: that's the whole point.'

A note of triumph, small but unmistakable, sounded in Sarah's voice.

'No. I forgot.' Chris said the words very slowly, as if the same foreign tourist he'd been addressing minutes before had now revealed that they didn't know the difference between left and right.

'There's no need to talk to me as if I'm completely stupid,' said Sarah hotly, 'just because you can't remember the name of some dead author. I mean, you're the one who's forgotten. Not me.'

'All right, all right. Don't get so worked up about it. It's not important anyway,' said Chris reasonably. In the armoury of their marriage, being reasonable was one of his most potent weapons.

They drove on, not speaking. Hannah was still singing: 'So long, farewell, a weasel den, goodbye . . .'

Tom's patience had worn out. 'Shut up, Hannah,' he said.

'No, I'm not. So long, a view, to you and you and yooooo.' Hannah stopped singing and there was a moment of silence before a high-pitched wail of indignation and woe. The baby woke up and joined in.

'I can't stand it!' railed Sarah. 'He's only been asleep for twenty minutes and now you've woken him up. He'll grizzle now for the rest of the day, and it'll all be your fault.' She swivelled round, furious, to accuse her children.

'It wasn't my fault,' said Tom. 'It was her. She's the one who made the noise.'

'He hurted me,' wailed Hannah.

'Never mind, we'll soon be there, then everyone can have an ice lolly,' said Chris, soothingly.

'No they can't,' snapped Sarah, 'I don't want them filling up with sugar so soon before lunch or they'll get hyper. They'll have to wait till this afternoon for lollies.'

'Oh, Mum!' whined Tom and Hannah, momentarily united by their sense of injustice. 'That's not fair. Daddy said we could.'

'Well, you can't. You can have one after lunch.'

'Not fair,' muttered Tom. Hannah began to cry again. The baby howled.

'Now look what you've done!' Sarah turned on Chris. 'You've got them all wound up about stupid fucking ice cream. We're supposed to be going to the zoo to see the animals, not to stuff our faces with more bloody junk food.'

'There's no need to swear in front of the children,' said Chris.

'Mummy said a rude word,' crowed Hannah.

'Shut up, Hannah,' said Tom.

'All of you shut up,' said Sarah.

They arrived at the zoo. Chris, his face already set into a mask of contrived pleasantness, took Tom and Hannah ahead to see the tigers while Sarah stayed to feed the baby in the car. She would join them at the ape house in twenty minutes. Sarah was tired. She was tired of being angry all the time.

She didn't feel herself. She had the sense that anyone could have taken her place – any woman off the street – without her husband or children even noticing the substitution. Sometimes it seemed to her that she had lost her personality altogether, that she was a robot pre-programmed to issue only negative commands: Don't do that. Put it down. Stop it. Get down. Be quiet. No. No.

She finished feeding the baby and strapped him into his buggy. In the ape house an adolescent orang-utan stared dolefully at her through the thick glass.

'Look at the big monkey,' said Hannah.

'It's not a monkey, silly,' said Tom.

Chris raised his eyebrows in mock comedy, and Sarah gave him a watery smile in return. The children seemed to be the only thing they had left in common with each other. Their conversation was always about the children now; their observations made with a sort of laden irony, as though everything they said was in inverted commas. As if being arch made their parental pride less smug.

They traipsed through the reptile house, the aquarium and the marsupials. Chris always insisted on visiting every part of the zoo – it was educational, after all; and they wanted to get their money's worth. But the children only seemed to like the meerkats, and the small monkeys. Even the elephant didn't excite them. Chris pointed enthusiastically to the pygmy hippos, but no one seemed interested.

In the tropical bird house Sarah looked at the bleeding heart pigeons. They had great splashes of red on their chests which looked like gunshot wounds. But what caught her notice was the noise they made, piercing and remarkably plaintive. Sarah thought that, if she was a bird, she'd make exactly that sound herself.

Tom and Hannah ran ahead towards the tall narrow

building, like a double-decker bus garage, which marked the centre of the zoo. When Sarah and Chris and the baby caught up with them they saw that the giraffes were outside, lumbering about, their hooves slipping noisily on the concrete floor. The giraffes usually just stood about, occasionally dipping their long necks towards the ground; their movements seemed clumsy and out of character. Then the male – a good eighteen inches taller of the two – circled to the female's rear and began an attempt to mount her. His movements were jerky and graceless. Just as he appeared to have gained purchase, the female stepped forward, and his front hooves skidded and clattered along the ground. The male was left in amorous limbo, his grossly distended genitals hovering in mid-air.

'Come on, you two, let's go and see the funny tapirs,' said Sarah, taking Hannah firmly by the hand.

'No. Don't want to,' said Hannah, slipping free of her mother's grasp. She stared at the giraffes. The male began to repeat its mating dance, its hard long penis trembling slightly.

'He's got a willy,' said Tom.

'That's right, Tom,' said Chris.

'Willy!' exclaimed Hannah delightedly.

'What's he doing, Mum?' asked Tom.

'He's trying to get married,' said Sarah.

'He's trying to mate,' said Chris, 'To make the lady giraffe have a calf.'

'How?' said Tom.

'Let's go and see the other animals now,' said Sarah.

'He wants to do a pee-pee,' announced Hannah.

'Come on!' said Sarah, fiercely.

The male giraffe continued its attempt, but the children had lost interest. They all wandered off towards the seals. Chris's face had coloured slightly as it did when he was aroused. Sarah wondered whether the spectacle of the giraffe's inept coupling could have turned him on.

'I want a divorce.' The thought came to her out of the blue, and she felt giddy from the impact of it. She was overcome with an urge of destructive power, or the desire for freedom, she couldn't tell which. Divorce was taboo. Chris had read an interview with some old couple in a Sunday colour supplement in which the man had said that divorce was a kind of murder. And Chris concurred with that; they both did. He and Sarah had often agreed that it was simply not an option; not for couples with children. You had to put the kids first. If there was domestic violence, then divorce was acceptable, but for average, middle-class couples who were merely restless or bored it was unforgivable. It was out of the question.

Sarah sat down on a bench by the penguins, the baby on her knee. The others wandered on, laughing at the birds and holding their noses at the sour fishy smell. Sarah looked at Chris and felt an indifference that seemed even more poisonous than hatred. She looked at her children, and they just looked like ordinary children. They could have been anybody's. It occurred to her (and she flushed with guilt even as the thought came) that divorce would enable her to spend alternate weekends – even whole weeks, during holiday times – away from them.

A few months back, soon after the baby was born, Sarah had been helping Tom to look up a map of Europe in the atlas. His class were doing a project on geography. Flicking through the atlas, her eye had alighted on the pages which depicted Canada. Sarah noticed that most of the country was shaded in beige, which denoted a population density of less than twenty-five people per square mile. Above this southerly ribbon of beige was a huge area – bigger than Europe –

shaded in palest yellow; in this enormous region there were only two people to every square mile. Most of Britain, apart from the very tip of Scotland, had 250 people per square mile. Canada was virtually empty.

Sarah got a guide to Canada out from the library. It was one of a series of travel books called the *Lonely Planet* guides. If the population of Canada was distributed evenly across its vast surface, there would be an interval of 880 yards between each person who lived there. She imagined herself standing in a field in Canada, waving her arms about, with the nearest person – half a mile away – not being able to see or hear her. If there were only two people to every mile, you could do whatever you liked and no one would notice; you could scream at the top of your voice, or sing to yourself; you could never cook hot food, or clean the bath. No one would know.

When the *Lonely Planet* guide had to go back to the library Sarah went to the travel agent and got a heap of leaflets about holidays to Canada. While she fed the baby she leafed through them, staring at the pictures of mountains and forests and lakes. It looked miraculously beautiful, clean and spacious. One evening Chris spotted a brochure on the sofa.

'What's this, darling? Planning a holiday for us?' he asked.

'No. No, it's nothing.' Sarah scooped the pamphlet out of his hand.

'Hey, I was going to have a look at that! See if there's anything interesting about Canada, or if it's all maple syrup and Mounties. And ice. I've always thought it sounded one of the most boring places on earth.'

'I like the idea of it. It's not boring at all. It's incredibly unspoilt.' Sarah sounded even more defensive than she felt.

'Oh, sorry. Pardon me for breathing. Anyway I don't know what you're doing, looking at holidays to Canada when we're so broke. And you hate being cold. You'd freeze over there.'

'I wasn't thinking about a holiday.'

'What, you're emigrating, are you?' Chris turned towards the TV. 'Well, you can count me out. I don't want to go and live in an igloo, thank you very much.'

'Just leave it alone, will you? It's got nothing to do with you.' Sarah felt tears prick behind her eyes. She stared at her husband accusingly, with a now-look-what-you've-done expression. Chris wondered whether she was suffering from some kind of post-natal depression. Since the baby had arrived she'd been morose and snappy. He meant to be kind to her, but she looked so wounded all the time. And the texture of her skin had altered so that it looked dry and puffy, and yet almost moist at the same time. Touching his lips to her cheek was like kissing uncooked pizza dough. She even smelled slightly yeasty.

After that Sarah hid her Canada brochures in the kitchen drawer and only looked at them when Chris was at work. Looking at the pictures of blue sky and pine-clad hills calmed her. When the children clambered over her, claiming her flesh, she imagined herself alone in a wooden cabin at the side of an empty Canadian meadow. Even the idea of being cold appealed to her; made her feel self-sufficient and strong.

Now, at the zoo in the muggy heat, she tried to summon up the soothing image of Canadian solitude. She pictured the long grass of the imagined meadow, and the distant slopes, and the song of birds in the uninhabited wild. She saw herself, standing alone on a wooden verandah, with no husband, no children, no neighbours. Nothing. No one to want anything from her, no one to expect more of her than she could give. No one to feel she had let them down.

'Come on, Mum. Lunchtime.' Tom stood in front of her, his hands on her knees. He seemed so innocent; there was some germ of courage, almost of valour, in him which moved her. Once again her son appeared radiant, pure and unique. She stood up and took his hand, and they went towards the café.

After lunch the children said they'd had enough of animals and wanted to play on the big slide in the zoo playground instead. The baby refused to be strapped back into his push-chair. Chris insisted that they at least walk through the birds of prey, but Hannah whined and Tom looked theatrically bored, even at the gory furred carcass which the crested eagle was picking at. The baby, now being carried by its father, began to grizzle and wouldn't keep still, thrashing its limbs and becoming red in the face.

'What does he want?' said Chris, exasperated.

'I don't know,' said Sarah.

'You take him. Look, he's quieter with you.'

'I'm tired of carrying him. I've had him all day,' said Sarah, reaching out her arms to receive the kicking bundle.

Their parents stood side by side, unspeaking, while Tom and Hannah went up and down the slide, time and time again. The children kept glancing towards their parents to make sure they were looking. They seemed to be enjoying the play area much more than they'd appreciated the animals. Chris wondered if it was worth bringing them all this way – there was a virtually identical slide at the park five minutes from their house. When he called out to them that it was time to go home they both began to cry.

'Come on, you lot,' said Sarah, trying to sound both coax-ing and authoritative. She wondered how many times she'd said those words.

'Can we have our ice creams now?' said Tom.

'Yes, my darling,' said Sarah.

'Not in the car, they don't,' said Chris.

'But you promised, Daddy!' said Hannah.

'On the grass, then. But you'll have to finish them up quickly.'

Once they'd been on the road for a quarter of an hour, all three children dropped off to sleep. Sarah looked out at the suburban houses on the outskirts of the city and felt a stab of envy at other people's lives: their neat hedges and comfortable armchairs and office jobs. Some of them probably had wonderful sex, and went to the cinema and had grown-up children. Their lives were ordered and manageable. She felt tears slide down her cheeks.

'Do you ever think that we might be so strongly anti-divorce because we'd really like to be divorced ourselves?' she asked Chris.

'What do you mean?' he said. 'No.'

'But we do go on as if divorce is a criminal act, when in reality it's an everyday occurrence. I mean, I wonder if we protest too much,' said Sarah.

'I don't think so,' said Chris. 'I just think that lots of people don't take their commitments seriously enough. If you marry someone and you have children together, you shouldn't up and off at the first whiff of trouble.'

'But I mean, the way we were so outraged when Tony left Laura, as if no one had ever done such a wicked thing before. It's not as if theirs is the only marriage ever to have gone wrong. One in three marriages end in divorce these days. Maybe they both tried their best, but they just couldn't do it any longer.' There was a note of appeal in her voice.

'You know it wasn't like that,' said Chris reasonably. 'Tony'd been seeing Isobel for eight months. The split certainly wasn't Laura's fault. And I think it was very wrong of him not to knock the affair on the head before it threatened his wife and kid.'

'What, it would have been OK for him to have had the affair, as long as it didn't mean leaving his home? Is that what you're saying?'

'Don't be silly, Sarah. I didn't mean it like that.'

'Well, anyway, I wish we could get one.'

'One what?'

'A divorce.' She meant what she said, but the words came out wrong. She sounded sulky and unconvincing, like a petulant child asking for something in a toyshop.

'Look, I know you've been feeling really down lately,' Chris tried to sound patient, 'but I think you're more than a bit worn-out.'

'I am. I'm just so tired of all this.' Sarah began to cry in earnest.

'Well, I think you should go to the doctor on Monday and see if he can sort you out with some tablets or something. Something to make you feel more able to cope.'

'I don't want to go to the doctor,' wailed Sarah, 'I want to divorce you.'

Chris took no notice. 'I honestly think you might be suffering from depression. You haven't been yourself for ages now. You always seem to be tense, in a bad mood. I think it'd be worth visiting the doctor.'

Sarah was sobbing now, and rummaging through her handbag for a Kleenex. 'It's living with all these people on top of me, never having any time on my own. I can't even have a bath without one of you coming into the room because you want something. I just can't stand it any more. I didn't think it would be like this – I always wanted to get married and have my own children – I thought having a family and a home was supposed to make you happy. I didn't know it would be so bloody awful. It's not depression that's wrong with me – it's disappointment.'

The notion of disappointment hung on the air between them, acrid and pervasive as the smell of stale beer. The car seemed stuffy with rancour.

'Yes, well we're all disappointed with some aspect of our lives. It doesn't mean you have to walk out on your children.'

'I'd never do that! I'd never leave the kids,' said Sarah.

'Well, I wouldn't let you take them, so you'd better have a serious think about what you're saying.' Chris's lips had lost their colour.

Sarah wished she hadn't said what she'd said. She knew she'd gone too far, but it was too late to clutch back the words. She blew her nose and looked straight ahead at the road. She imagined herself unencumbered, other; but when she tried to journey north in her mind, her refuge – the dream of lush meadows and green mountains – had evaporated. She suddenly found herself picturing a harsher terrain: a lonely house on dark rocks overlooking an angry sea of battleship-grey. She imagined laundry dried stiff and rough from the salt breeze, and the tar and turpentine aroma of pitch on rough wooden floors. There would be small clumps of coarse grasses, and shingle everywhere, and no flowers. There would be a small black stove, with a pot of bitter coffee by it and one tin cup; and this would be her home, in northern New Brunswick, perhaps, or on the coast of Ontario. It would be cold, and she would be quite alone.

The Pleasure Gardens

Decimalisation came in the year after my mother died, the year when Kathryn and I both turned thirteen. It was just another of the strange new things we had to get used to; not as hard to come to terms with as the sadness which engulfed my house, nor anywhere near as exciting as entering our teens. People like my father, who were sticklers for the way in which things were said, would tut with irritation at the ugly new word: 'pence' instead of the old 'pennies'. But Kathryn and I saw opportunities in the new currency. It was a chance for me to get a rise in my pocket money, to round up the sum from five bob to forty pence – an increase of three shillings, which my father agreed to with scarcely a murmur of protest. At that point, he would have probably agreed to anything. It was different for Kathryn. She didn't get pocket money from her parents. She did a paper round on a Thursday, when the local newspaper came out, and then often, after school, she showed her bare bottom for sixpence a time.

I acted as her manager. She would wait by the wall at the back of the churchyard, screened by laurels, while I took the sixpences from the boys who wanted a look, and kept watch. The vicar never came into this part of the churchyard, only a deaf old lady with an indignant-looking Pekinese dog, and she was under the impression that we were dear little girls. Occasionally she delved into her stiff, box-like handbag and gave us sixpence apiece.

Kathryn's passion in life was her menagerie, which at that time consisted of a pair of guinea pigs (both male, though we didn't know that until later, when their puzzling absence of offspring caused us to inspect them very thoroughly), a hamster and a refuge for garden snails. Kathryn was an animal rights activist before her time. As early as 1970 she had realised that garden snails didn't stand a chance when confronted by the probing beaks of hungry birds, and she had formed a sanctuary for them in her bedroom, made from shoeboxes. (A similar refuge, for earthworms, had not been a success.) Her secondary hobby was the creation of very tiny animals, which she made out of felt. She made miniature pigs and sheep and dogs from scraps of material, and she knitted their teensy garments on dressmaking pins, using sewing cotton as yarn. She really had a gift for it.

Even activities as modest as these needed funding. By the time she was thirteen, most of the boys from the grammar had already seen Kathryn's bottom, and business seemed to be floundering, until one boy asked for a look at the front part too. She didn't mind: Kathryn wasn't yet interested in boys in a romantic way, and she was able to reveal her all to them for this very reason, because she could do so guile-lessly. Boys sensed this, and because they didn't feel threatened by her, were able to reveal their curiosity unabashed. She put up her rates from sixpence (old money) to five new pence – double the price. But a good look at a girl's naughty bits was worth the money for them – they needed something to masturbate about, and here it was, for a shilling. No touching allowed.

Most of her earnings were spent on her animals, either the living ones, or the kind she was always making. Kathryn wanted to be an occupational therapist when she grew up. She had always wanted to be an occupational therapist, just as her sister Lisa had always known that she would be a beautician. I didn't know what I wanted to do, but I did want to be as much like Lisa as possible.

Lisa was fifteen. Next summer she would be old enough to leave school. She was the first in her year to own a hairdryer, and a pioneer also in gadgets for the styling of hair. She had a scissor-like apparatus for curling eyelashes, and heated electric tongs to add a teasing lift to the many layers of her feather-cut. Hair was Lisa's speciality, almost her vocation. She had tweezed her eyebrows into perfectly symmetrical pencil-thin crescents, which sat strangely, high above her eyes. She had begun to wax her already alabaster smooth legs well before the onset of her first period. She used a foul-smelling cream to remove the minuscule quantity of fluff which marred the pale surface of her underarms. She was not at all hirsute, yet the dying, styling, curling and removal of hair occupied most of her time. Kathryn and I both looked up to her with an awe which felt a little like veneration; the fact that she had decided to become a beautician weighed heavily upon us, who were nearly three years younger; it was like being in the company of someone who had been chosen. I was especially solemn in her presence, and a willing handmaiden to her art. To be allowed into Lisa's bedroom was an honour we were very seldom permitted, but whenever I spent time in Kathryn's bedroom – which I did almost every day – I hoped that Lisa would come in and summon us across the landing. Her room had a curious chemical odour, made up of nail-polish remover, dry shampoo and singed hair. Her dressing table was a console, a shrine. She had a Saturday job at a hairdressing salon near the pier, and from her work she had amassed a large collection of free beauty products: aerosols of mousse and lacquer; gels and setting agents. Much of her wage was spent on make-up (her favourite range was called Number 17) and she had a whole basket, of the sort used to serve bread rolls in restaurants, full of make-up pencils for lips, lids and brows. She herself wore dark blusher, dusted in dramatic stripes across her cheekbones; it was the early nineteen seventies, and all of us were under the influence of David Bowie's make-up and Suzie Quatro's layered hairstyle.

Despite Lisa's allure, she didn't have many friends. Most evenings, after school, I'd escape the emptiness of my own house by going up the road to the Robards'. But no one else ever did. Mr Robards didn't like the girls to bring their friends to the house, and I think he only allowed me to go there because I lived so close that I could be ejected at a moment's notice. He and his wife never had friends round. They didn't even seem to have any relations. Mrs Lawrence, who came to our house to clean and do a bit of cooking after mum died, said that Mrs Robards had married beneath herself, but I didn't know what she meant, because Mr Robards was a good fourteen inches taller than his wife.

Up in her room, Kathryn and I used to clean out the animals' cages and boxes, and then we'd practise our dancing in front of the full-length mirror on her wardrobe door. We'd put several singles on at once – mostly paid for out of my pocket money – and then start dancing, without pre-amble. In the silences between songs we'd stop and stand about, while the needle swung out and another record plopped down on to the top of its predecessor. We had perfected various styles, each one tailored to its own song: Bay City Rollers, Rod Stewart and Mud; Slade, Mungo Jerry and T-Rex. We were the queens of the disco, except that we never really went to discos. We had only been to two, both of them in the youth hall near our school, and Kathryn had, in the event, been too embarrassed to dance in public. But we fervently wanted to go to more.

And while we were earnestly practising our dance routines – there was more concentration about it than enjoyment – Lisa would be in her bedroom, getting ready to go out. This was a daily ritual. She would sit at her dressing table and slowly and thoroughly cleanse, tone and moisturise her face. She would squeeze any blackheads which had appeared on her chin, and deftly pluck out any eyebrows which had strayed from their regimented lines. She would apply her make-up, and spend a long time doing her hair. But Mr Robards almost never let her actually go out. It was rare for either of the girls to be away from the house after seven o'clock in the evening, even in the summer.

Mr Robards worked for British Rail and he kept irregular hours. When he laughed it sounded like the laugh of Sid James: raucous, chesty and abrupt, ending as suddenly as it had begun. His laugh was loud, but his voice wasn't. Many of his teeth were missing, and he slammed doors. You could always tell when he was at home, even if you didn't see him; the atmosphere in the house altered when he was there. The girls tended to keep out of his way, especially when he was what they always called 'in a mood', and I was frightened of him. He tolerated me, and he didn't often get in a mood with Kathryn, but to Lisa he was often surly. She avoided him by staying in her room, painting and repainting her toenails or applying cuticle cream. She was always busy.

I supposed that her dad hardly ever let her go out because he didn't want her mixing with boys, and getting into trouble. But, despite the fact that she spent all her time adorning herself, Lisa wasn't interested in boys. For her, clothes and make-up were an end in themselves, and boys were just an excuse for her true purpose, which was to get dressed up. But she wasn't getting dressed up for them. Lisa was pretty, with small features and neat limbs and very pale skin. She had fluffy hair which, although it was light in colour, couldn't actually be described as blonde. People called her petite. Even at fifteen, she had already planned her ideal lounge, her dream kitchen units. More than anything, she longed for a home of her own, a place where she might extend her make-up routine into an equally strict regime of housework, and her buying of clothes into the choice of luxury soft furnishings. She accepted that she would need a man to help her realise this scheme – and he would have to be a husband, she wasn't going to just give herself away to the first bloke who came along, without the guarantee of marriage – but the man was secondary to the house. She wanted central heating and a leather three-piece suite. She definitely didn't want children.

It was imperceptible at first, but during that summer things between Kathryn and me began to change. A hairline crack appeared in our friendship. We continued our dancing with the same perseverance – there was a disco coming up, at the beginning of August – but I wasn't so interested in her animals any more. I was more interested in Karl Bevan.

I had been in love with Karl since I started at the high school when I was eleven. At first I had been happy to adore him from afar: the devotion I felt towards him didn't, at that time, extend to any interest as to what he might be like as a personality, as someone to actually talk to. Let alone to kiss. Karl's dad worked for the council; outdoor work, mostly, including the upkeep of the cemetery just down the street from the school. They lived in a house which went with the job, a Victorian gothic building, half red brick, half flint, just by the cemetery gates. Karl went to the boys' grammar school, which didn't start until ten past nine in the morning. But high school began at nine, which meant that each day, when the bus pulled up to deposit us girls there, I stood a good chance of catching a glimpse of Karl. Once, unforgettably, he was standing at an upstairs window – it could have been his bedroom – staring out and knotting his tie.

Other girls at my school loved Karl, but I knew that no one loved him as much as me. Sometimes, after school, before my father got home from work teaching biology at the private boys' school on the far side of the golf course, I would shut myself in the lounge and enact, in my mind, the drama of my doomed romance. I didn't, like Kathryn, have a record player in my bedroom; the gramophone at our house was for communal use, which meant that I never used it unless there was no one else at home. Then I would play 'The Leader of the Pack', by the Shangri-Las, on repeat, and imagine that its tragic story was my own. How the other girls at school would respect me, when they saw Karl's ring, glittering on my finger; how they'd envy my suffering when he met his untimely end. I pictured Lisa as the head bridesmaid of my grief, holding my arm as I – dressed in gauzy black – led the mourners to Karl's graveside; how the others would marvel at my courage, my brilliant dress sense and the depth of our lost young love. The actual proximity of the cemetery to our school made this fantasy especially piquant: my imaginary audience was huge.

Some months after decimalisation my periods started, and after that happened I began to think about Karl in a less abstract way. The sight of the little gold ring in his ear started to trouble and fascinate me and I found that I longed to touch his hair, which fell in black curls around his collar. I noticed that his mouth looked cruel, and yet sort of wounded at the same time. I wondered what it would be like to kiss and be kissed by that mouth. These feelings I could not share with Kathryn, and dared not voice to Lisa.

Lisa had tried snogging, and she didn't recommend it: a boy's cheek when he kissed you was like having an emery board rubbed against your face, she said, and it made your neck sore too. Your teeth clashed against his and it made a terrible noise; it tasted revolting. It was ever so embarrassing. Kathryn had her animals to think about, and she didn't want a boyfriend anyway. One of the lads she'd shown her bum to had grabbed her, once, and forced his tongue, which had seemed strangely thick, into her mouth. It was horrible. He hadn't had a chin like sandpaper; it was worse than that. He'd had a tiny drift of a moustache, soft and thin, and his breath had been very hot in her mouth. But despite what the Robards sisters had to say – and it was a dreadful testimony, I was forced to admit – I still wished, in my heart, that Karl Bevan would look unsmiling into my eyes and kiss me.

My father had started applying for jobs up in the Midlands, near to where his sister lived. The idea of moving had possessed him very suddenly, as if it could provide the only possible answer to a question which was too urgent even to be formed. He announced that he was hoping to get a new post which would commence at the beginning of the autumn term, and to fix up a new school for me at the same time. He'd told me that we'd be moving, with any luck, in the first week of September; but it seemed so remote, so unreal an event that I didn't believe it could actually happen. All my friends were here, and all the people I knew and had always known; mum had lived here with us. The sea was at the bottom of our road. We had accounts at the newsagent and the butchers, and we knew all the bus routes. And there was Karl Bevan. It didn't seem possible that all this could just be left, abandoned. It would be like leaving your whole life behind.

Every Saturday I went along the seafront with Kathryn, or with another girl in our year, Fiona Walters. That summer Kathryn had not been coming with me so often, although I much preferred her to Fiona, who was a very overdeveloped girl with heavy breasts and startlingly thick pubic hair, stiff and proud and rust-coloured, like dead bracken. I knew this because I had spotted it in the changing room one afternoon after netball. Boys were attracted to Fiona, because of her womanly physique, but her face was rather horselike and she suffered from a maddening surfeit of confidence. She was the baby of her family – her older sister was fourteen years older – and she only laughed at her own jokes. But she was kind-hearted, and willing for adventure.

Our town, despite its long beaches and the fame of its many hours of daily sunshine, was not popular as a holiday resort. Most of its population were retired people. Even at the height of summer it was possible to find a whole beach – more than thirty feet across, sandwiched by tarry wooden breakwaters – with no one on it; and the café and pleasure gardens at the far end of the esplanade, where the cliffs began, were usually deserted. These were our destination. Every Saturday we'd start from the pier and walk the entire length of the pink-paved promenade; the big hotels on the front like a series of dusty, giant wedding cakes on our right, and on our left the sea. There was a slight shimmer in the paving slabs, which caught in the sunshine and made the promenade look like a hard crust of sugar icing. We'd walk all along it; counting the breakwaters, watching the bathers, looking for boys. When we reached the end we'd go for a milk shake

– tepid, made not with ice cream or syrup, but with a cheap powdered flavouring – at the café below the pleasure gardens.

One Saturday in early July it happened. Fiona and I were sitting sipping our synthetic pink milk drinks, when a group of four boys appeared at the café, among them Karl Bevan. They pretended not to be looking at us, and we pretended not to be looking at them. This went on for several minutes, during which time conversation between myself and Fiona – rarely very scintillating – became especially strained and monosyllabic. At last they shuffled over and asked if either of us had a light: all the boys we knew smoked as much as they could. To have a finger stained yellow with nicotine was to be accepted as hard, as one of the lads; and they all inhaled very sharply, eyes narrowed, from the Embassy Regals which they held between thumb and third finger, the lit end facing inwards, towards their palms. Asking for a light, in our circle, was tantamount to a declaration of undying love: all the boys had their own evil-smelling paraffin lighters, which they were never without.

I could not bring myself to look at Karl. The boys sat down next to us and they all drank cups of tea with a lot of sugar, and smoked and talked among themselves, but with half an eye on Fiona and me. Then, abruptly, they all stood up and asked us if we were coming – which of course we were – and I found myself standing alongside Karl Bevan and then falling into step with him. The other three boys were walking on ahead, back towards the seafront, teasing Fiona about something. 'Let's go,' said Karl and he turned away from his friends and towards the pleasure gardens. We walked across the apron of grass and to the left, where wooden steps cut into the cliff rose up to a path which encircled the pleasure gardens below. In the gardens was a covered shelter, with roses growing up it and a bench inside.

I thought that Karl would go there, but instead he walked on, not speaking, and up the steps with me behind him. Above the steps and on a little way further was a wooden bridge, suspended in the air: it was level with the tops of the trees and you could see the sea through the leaves, and the light there was green. Karl stopped walking when he reached the bridge and I leant on the creosote-smelling balustrade with my back to the view. And then Karl Bevan put his hands on my neck and kissed me.

At first there was only the sensation of his lips on mine, kisses as gentle and as dry as my mother's had been, on my cheeks when I was small. But at last his tongue entered my mouth and darted across the surface of my teeth like a small fish and made me shiver; I realised that his hands on my throat were very cool, despite the heat of the afternoon and that his breath, also, was almost cold inside my mouth. The chill of him was intensely exciting and mysterious. Perhaps it was because he lived so near to the graveyard.

After this I could think of nothing except Karl Bevan, and how to make him want to kiss me again. We'd parted by the wall just outside my house, where he'd walked with me, in almost total silence, after our embrace at the pleasure gardens. But he hadn't asked for my phone number, nor made any suggestion that we meet again. Perhaps I'd been too easy. Perhaps he liked someone else. These torturous questions preoccupied me to the exclusion of all other thoughts. Even Lisa's beauty regime began to seem trivial, shallow, by comparison. I dared not confess to Kathryn, much less to her sister, that I had tried French kissing. If I told them about the kiss, I'd have had to confess, too, that I lived only for the moment when I could repeat it. There was obviously something very wrong with me. No one liked snogging. It was just something that you had to allow boys to do – under sufferance, always – to reward them for taking you out often enough for your friends to realise you had a steady boyfriend. I wondered whether Karl had sensed my unnatural delight at his kiss; whether my response might put him off.

The only way I could think to win his attention back was by a virtuoso display of dancing at the next disco. This meant redoubled practice. Kathryn and I danced and danced, singing along to all the songs and giggling together, just as we always had. When we were busy we were as close as ever – it was only when we were idle in each other's company that I felt an absence develop between us. There was a vogue then for songs about dying teenagers, some of them old songs: as well as 'The Leader of the Pack' there was 'Terry', which also featured a road accident; there was 'Honey', and there was the deliciously mawkish 'Seasons in the Sun'. Kathryn and I had made up a rude version of the song's stirring chorus, substituting our own words, which included sessions in the sun, tits and bums. We thought it was the funniest thing we'd ever heard.

Lisa had a new obsession, precipitated by meeting a man called Gareth, who was twenty-three. She had only spoken to him twice, but their brief acquaintance had already convinced her that he was suitable husband fodder. He had told her that he worked self-employed as a taxi driver; that he had wall-to-wall carpets – and that he had been sterilised. She wasn't about to fall in love with him – she wasn't completely stupid – but he was her dream man, even so.

Since meeting Gareth her fondness for hair treatments had been supplanted by a mania for deodorising products. She amassed an impressive collection of underarm anti-perspirants, both aerosol and roll-on. Then she had a Dr Scholl foot-freshening spray which she used, with some panache, through her (so-called) flesh-coloured tights. Flesh-coloured if you had skin the colour of Lucozade. Most daring and new were vaginal deodorants, which weren't called vaginal at all, but were marketed as products for 'intimate' or 'feminine' hygiene. Only the initiated could have guessed their true purpose. Lisa had purchased every brand available. They came in discreet pink canisters with blurry pictures on them, of hot-looking women standing amid thick foliage. There were also modest little boxes full of moisturised sachets, which were designed to revive feminine freshness on long journeys. Lisa always slipped several of these into her clutch bag before she travelled the half-mile to the town centre.

It was nearly the end of July. My father's attempts at finding a teaching job up in Warwickshire had not been successful, and he was thinking, now, that we might make the move at Christmas instead. It would give us longer to find a nice new home, he said, and by then our house would be sure to have sold, so he wouldn't have to take out a bridging loan. I didn't care about loans. All I cared about was where we lived already. When I said so, dad looked away. He said the move would be for the best, in the long run. I wanted to know why. Best for who, I asked him, but he didn't answer. I overheard Mrs Lawrence talking to my father in the kitchen one day, saying that it was a shame; that children of my age were always so tricky, such a difficult stage; as if he didn't have enough on his plate already. He didn't agree with her, but he didn't disagree either – he just said nothing. His silence then made my eyes smart, but I wasn't about to cry from sadness, or from loneliness, or even from missing mum; it was the injustice of it. It was a kind of betrayal. I didn't think I was being difficult about wanting to stay; I was only making my side of the situation known. What gave me a shock was the sudden understanding that it made no difference what I felt. This was the first time I'd realised that what children want had no effect at all on the choices which parents made. Up until then, I'd always believed that my father would take me seriously, would listen to me; that he would be, fundamentally, on my side.

It was a stay of execution, at least. I was spending more and more time at the Robards' house by then, partly to perfect my dancing for the forthcoming disco, and partly to keep out of my father's way. By unspoken consent, I generally left before Mr Robards came home which, because he worked shifts, was frequently as late as nine thirty at night. I often stayed right up till then, thereby succeeding in avoiding my father's company for all but a few minutes before bed. Kathryn and I would dance for a while, then sit chatting on her bed. Sometimes, when the gramophone had gone quiet, Lisa would call out to us to join her in her room and there she would instruct us in cuticle control, or the correct procedure for eyebrow shaping (always pluck from under the brows – never, ever from above, or you'll ruin the shape), or whatever small ceremony she herself was engaged in.

One night Mr Robards came home early. I was still upstairs with Kathryn when he arrived, and it was obvious from his exaggerated tread and from the slamming doors downstairs that he was in a temper. I stood up to go just as his voice – loud and yet still husky, like a roaring whisper – came up the stairs. He was shouting his daughters' names – Kathryn, Lisa – but neither of them responded by leaving their bedrooms. Kathryn's face went a funny colour, white but with the memory of colour beneath the surface, like an uncooked chicken portion. Mr Robards called their names again.

Kathryn spoke very quietly. 'My dad's in a mood. Get under the bed.'

It didn't even occur to me not to do as she said. She had a dusty pink candlewick bedspread which came almost to the floor, and I scrabbled to conceal myself under her bed beneath it. I could still see her slippered feet, and the door open on to the landing. Mr Robards began to come up the stairs. He had stopped shouting his daughters' names, but his breathing was still audible, and it sounded as if his own menace had somehow constricted his windpipe, as if his rage was suffocating him. When he reached the top of the stairs I felt the floor vibrate with his steps. It reminded me of a story from long ago, a story my mother used to tell me when I was young, where an evil giant stalked his castle, searching for small children to eat for his dinner. I had a sudden urge to laugh as I lay there, terrified, on the cold red lino of Kathryn's bedroom floor.

He came into the room. His boots – round-toed, scuffed – were level with my eyes.

'What are you doing, then?' he asked Kathryn.

The question was a threat. I knew for certain that she had to answer him correctly; that something awful could happen if she got it wrong. And I also realised that it was a question he had asked her, in exactly this same coded way, many times before. She told him she was just cleaning out the cage of her guinea pigs. He stood still and did not speak while she brushed the damp wood-shavings from the floor of the hutch. Two or three little pellets of hard round guinea-pig dung rolled across the lino towards me. Neither of them spoke, but I could sense the restrained urgency with which she enacted her task, as if her life depended on it. Mr Robards remained in her room for what felt like for ever, his breathing harsh and rasping, and then he walked out leaving the door open behind him. I expected a sense of relief to become palpable when he left the room, but Kathryn still exuded the same contained dread as she had when he'd been standing over her.

I heard Mr Robards trudge across the landing and enter Lisa's room. I heard him say the same thing to her: 'What are you doing, then?'

His voice was low. She answered thinly: 'Nothing, Dad.'

I understood that, for reasons I could not fathom, this was the wrong answer, the wrong thing to say.

'What do you mean, nothing? Didn't you hear me? I said, what are you doing?'

'Dad! I'm not doing anything. I'm just sat here.'

'Oh yeah. I can see that. And what do you think you're doing, then?'

She was silent.

'Can't you hear me? Are you deaf or something? I said, what do you think you're doing?'

Still she didn't respond.

'I said, what do you think you're up to, you little slag? Do you think you're going out tonight, then, do you? Think you're going out to meet your boyfriend, then, do you? You little whore. You filthy little slag. Can you hear me?'

Then Lisa spoke, very softly: 'Please, Dad. Please.'

But it was as if he hadn't heard her, because he went on: 'You know what I do to filthy slags, don't you?'

For the next few moments there was no sound from Lisa's room, although something in the silence made it clear that Mr Robards had not finished with his daughter yet. Kathryn was still fiddling about with the guinea pigs; filling their bowls of seed, padding about the room to replenish their water from the tap in the washbasin by the window. The clean smell of fresh sawdust came to me under the bed.

Then it started: a low, rhythmic noise came from Lisa's room; a noise which seemed to combine slapping and groaning and another sound, which was like a piece of old furniture being dragged across a floor. None of these came from Lisa herself. I couldn't hear her at all. Words began to punctuate the groans which Mr Robards was making, and his voice became louder and louder until he was shouting and puffing and wheezing and grunting all at once, like a barnyard: 'You – filthy – slag.'

The words came again and again. And then the noise ceased as abruptly as it had begun, and I knew that whatever it was that he had done to her was over. I heard Mr Robards walk out of her room – very much more quietly than he had arrived, almost as if he was walking on tiptoes – and go back down the stairs.

I was too frightened to move from under Kathryn's bed. It was only some time later, after we had heard the front door click shut, and the transit van start then fade away up the road heading away from the sea, that I dared even whisper to her: 'Can I come out now?'

She said I could, but to go out of the house quietly, because her mum was downstairs and she didn't want her to know I'd been here this time. This time. The matter-of-fact, flat way that she said it was awful. I left her in her room and went out on to the landing. The door to Lisa's room was open and as I looked in I saw her, lying on the floor at the foot of her bed. I wanted to say something, to reassure or comfort her, but I didn't know how to. I just stood there, looking at her.

Then she glanced up, as if she'd realised she was being observed, and for a moment her eyes caught mine. Her cheeks were blotchy and her eyes were small and swollen from crying. Her hair was sticking up, and it was damp in patches across her skull, like the fluff on a newly-hatched chick. Her expression seemed to have lost all of its self-containment, as if her composure had been liquefied, then smudged crudely back across her features, like a familiar garment put on in haste, back to front and inside out. When she looked at me for that second, it was not with complicity or despair or hopelessness with which she was regarding me: it was a look which consisted only of hate. And then she sank her head back on to her arms, and I went down the stairs and let myself out of the house, and walked home.

Our house found a buyer in late October and the move was planned for the beginning of December. I was going to miss the last fortnight of the autumn term, but my father – unlike his usual, schoolteacher self – said it didn't matter, since I was leaving anyway. He had a new job to go to in January, and we drove up to Stratford together several times during those autumn months, to house-hunt and visit schools for me. We got on well, when we were in the car, much better than when we were at home. Driving relaxed us and it was during those long car journeys that we laughed and joked together for the first time since mum died. We visited three schools and chose the largest of them, a mixed grammar; and my bedroom in the new house was much bigger than my old one, so dad said I could have my own desk up there, and the gramophone too, if I wanted. I liked the look of Stratford, with its unfamiliar black-and-white buildings and its sleepy river, but I knew that I would miss the sea.

Kathryn and I had gone to the disco in August as we'd planned, but again some awkwardness had prevented her from displaying her dancing skills in public. When I had seen that Karl Bevan was not there, my heart had gone out of the disco too, and we'd spent the whole evening standing at the side of the dance floor, awarding points to the other girls, who greatly outnumbered the boys and danced apart from them in nervous little groups of two or three. It had been more fun in her bedroom.

I still saw Kathryn every day at school, and she came to my house for tea at least once a week, but I didn't go round to the Robards' place any more. It wasn't that she said I couldn't. She still took her knickers down occasionally to earn a bit of extra pocket money, and I still chaperoned her when she did. We didn't talk about what I had witnessed at her house that night, and we didn't talk about me moving away; or about what either of us felt about these, and other, things. We just carried on caring for her pets and practising our dancing – even though we knew now that the dancing was only for dancing's sake, and not as we'd always pretended, for public performance and glory.

But Lisa never spoke another word to me.

A few days after the disco there was a knock at our front door. It was about three in the afternoon and my father had gone out to the shops, planning to stop and exchange his books at the library on his way back. I was upstairs in my room when I heard the door, and I almost didn't go to answer it – it was probably someone collecting for charity, because people didn't usually drop in on us, at least not since mum died. But I stirred myself and went downstairs to the front hall to get the door, and when I opened it there was Karl Bevan, with his cigarette and his dark hair and his earring, standing scowling on the step. He came in and we stood around in our sitting-room for a while, not saying much. I was anxious that my father would get back – not that he would have objected to finding a boy in the house, but the thought of having to introduce them to each other made me cringe – and so I suggested that we walk down to the seafront.

Once again we found ourselves at the pleasure gardens,

and once again we fell in step and made for the wooden bridge, hidden in the tops of the trees high above the sea. Once again Karl Bevan kissed me, as intently as he had before; mirthlessly, as if it was important. He was always wholly serious. That day and other days we kissed there on the bridge, and later on we did other things besides, and in other places. But I didn't talk about Karl Bevan to anyone any more, not to Fiona nor even to Kathryn. It seemed to me that knowing things about other people didn't necessarily bring you closer to them; that it was even possible to know too much about another person. The things that you knew could build up and become like an invisible wall between you. I guessed that this was the reason that Lisa was unable even to acknowledge me any more, because of what I had seen and heard, that evening at her house. And I thought that perhaps it was the same with my father and me; that we couldn't comfort each other, not because we didn't understand how the other of us was feeling, but because we understood too well.

It was only when I was alone with Karl Bevan that I sometimes did what I was not able to do with another living soul: I cried about my mother, and about everything I felt I'd lost, and about going away. Whatever we told each other, it didn't seem to make any difference to the things we did when we kissed, and after. He didn't say much when I cried, but he let me cling on to his neck, and he didn't flinch when I sobbed directly into his ear. He let me blow my nose on his shirt. Once, not long before my father and I were due to move, after Karl had been exploring my body – and I his – all of one Sunday afternoon, tears began to drip down my cheeks and across my nose, and then I couldn't stop; I felt as though I would never be able to stop, and I heard myself crying: 'I want to go home.'

But the words sounded wrong, as though they were only an emblem of a feeling, and not a way to express the feeling itself. As if that phrase represented me, but only in the way that a flag represents a country – by instantly identifying a place, yet not revealing anything about its real character. And anyway we were already at my house, so I surely could not have meant to say that. It was as if the words were someone else's.

Greengages

I was stolen, when I was a baby. It used to be called baby-snatched. It wasn't in an empty street; it was broad daylight and I got taken away almost from under my mother's nose. I was nearly a month old when it happened, still a newborn. I couldn't even smile. It's the kind of story you read in the papers, the kind of story which makes the world seem disordered, fragile. It makes you feel that nothing is safe; that there is no hope, even for innocence. Perhaps especially not for innocence. But it's something you can't imagine happening to yourself. Even I can't imagine it very easily.

People always envisage it from the mother's point of view. I tend to picture my mother, not as she is now and probably not as she ever was, but as a sort of *Ideal Home* woman of the 1940s, with a neat perm full of kirby-grips, and a flowery frock and a kitchen of powder-blue formica. In actual fact our kitchen had red counter-tops, and I was born in 1958. Nevertheless, the picture I have formed of my father and her – placid but inconsolable – is one of them drinking tea out of the best porcelain cups, sitting up very straight, talking in low voices; as if their good, polite behaviour would some-how, of itself, bring their baby daughter back to them. As though manners would be enough to restore the *status quo*.

I see them sitting in a parlour, listening gravely to the wireless, like people in an old war film.

Of course I think about it all the more, now that I'm expecting myself. I try to imagine what she felt as she came out on to the pavement and found me gone. The panic, the wild grief and fear; people beginning to stare as she ran up and down in front of the shops.

She wheeled me into the town every afternoon in my big navy-blue pram. It was a long time ago. Everybody left their babies outside on the pavement in their prams while they shopped, then. Anyway, she told me, shop doorways were too narrow to allow prams through. She had no qualms about leaving the pram outside. Everybody did it. She had already been to the butchers. She'd been to get some postage stamps too. It was to be her last call, the greengrocer. She bought beetroot and carrots and then, on a whim, a pound of plums.

The plums weren't on her list. Perhaps it was during the time it took her to decide on those plums that I was stolen. Perhaps, if she had not bought the plums, it would never have happened. Because, when I think of it, I imagine that the abduction could only have taken place at the precise moment, and in the exact circumstances, in which it did actually occur. Sometimes I go over the sequence and see whether things could have been rearranged, edited, so that it wouldn't have happened. So that my mother would have been emerging from the greengrocer without her bag of plums, just in time to prevent the thief – my thief – from placing her hands on the chrome handle of the baby carriage. So that the woman would not have had the time to walk away with me. She'd only have had time to look at me with longing, before my mother claimed me. I play it over and over in my mind, like a home movie. Like a happy memory.

'When I came out, the baby had gone.' That is what my mother told me. From the first time she spoke to me about it I noticed that she called me 'the baby'; and every time it was referred to thereafter I was always referred to in the same way. I was never 'you'. It was always as if she were describing it to someone else. She never allowed me the sense that the child was me. Do you know what I said to Derek? I told him that I feel she excluded me from it altogether in her mind, as if it were a drama which had happened only to her. Even from this she managed to make me feel left out. It's as if it didn't happen to me at all.

★

I wish now that I had never told her about what happened when she was a baby. I can't see that it's done her any good to know, and I wasn't following my own instincts when I did tell her: I only did it because Paul said I ought. Everyone says too much today. They think they're being honest with each other, uninhibited. People don't spare each other any details, now, of what they're up to, or what they're feeling inside. They even say the bad things: 'I'm in love with another woman,' or 'I've always hated the way you only dab at the corners of your mouth when you use a serviette.' Even personal things like that. As if anyone can really change the little habits of a lifetime. As if it does any good to anyone to be criticised all the time, let alone to make such remarks; as if that's honesty in a worthwhile way. No one's any happier for all this confession – look at the divorce rate, look at the empty churches; and the crime. Everything's uniform now: the same stores in every high street, selling identical goods. You get the same egg sandwich in Edinburgh as in Bourne-mouth, no difference at all. And all the cars look the same, all the television programmes the same. And this telling of everything – that makes people all the same as well. Because there's nothing individual about being irritated by the way another person holds their cutlery, or sits with their legs too far apart. Everybody's shortcomings are the same, and everyone's annoyances are the same too, and sharing them around doesn't alter that. It's the good things about a person, and the secret things, which make them what they are. What makes people unique is what they don't tell. That's where people cannot be the same as each other, in their reserve, in their silence. In their secret hearts.

She'll never know the half of it, even though I've told her some of the details. She knows that she was taken, and for how long. But she'll never know what I went through, because she only thinks about it from her own point of view. It suits me that she doesn't think to wonder more, because if she did she might get to asking questions, questions that are better left unasked, and unanswered too.

To her, being taken is more significant than being born. Everybody is born, that's how she sees it, but hardly anybody gets snatched away from their mother like that. It makes her special to herself, as if she was chosen in some way – well, of course, she was chosen. It's almost like a fairy story. It's the most special thing that's ever happened in her life. The most unusual thing she's ever done. But the problem is that she can't remember anything about it. Sometimes I think that she's jealous of me, because I can remember. That's why I wish I'd never told her, because it gives her an excuse to feel aggrieved towards me and that doesn't do her any good, not at her age. It's one thing when they're in their teens, you expect it, but she's in her thirties now – forty, nearly – old enough to have a family of her own. Getting on for too old. She shouldn't still be harking back to when she was a child all the time; she should be living her own life, now, in the present. You can't turn back the clock.

She's always been like it, though. When I stop to think, I must admit that she was always looking for a peg to hang her grievances on, and learning about the abduction gave her that. She thinks it explains things. As if she's had a hard life, when she's had everything going for her: she's got brains as well as looks. She's the first person to've gone to university, on either side of the family. Paul and I were never strict with her, probably because of her being an only child. And because we both felt – although neither of us ever said so – as if we had to make it up to her; make up for the time when she was taken away from us. I'm sure he felt that, too.

She had a lot of love when she was growing up. We tried to let her have her own way about things. She and Paul were ever so close. It's not that I didn't love her as well, I did. I love her because she's my own girl, and I'd defend her to the death – of course I would – if any harm was threatened. But when we're alone together, she and I, we're not easy company for each other. We don't have a lot in common. I sense she's always on the verge of asking for something, something I'm not in a position to be able to give her. She's so wrapped up in herself, it's as if she's a bucket with a leak – however much you put into her, she's never full. I get exasperated by that, although I'd never show it. I keep my own counsel. Always have. I believe that you can love a person without necessarily liking them very much. Perhaps that is what I feel about Vicki. I don't often reflect on these things, not any more. I try to keep busy, keep myself occupied, now that Paul has gone. But if I search my heart, I'd have to admit that I'm not sure I do like my daughter very much. And when I stop to really think about it, that's what I felt about her father as well.

★

People always imagine we must be very close, what with me being an only child. If you're an only child people seem to imagine that the love you get from your parents is more concentrated than in big families. As if there was only so much emotion allocated to each household, and it could be diluted, thinned, by large numbers of people. When people ask me if I have brothers and sisters and I tell them no, I'm an only child, they always brighten and say: 'Your mum must have spoiled you, then.' They always say that. As if I was lucky.

It's true, in a way. She did spoil me. I was the first in my class at school to own a bicycle; the youngest to have a pet rabbit and the only one who owned a pair of roller skates. Nobody else had even heard of roller skates then. My dad got his sister in Canada to send them, specially. But I never really got the knack of roller skating: it required a totally smooth surface, or the little front wheels snagged the ground and you'd topple over. All the pavements looked flat, if you were only walking along them in ordinary shoes. It wasn't until you tried to negotiate them in roller skates that you realised how pitted they actually were. And I had a doll with growing hair – you could turn a key in her back and it would loop out of the centre of her head. When you turned the key the other way the hair shrank back into her tiny skull. But I wasn't unhappy as a child. I wasn't aware of being lonely.

They say people who snatch babies are unfulfilled, meno-pausal women who have no children of their own. As nature's time bomb ticks on, and they reach an age where childbearing is no longer a biological possibility, they start to roam the streets, searching in their misery for an unattended child to pluck. Like shoplifters, only worse. The general idea is not that these are wicked people, but that they are pathetic. They are to be pitied, not despised. That's how most people perceive them, I think.

In our house, the woman who took me was so hated – so feared, too, I suppose – that her name could not be spoken aloud. She was not menopausal; she was not childless either. Or not exactly. She was a girl of nineteen who had had an illegitimate baby the year before; her child had been given up for adoption soon after the birth. Her parents had apparently persuaded her to have the baby adopted, but they threw her out of the house, anyway, after it was born. She was living in a bedsit on the far side of town, beyond the railway station. She worked in the bed linen department at Bobby's. She didn't have a boyfriend, not any more.

All of this we know. It would have been difficult not to know about her: she only lived a couple of miles away from our house, even afterwards. She has never moved away from this area. The police told my mother her name, and a little about her; the rest came from the local grapevine. The story never got into the newspapers. Things were different then, in a smallish seaside town. People knew each other, they spoke to each other. People noticed things going on. The idea of reporters camping on people's doorsteps would have seemed as improbable as men walking on the moon. Newspapers then were about the people who mattered: politicians, sportsmen. Not ordinary people like us.

I've never seen her. I know that she got married eventually, and had a family – two or three children – and stopped working at Bobby's. But she still lives here, and it wouldn't be difficult to find her. Sometimes I have wondered what it would be like to meet her. Quite often. I've imagined what it would be like to walk up the path to her front door, and ring the bell, and hear the chime shrilling into the house. How my heart would be racing as her figure blurred behind the frosted glass panels. What it would be like when the door opened. But I can't really picture beyond that point. Would we introduce ourselves, or would she know who I was, instinctively? Would I know that it was her? I wonder whether we would like each other, whether she would be glad to see me again. Whether, in the end, I would have been glad to see her.

My mother doesn't know this, but I have told Derek: I don't hate my kidnapper. I feel close to her. She didn't mean me any harm – she didn't do me any harm, at least not consciously. The doctor checked me over when my mother got me back, and he said I'd been looked after beautifully. And I smiled a lot. When she took me I was too young to smile, but by the time my mother got me back I'd learned how. My mother always includes this detail in her account, just like she always includes the plums. As if accuracy will make amends, as if she's trying to prove what an observant, careful person she is – not the sort of person who'd be absent-minded or scatty; not the sort of person whose fault it would be if their baby was snatched. And her voice always catches when she says: 'The baby was so young – not even smiling.' She never actually breaks down, there's never a tear. But her voice gets a notch higher, snags, at the same point every time.

I get embarrassed, then. Actually I feel more annoyed than embarrassed, but it's the getting irritated which embarrasses me. I wouldn't want her to know that it makes me angry when she goes on about me smiling. It must sound harsh, I know. But I see it differently to her. To me, the fact that I smiled a lot when she got me back is a cause for celebration, of a kind. At least it shows that I must have been well treated, while I was away. I must even have been quite happy.

Come to think of it, perhaps that's exactly why it almost makes my mother cry.

★

She's been around here again today, going on to me about it all. I can't tell her any more than she knows already, and even that's more than she should know. I wish Paul was here. It upsets me. After she's been round I can't settle, can't get on with anything. So much goes round and round in my head when she's gone; all the things which she never thinks to ask, all the things which never seem to occur to her. All my old feelings come back.

I don't know why she keeps on about her childhood so much lately. Maybe it's because of this Derek encouraging her; or maybe it's because, now that Paul's gone, she's realised I won't be here for ever to ask. The funny thing is she's only interested in it from her own point of view. She never wants to know how I coped, or what Paul went through. She asks what I did when I came out of the greengrocer and found her gone. And I tell her that. But she's never stopped to wonder what happened afterwards, what happened when I got home. How I had to break the news to Paul, how I had to face the sympathy of the neighbours; how I had to carry on with the little things, peeling the potatoes for our tea, knowing that neither of us would have the stomach to eat it. How I hated Paul, even knowing it was unreasonable of me, when he did eat. How I felt as if even God had deserted me. She asks about when we got her back. But the time when she was actually missing – that's the bit she doesn't want to know about. I suppose she isn't interested in that part, because she isn't in it herself.

I've never lost the shame. Because that's what I felt when my baby was taken: ashamed. I thought it was my fault, that I was being punished for the wrong I'd done. And I knew that I deserved to be.

But it wasn't only the worry and the shame and the fear – there was the physical side to it as well. I was feeding the baby myself. To this day, if I hear on the news that a baby's been abducted, I still get a pricking sensation in my breasts. When I see those poor mothers on the television – thank heavens it isn't often – I know what they're going through in their bodies, not just in their hearts. People tend not to think of that side of the tragedy, but to me it was the very worst part of it, the thing that upset me most. It was that my breasts carried on producing milk to feed a baby I didn't have. My breasts became more and more swollen and sore, so that I couldn't rest at night – I doubt that I'd have been able to sleep, anyway, with the worry. But with such full breasts I couldn't even lie still; it was like having enormous chilblains all over my chest. And my nightclothes became drenched with milk, warm at first, then cooling on the cotton of my nightie. I had to keep changing my things. I didn't know what to do. The next day the doctor came out and told me to bind my chest as tight as I could, and not to drink too many fluids. He said that would stop the milk. But I didn't want to stop it. I thought I'd need the milk for when the baby was back with me. She was my first baby – I didn't know I'd not have any more children – and it meant a lot to me to be feeding her myself.

It went on for days. The milk made dark patches on my blouses as it seeped out, and I felt it running down my side. When I was in the bath it seemed to get worse; whether from the warmth, or the pressure of the water. The bath water would turn all cloudy around me and my breasts would throb and hurt. All the veins in them were raised and they were hard, like upturned pudding basins. In the bath I'd squeeze them ever so gently, to try and take away the pain; but that made more milk come, and I'd sit there and cry and cry. It felt as if my leaking breasts were crying too. Weeping tears of blue-white milk for my lost baby.

This may sound barmy, but I used to listen out for the milk float, coming down our street at four o'clock in the morning – I'd think about milk then, and where it came from. The clink of the glass bottles on the brick step comforted me, made me feel less alone. I used to lie awake and think about the cows which had produced that milk, that got delivered in the half-dark. My father had grown up on a dairy farm, and I remembered him talking about it all: how the bull came from a neighbouring farm to impregnate the heifers; how, later, the little calves were removed from their mother's side. The calves got fed with some sort of powdered milk, so that the cows' milk could be kept for the dairy. And when the calves were taken away, the cows bellowed and bellowed for their young. Sometimes they went on for days on end. They never learned that it didn't make any difference; it never worked. The calves were never given back to them. After a few days they'd grow quiet again.

My baby couldn't even smile when she was taken. That's how little she was. Someone who hadn't had a child of their own couldn't guess what it meant to me to have missed her first smiles; to have had them stolen from me. I hated that woman for that. I hated her more for stealing her smile than I did for taking Vicki in the first place. But the fact that the baby had smiled for her, it meant that they'd got along fine together; it meant that the baby hadn't needed me in order to show that she was happy. To be happy. It was as if they had shared their own little jokes together, their own secrets; and the thought of that made me feel sick. Of course a tiny child like her doesn't know anything about betrayal; they don't care who looks after them, so long as they're fed and cuddled and dry. But it was as if the baby had betrayed me – there she was, smiling and cooing, all for her. Everybody else was thrilled about it, when we got her back. As though the fact that she smiled meant no damage had been done to her. But the damage was done to me.

★

I wish my dad was still alive. I could have told him about the baby; I know he would have been happy for us. It's harder with my mother. It's not that she's a dishonest person, but she is what you might call economical when it comes to disclosing things. She's cagey, and I suppose that's why I tend to go the other way – it's a reaction against her. Not that I tell everyone everything, of course, but with the people I'm closest to I don't like to have any secrets. Derek thinks it's a generational thing. He reckons that people of my mother's age were raised during wartime, when there was propaganda against gossip – careless talk costs lives, all that. The telephone only being used for emergencies. They didn't just sit around and talk, like we do now.

I can't face her nagging me about not being married, not that she would nag, that's not her style. She'd just act reproachful. But Derek and I aren't ready for that step right now, and I'm not going to be pushed into it just to please her. Her value system is pretty antiquated – she's very fastidious, too. She's a very neat person, very modest physically. I can't ever remember seeing her naked, when I was growing up.

That's what I'm getting to. I still have my key to the house, even though I moved out years ago. But when I go round to see them – her, now – I always use my key. So the other day I went over to pick up some of my old books from college; it was about seven in the evening and I let myself in as usual, without even thinking about it. My mother would normally be watching TV around that time. Anyway, I called out hello as I went in, and I heard the noise of the television, so I assumed she was in the lounge. I didn't go straight in to see her, because I wanted to spend a penny. So I went straight up the stairs to the bathroom. And just as I got to the landing, she came out of the bathroom herself. And she had nothing on.

She'd been having a bath. I don't know why she'd left the TV on if she wasn't watching it; maybe for the sound of voices, for a bit of company. I don't know if she feels lonely since dad died, it's not the sort of thing she'd talk about. Too personal. But the thing was, seeing her without her clothes on gave me – not a shock exactly – a fright. My mother is in her early sixties, but I suppose she looks a fair bit younger, even dressed. Her hair is dark, still, and she wears it short; she's quite dark-skinned, so she tends to look healthy all the year round. She's always walked a lot. She goes on walking holidays – to the Lakes, or Wales – she used to go alone, even before dad died. But it had never occurred to me before that she was attractive.

Seeing her there, naked, she suddenly looked completely different to me; almost as if she were a different person. She was quite unfamiliar, and she was beautiful. It isn't that her figure is good, because her breasts aren't firm and her hips are too broad. So it isn't that she truly is lovely. But she looked lovely, then, to me. Seeing her like that gave me a sharp sense of her as a woman, unconnected to me; somebody who'd grown up and married and had a child; somebody who'd suffered and been widowed and now lives alone. I don't think I'd ever seen her in this light before, as someone so other from myself. As a separate person, who could be vulnerable, imperfect, human. As an individual.

It can only have lasted a couple of seconds, this encounter on the landing. Neither of us had time to say anything. My mother isn't the sort of woman who blushes readily, but I could tell that she felt awkward about my seeing her like that. She went quickly into the bedroom, and I brushed past her, into the bathroom. While I was in there – it was still fugged up from the steam of her bath, and her towel was folded on the rail – I felt nervous, suddenly. I had the same sensation I'd had as a child, when I knew I had to confess to something – breaking a piece of crockery, or getting into trouble at school. It was as if the time had come for me to own up.

I stayed in the bathroom longer than I needed to, unready to face my mother again until I'd made up my mind what to do next. I felt confused. That glimpse of her nakedness had made her seem like just any other woman, not so different from me; but it wasn't like the sense of equality – the liberating sense that communal nakedness brings – you might get in the changing room at the swimming baths, because I was still clothed. She was the one who was exposed, and that created a moment of imbalance which I found very unsettling. Seeing her without any clothes on had made me aware of the love I have for her, and how seldom I've expressed it to her openly. I'd never felt protective of her before, not even at dad's funeral. She's always been in control, guarded; a bit unapproachable. I had the strongest sense, there in the bathroom, that this was my chance to redress the distance between us; that I should seize this moment, now, to get closer to her. Open up to her, tell her about my pregnancy and how much I miss dad. I felt I might never have the opportunity to be intimate with her again.

But I couldn't do it. I came out of the bathroom and went downstairs and mum appeared and offered me a cup of coffee – she always drinks coffee in the evening and tea during the day – and I knew I wouldn't be able to say anything after all. I just couldn't. The gulf which seemed to have closed when I saw her naked on the landing suddenly seemed wider than ever, once we were back to normal, downstairs with our cups on our laps and the TV covering up our silences. The moment had passed.

★

There are things I know that will die with me, things no other living soul has any idea of. Some big, some small. Some are a burden to me, but some are a kind of solace.

When I came out of the greengrocer and saw that the baby had gone, my first thought was that her father had taken her. I was calm because I didn't think anything could come of it; I knew where she'd be, so I could simply go and fetch her back. Paul was not her father. She doesn't know, of course: it would break her heart; and if Paul ever guessed – I sometimes wondered if he did suspect – he never raised the subject. Anyway he was devoted to Vicki, they were ever so close. And he wasn't one to rock the boat, Paul.

I was engaged to her real father when I met Paul, and it was Paul who picked up the pieces when the engagement was broken off. He was a good, kind man. Steady. We married less than a year later – I didn't really stop to think what I was doing – on the rebound, I suppose. I'd not long been married when I met up with him again, and we started seeing each other regularly after that. More than seeing each other. I think he liked me better the second time around, when I was safely married to someone else – he liked the element of wickedness. So did I. When he found out that I was expecting he begged me to leave Paul, but I'd already been so hurt by him before, I didn't feel I could trust him again. I didn't think he'd stick by me. And Paul had never shown me anything but kindness – he didn't deserve to be discarded, like an old suitcase. So I told Vicki's real father that I could not see him any more. He knew I'd never tell a soul about the baby, and I never have.

I gave him up. I hadn't seen him at all during the time I was expecting, but when the baby went missing I still felt sure it was him. I ran up and down the pavement in front of the shops, thinking I might catch him up. I didn't even think to search for anyone else with a baby. I didn't ring the police. I just went to the bus stop and waited for a bus to take me up to his place so I could go and get her back. Of course I did feel anxious, apprehensive. But the truth was that I felt excited, too, in a not unpleasant way. Him taking her proved that he must have still had strong feelings for me. And it gave me an excuse to see him again. To this day I am ashamed to have thought of that.

He was at home; he answered the door. He said the baby wasn't there. At first I thought he was having me on; that he had taken her, not in order to get me back, but to keep her for himself. I started to cry, telling him to let me in, give me back my baby. I began screaming and scratching at his face with my hands. He took me inside, into the living-room. He kept saying: 'She's not here. She's not here.'

I was starting to panic, then. I couldn't think of another reason that she'd have been taken; I couldn't imagine that anyone other than him would have a reason to take her. There didn't seem to be any alternative: it didn't make sense. But he told me I must calm down and ring the police.

'She's not here,' he said, holding my arms and looking at me. Then I believed him.

Even in that distress I felt I shouldn't make the call from his place; the police would have asked me where I was phoning from and of course I couldn't give his address, or Paul would find out I'd been there first, instead of coming straight home. I thought the police would have traced the call. I had to telephone from home. So he drove me to the end of our street. I didn't say goodbye to him, I've always remembered that. I hated him at that moment, as I got out of his car and walked up the road. So then I let myself into our house, weeping, and I made the telephone call. I thought it'd be only a matter of a few hours before they brought her back. I never thought she might die, or be harmed at all; I always knew she was all right, safe, I don't know how. When I've seen other mothers whose children have been abducted, when that happens and they're interviewed on television, I can always tell the ones who know their baby's safe. They tend to be hysterical, crying; whereas the ones who guess it's already too late seem wrung out, spent. And they sound flat, as if having no hope had somehow removed all the intonation from their voices.

By the evening I had begun to feel angry with the police for being so slow. What was keeping them, anyhow? I was still convinced that I'd have her back the same night. In the end it was nearly five weeks before they found her. They'd gone through all the local hospital records to search for women who had babies that had died, and they'd found one who had moved up north the year before, shortly after her son was stillborn. She still had relatives around here that she visited from time to time. They weren't able to trace her immediately, but they were convinced she was the woman responsible. When they did find her, she was living up near Leeds somewhere, but she didn't have Vicki. The police never looked into the whereabouts of the girl who really did have my baby. Her baby had been born healthy and the adoption was arranged privately – through their church apparently – so the hospital had no record of the baby having been separated from the mother. No one had any reason to suspect her of anything. We heard later that her parents weren't speaking to her, so they couldn't have known she was harbouring a newborn. She'd phoned into work saying she was sick, but she was off for such a long time that the manager of the department worried and went round to see her; check she was all right. When she saw the baby with her she knew, or anyway she guessed, that something wasn't right. She notified the police. Apparently the girl didn't put up a fight when the officers came; she just cried.

So then they brought the baby back. I knew she'd be unharmed, but I hadn't been prepared for the difference in her – how much she'd grown, and how she smiled, and how she smelled. I threw away the clothes they brought her back in and I took her into my bath with me, that evening, so she'd smell like home again. But it was difficult to get back into a routine with her – I'd lost the thread of it all. I didn't know what her habits were – babies change so quickly – and she didn't seem to sleep as much as she had before. Which was natural, really, because she wasn't so tiny any more. And I had to get used to making up bottles of milk for her.

It was months before I slept well again, a long time after she was sleeping through the night herself. I used to get up from my bed at all hours and go into her room and just stand at the end of her cot and look at her. Listen to her breathe. Sometimes I'd bend over and sniff the top of her head. And when I was washing her little things, while she had her afternoon rest, I'd often lift them up to my nose before submerging them in the soapy water. I didn't do it deliberately; it was as if I had to, like needing to drink when you're thirsty. I'd lift her cardigans and gowns up to my face and inhale as deeply as I could. And sometimes the baby's smell on the clothes – sweet and dry, like the smell of Rich Tea biscuits – would make me weep; and I'd stand at the wash-basin then with no one to hear me and cry out loud with the sorrow of the time I'd lost with her, and the relief of having her back.

★

Sometimes I wonder whether we could have been closer, if it hadn't been for the abduction. I do wonder that, but knowing my mother's temperament I don't really think so. I suppose I take after my dad more than I do her. It's not that she's not kind. But if the world was divided into people who are like dogs – spontaneous, untidy, loving – and those who resemble cats – aloof, self-contained, scrupulous – then she'd be in the cat category. Derek and I have even thought of getting her a cat, now that dad's gone, but when I stopped to think about it I realised that she's too feline herself to want the dependence of a pet. She's too like a cat to want a cat.

It's hard to imagine her when she was young. When I got over the minutes leading to my abduction my picture of her is always vague, even though all the other details seem so vivid. I can almost see the polished chrome of the pram's handle, the autumn sun on the pavements. The brown-paper bags hanging from a circle of string on a hook above the greengrocer's scales. How the shopkeeper would have pulled a bag down and tipped my mother's plums into it from the shiny metal basin of the scales; then twirled the bag over once, twice, with a small but practised flourish, so that its corners would form little twists like squirrels' ears. The exchange of coppers, the smiles and thank-yous. And all the while, me being taken away.

Once I saw a cashier at the bank wearing a name badge with her surname on it. The name of the woman who took me, I mean. For a moment I thought it was her – it was several minutes before I realised that it couldn't be, that the bank clerk was much too young; and anyway the woman was married now and had a different name. But for those instants I did believe that I was coming face to face with her, at last. I felt almost excited at the idea of our meeting. I do feel a bond with her, I can't help it. After all, she really wanted me: she chose me, she picked me out. She taught me to smile.

★

There are other things I've never spoken of. How her real father used to telephone, sometimes, to ask after us. How disappointed I was – relieved, too – when his calls stopped. How it was as though I lost something when the baby was taken, something of myself, and never got it back. My gaiety and optimism. Every life has its secrets, every marriage too. You need to hang on to some things, when you live in a family; otherwise you have no privacy. And I can't bring myself to mention the greengages.

Whenever we talk about the abduction, I always tell Vicki that I was in the greengrocer when it happened; that I went in to buy carrots and beetroot – Paul was very partial to beetroot – for tea, and that while I was in there I also bought some plums, on a whim. It isn't untrue. It really did happen like that, as I've told her. Only they weren't plums, or at least not plums proper. They were greengages.

I don't know why I didn't tell her this from the start. Maybe I thought it would have sounded as if I was thinking only of myself, and what I fancied to eat, instead of remembering the baby outside in her pram. Greengages seem sillier, more frivolous, than normal plums. I'm not usually a self-indulgent type of person. So I half had it in mind that perhaps she would have blamed me if she'd known about the greengages; she might have thought I was being spoilt, or greedy. Then there's the fact that telling her about the abduction wasn't my idea in the first place, but Paul's. I didn't want

76

her to hear about it, I thought it would only upset her. I didn't see the point in raking over the ashes of it, especially since she never could be told the whole story. So maybe that's why I held my tongue about the fruit.

Or it could be that I wanted to keep something back, to keep something just for myself. It would be foolish to put her right about it now, when she's got the idea of the plums stuck in her head. I couldn't tell her now. Anyway, you hardly ever see greengages any more – she might not even know what they are. They are smaller than the usual plums, more the size of biggish damsons, and they feel, I don't know, tighter, more dense than other fruit. But the main thing, of course, is that they have a lovely flavour; they're sweeter than a Victoria plum, but just a little less juicy. And they're not plum-coloured. They're green, and it's a very cool, pure sort of green; the kind of new-looking colour that you expect to see at the beginning of spring rather than the end of summer. They're the kind of colour that reminds you of clear, thin sunlight and cool rain and young ferns; of waking up in the countryside when you were young, opening the window and leaning out to breathe the fresh inviting smell of the earth as the first light fell across it; when it was still very early in the morning and you could be all alone, before anyone else was yet awake.

Granville Hill

My father came into my room after the lights were out and knelt on the floor by the side of the bed. I should have been asleep – it was quite a while since bedtime – but I wasn't. I was lying there, thinking about things: thinking about school and my friends; trying not to think about what was going on at home. When my dad came in I sensed him rather than saw him, because I preferred to lie with my face towards the wall. I'd got some pictures, there, that I'd put up with Sellotape, pictures of things I liked: guinea pigs and ponies and a girl in a ballet dress. My mum used to tell me not to use Sellotape because it was bad for the wallpaper, but lately she'd forgotten about stuff like that. Little things. She didn't even tell me off when I left my school uniform on the floor, or when my library book was overdue and she had to pay a fine on it. She didn't seem to notice so much. But then she'd get angry about something really tiny, like if there were empty crisp packets in my satchel that I hadn't thrown away, or if I left the plug in, after my bath. Then she'd really get sharp with me, as if I'd done something terrible. But she never told Caitlin off any more.

My dad didn't usually come into our rooms, except to wake us up in the mornings. It was mum who tucked us in at night and switched the lights off and made sure we'd brushed our teeth. So I knew he wanted something; I could just tell from the sound of his breathing by the back of my head. He was so close to me that I was frightened he'd be able to hear my heart beating; it wasn't that I was scared of him, but I was apprehensive about what he might expect from me. When he said my name I thought of pretending to be asleep. But I didn't. I was nine years old, I was tired, I was used to doing as I was asked.

It was about Caitlin, of course. Everything was about Caitlin. Dad said there was something else that could be tried, something which could maybe make her better, if I would help.

'You do want to do that, don't you, Jen? You do want to help your sister?'

'Yes, Dad,' I said. I was ready for sleep. I didn't know what I was saying yes to, but in any case I would have done almost anything, then, to have made the problem which my sister had turned into go away. To get our family back to normal. I didn't want her to die, but quite often I wished that she could just disappear, so that it would stop. I wanted – more than I have ever wanted anything since – for Caitlin's illness to be over. I can't imagine that I will ever want anything so much again.

There's a hierarchy, when someone's ill; a tiered system and my parents had exclusive occupancy of the high ground. They prayed and wished for Caitlin's recovery with such unalloyed zeal, such single-mindedness, that there was no room for anyone else on the platform. Everyone who came to the house deferred to their suffering and hope: it was their little girl who was poorly, their baby who might die. Their tragedy in the making. In the eyes of the world there is no fate more awful than to lose a child. No one thought of

Caitlin's illness as something that was happening to me, too. People saw me – the older daughter – and thought I was the lucky one, the one who'd got away. Illness had cursed us like the bad fairy at the christening, and Caitlin was the child who'd pricked her finger on the spindle. She was the sleeping beauty, the sick princess.

I was too young, then, to question what words meant. But now, looking back, I understand the expression 'rude health'. In that house my vigour, the pinkness in my cheeks, became an insult to my sister's pallor and bouts of weakness. There was nothing wrong with me; I had no cause for complaint. I should be thankful and try to help my mummy and daddy – that's what my grandmother told me. I didn't feel thankful, though. I felt frightened and jealous, and ashamed. Sometimes I hated my sister with her new funny smell – musty and yet sweet, like an old lady's powder compact – and her chalky skin and everyone fussing around her all the time. I was scared when I heard her sometimes in the night, vomiting and crying while mum tried to comfort her. And most of all I was afraid that I would wake up one morning and she wouldn't be there any more; that I'd go into her room and her bed would be empty: there'd just be sunlight and no Caitlin, and I wouldn't have had the chance to say goodbye.

It all seemed to have been going on for so long that sometimes I could hardly remember what it had been like before she became ill. She had just turned eight – there had been piles of presents and smiling visitors, but I saw my mum's hands shaking as she struggled to fit the miniature candles into their plastic flower-shaped holders, then embed their tiny stiletto heels into the earthy chocolate surface of the birthday cake. Caitlin had barely been six when it started. She was born only fourteen months after me, although people often took me for much older because I was tall for my age. We didn't look very alike, despite being so close together. I was always envious of her: she was the pretty one. People made a fuss of her, even before she got sick, because she was little and she looked so sweet.

I was always clumsy, but Caitlin was dainty and her gestures were neat. She had a lovely straight back – everyone admired her good posture – while I was a slouch. But she wasn't as perfect as she looked. That's what I loved best about her, her naughtiness. She was much less obedient than me; she did things we were never supposed to do, like lighting matches and letting our pet rabbit run loose around the sitting-room – leaving tell-tale droppings on the best rug – when mum wasn't looking. She raided the biscuit tin when it was nearly lunchtime. She went into mum's jewellery box without asking and took her pearl necklace for dressing up. She was always dressing up: as a circus lady or a vet or an orphan. Playing orphans was her favourite game. 'Pretend we haven't got any mummy or daddy,' she'd whisper fervently, up in her room. 'Pretend we live in this house all alone with no one to take care of us and nobody knows we are here and we have to make our own food and put ourselves to bed when it gets dark, all by our own.' We would shiver with the delicious fear of it, the vertigo of our independence.

The game evolved. Sometimes we were orphans out of history, who wore long ragged dresses – old evening gowns which had belonged to dad's mother, the one mum called our grand granny, whose own father had been a Member of Parliament – and lived in a gloomy abandoned castle. Sometimes we were circus orphans, with an entire menagerie of lions and ponies and dancing poodles in our care. Caitlin loved this version, but it was quite joyless: the responsibility of the animals weighed heavily upon us. There was a lot of illicit fetching and carrying of breakfast cereal up the stairs to the big top, and we heaved great bowls of slopping water from the kitchen; it never occurred to us that we could more easily have filled the pudding basins from the bathroom, just along the landing. The animals required constant feeding and attention. I preferred the freedom of playing gypsy orphans, when we would take over the covered concrete area behind the garage – the site of the washing line – and perform wild ritual dances. Sometimes we smeared earth from the flower beds on to our faces. Very occasionally, when we were sure the coast was clear, Caitlin lit a fire in a flowerpot and we'd pretend we were cooking hedgehogs for our supper.

She was braver than me. I was frightened of nearly everything – ghosts and witches, the dark, Captain Hook – but she was fearless. She didn't even have to cover her eyes, in the cinema, when the horrible stepmother in *Snow White* came to the seven dwarfs' cottage, disguised as an old woman. If it had been the other way round, if I had been the one who got sick, I would have been terrified. As it was I dreaded visiting her during her stays in hospital – the smell in the shiny linoleum corridors made me feel sick with fear, and I was afraid of the doctors and nurses, even though they appeared so smiley. To me their medicine seemed like Snow White's rosy red apple: they were pretending to cure Caitlin, but really they were poisoning her. I could tell. That was why her gums bled when she brushed her teeth, and her breath smelled toxic, chemical. Her hair fell out in clumps, clogging the wooden hairbrush.

Once my dad was driving me to a piano lesson – it was just the two of us – and I noticed that the back seat of the car was covered in strands of my sister's wispy fair hair. The hairs showed up against the dark upholstery like a giant cobweb. I clambered into the front seat, then. I felt as if I was suffocating. I opened the window as wide as I could and put my head out. My dad asked if I was feeling carsick, but I didn't say anything. I didn't know what to say. I just started crying. Then my dad stopped the car – just pulled over and stopped, not in a lay-by or anything – and asked me what was really wrong and I told him that I knew the hospital were trying to kill Caitlin, but no one seemed to have noticed except me. It was so obvious. Every time she had treatment she got worse, not better. When she first got ill all she had was a temperature which wouldn't go down and some bruises, but now she was nearly bald and she was sick all the time. She couldn't go to school. She wasn't supposed to even see people in case they brought germs. The doctors and nurses were probably trying to make her worse so they could kidnap her; they might be evil people who take children from their families by poisoning them. So then he explained about the treatment, how it worked by killing cells and how it killed some of Caitlin's good cells, too, in the process. Especially the ones with the fastest turnover, like hair follicles and the ones inside the tummy, the ones that made her be sick and lose her hair. But these things didn't mean she was getting worse. They probably meant that she was actually getting better.

I felt a bit safer about the doctors after that. I had long hair, too, though not as long as my sister's had been. I asked my mum to cut it short, so that me and Caitlin wouldn't look so different. Having hair like a boy was good for pretending games, anyway. It meant we weren't always arguing about who was the princess and who was the handsome prince – after my haircut we just took it in turns. In our dressing-up box was a bright yellow plait, made of the same kind of bright, coarse artificial fibre as doll's hair. It was about sixteen inches long and I think it may originally have been the tail of a wooden toy horse. We would tie one of mum's scarves around our heads and then wedge the plait into the back. Sometimes we used it to play Rapunzel, but more often it was the Sleeping Beauty. I liked Sleeping Beauty games because I was interested in kissing. I actually preferred taking the prince's part after my hair was short, although I didn't let on to Caitlin. I liked her to think I was being generous, letting her be the Sleeping Beauty. She would lie still with the plait arranged over her chest, and my heart would beat very fast with excitement as I approached her, ready with my reviving kiss. Then I'd press down really hard with my mouth on hers. Once or twice I even experimented with putting the tip of my tongue between her lips, but it spoilt the game then because Caitlin screeched at the sliminess of it.

I think they must have known before her eighth birthday that she needed more treatment. They must have decided to let her celebrate without the threat of more hospital hanging over her. Because it was only a couple of days later that my dad came into my room to ask whether I'd help Caitlin with a different kind of treatment. But after that it wasn't mentioned again for several days. I kept expecting mum or dad to say something about it, but they didn't. I even started wondering whether his night visit had been a dream of mine, whether I'd made it up.

Then at breakfast one day the following week mum said I didn't need to put my uniform on for school, because I was going to go up to the hospital instead, for tests. It was nothing to be scared of, she said, only a little needle prick to see whether my blood might be the same as Caitlin's. She and dad had already had the same test, and it hadn't hurt them at all. When we got there the nurse was nice to me. After I'd said I would help my sister everyone was nice to me, for quite a while. The nurse gave me a boiled sweet. She let me rummage in the packet until I found a purple one. After that we went home and then when the result came everything started happening quickly: once they'd found out that my blood was like Caitlin's they were in a hurry to give her the treatment. I felt quite proud of the fact that I was the best possible match for her. It meant that I would go into the hospital to stay for a few days, and I would be off school for a whole week, maybe two. And before then they'd take some blood from me to put into Caitlin, afterwards.

When doctors are going to hurt you they say: 'This may feel a bit uncomfortable,' or 'You may experience some discomfort.' They never mention the word pain. Maybe they think it will put the idea of it into people's heads. So they told me that they were going to give me something to make me go to sleep and that, while I was sleeping, they would take some liquid out of me, from my hip. They said I might have a little bit of a sore back for a week or so: nothing to fret about. And after it was finished I'd stay in bed for a couple of days and my mummy would probably bring me some comics and Lucozade if I was a good girl. Then I'd be able to go home.

I didn't like going on the trolley down to the theatre. I wanted to walk down the stairs, but they wouldn't let me. I had to lie on my back and the papery gown they'd put me into didn't feel big enough; I thought the nurses might be able to see my bottom and I didn't want them to. We went in the lift and it seemed to go on for ever, as if I was descending into a cave. Then we were in a little cupboardish place with no windows and lots of bottles on shelves above my head. The anaesthetist was there and he smiled at me and rubbed the back of my hand. I'd seen him before, when he'd come to talk to me in the ward. His lips were the same colour as the rest of his face: his mouth looked like the imprint of a thumbnail in a piece of plasticine. I felt something cold in my hand and he said: 'By the time I count to ten you'll be asleep' and I realised he was a bit creepy, like the Cheshire Cat, and I felt as if I was being pushed under water, held down, and I only heard him get to three before I couldn't remember anything any more.

When I woke up I felt sick. During the next few days I kept feeling woozy and I got a huge bruise on my hip, which looked like a stain from a spilled cup of tea. I had to use a bedpan. Most of the time I felt too tired even to look at a book, and usually I loved reading. Caitlin was in the same hospital, but she was in a different bit and I wasn't allowed to go and see her because she was having her treatment and she wasn't to be subjected to any risk of infection. It felt funny that she was able to have my bone marrow and blood put into her body, but that she wasn't able to actually see me. I would have liked to be with her, then. Now that I knew what hospital was like I didn't feel she was so different from me any more. And now that I was doing something myself towards getting her better, I started to want her to get well again. I let myself hope.

I had to stay off school for three weeks because I felt so tired. My grannies took it in turns to stay with me, at home, while mum went up to the hospital to be with Caitlin. I liked it when my dad's mum was there. She had long thin hands, like a whippet would have had, if dogs had hands. She played card games with me and sometimes we ate tinned peaches for lunch, just by themselves. She wasn't interested in cooking or clearing up, or stuff to do with the house. She liked to listen to classical music on the third programme and she was very interested in horse racing. At her flat she got a special newspaper delivered which was only about horses and she read it most carefully. Looking at this paper was called studying the form and she didn't like to be interrupted then. She had a paper bag full of mint imperials which she kept in her handbag, and while she studied the form she'd produce the mints and let us eat them, as many as we liked. Even so, Caitlin didn't like this granny as much as I did; she preferred our mum's mother.

Although my sister had been ill for two years, there wasn't always something happening. She wasn't forever running a high temperature or having treatment or tests. Sometimes there were weeks on end when things seemed almost ordinary. Almost boring. There were times, lots of times, when I forgot about it altogether – and I think Caitlin did, too – and we'd play just as we always had. I didn't know then that such periods of apparent stability were the worst of times for my parents; how they were always apprehensive, always waiting for the results of the next test, then the one after. How they'd watch for signs of health to return to their daughter's face; how anxious they were if she became over-tired, or feverish. My sister's illness was like the crocodile in *Peter Pan* with a clock ticking loudly inside its belly. All they were waiting for was the day when the doctors could tell them for definite that Caitlin's blood was clear.

I was jealous because she got a bicycle for her birthday. I hadn't got a bicycle, and I was older than her. She didn't even want a bike like I did; she was more one for dressing-up clothes and dolls. The bicycle was dark blue with pale-blue trim and it had a white plastic basket at the front and a white pump for the tyres; its white saddle came encased in a transparent bag, to keep it clean while it had been in the shop. It was so smart. When we took the bag off, the saddle smelled like pear drops. Our road was mostly on the flat and there weren't too many cars. Between her birthday and the start of the treatment, we took it in turns to ride up and down while the other ran alongside. Caitlin had to promise that she wouldn't leave the bike outside, because it would rust if the rain got at it. The bike had adjustable handlebars and saddle height – it was quality, built to last. She was to take care of it and keep it in the garage so she could get years of use from it.

Maybe they really did believe that she had years. In the autumn, after she died, I rode that bike furiously. No one ever said that the bike could be mine; I suppose they had other things on their minds. I went for long rides on it anyway, on my own. I didn't actually like the bike any more. I almost hated it. I liked the way it made me feel, freewheeling, going fast. But I didn't like the metal and chrome of the bike itself, not now. I often left it on its side on our driveway and I didn't care that the mudguards got dented and the paint scratched. No one else seemed to mind either.

There was a hill we weren't allowed to go down, at least not on wheels: Granville Road. We always called it Granville Hill. In cold weather my dad didn't even go that way in the car. It had a red sign at the top which said 1/6. It was so steep that to walk up it made the backs of our calves hurt for days. I took to riding the bike along our road to the top of the hill, then plunging down with my legs stretched out in front of me, my feet above the spinning pedals. The game was to test myself by seeing how far I could go before I put the brakes on. It was deceptive, because the road shelved suddenly just near the bottom – brake too hard and you could easily go right over the handlebars. But if you didn't brake at all you could shoot straight out into Silver Dale Road and under the wheels of a car.

I'd never done anything like that before. Caitlin was the

daring one, the one who could climb trees, the one who'd clamber along the slippery breakwaters as the tide was coming in. I suppose I wanted to be like her. I knew that nothing would happen to me, that I wouldn't come to any harm. God wouldn't let my mum and dad lose both of their children, it wouldn't be fair on them. I could do pretty much whatever I wanted. Anything. So I rode the bike down Granville Hill and sometimes I climbed over the flint wall at the bottom of our garden into the deserted grounds of the Victorian mansion which had belonged to Mrs Prendergast, something I'd always been too scared to do until then. I went all over Mrs Prendergast's forbidden, empty garden: I liked the sadness of the place, the stillness. It was like the Secret Garden. Later it became a close of thirty, almost identical, houses, each with a shiny new car parked outside, like toytown. But then it was still dark with rhododendrons and laurel, and sandy paths edged with brick-flanked occasional beds of stiff hybrid roses. The glass was still intact in the mildewy greenhouses and fading unopened seed packets were stacked on a slatted shelf in the wooden shed, which smelled faintly of tar and paraffin; old-fashioned smells, like in a hardware shop. I hoped that I might see a ghost there, but I never did.

I wasn't supposed to cry. My granny – my mother's mother, it was – said I had to be a good girl and be brave for mummy's sake, and keep my pecker up. She told me that I had a special responsibility, now, to look after my mum. People all seemed to think that Caitlin dying had only happened to my mum. It was her loss first, then dad's. At school in assembly they said a prayer for the family of Caitlin Taylor, but I couldn't join in as if I was just one of her classmates. I hated it when they said her name like that, out loud in front of all the teachers and children. It was like putting a full stop after her. I realised that I couldn't remember a time ever in my life without my sister: she had always been there. Mum and dad had years and years behind them that they could remember, before we girls were born. They had other times they could think about, but I didn't. I didn't realise then that when a child dies, it takes away all the hope for the future. I was still young enough to think we were grieving for the life Caitlin had led, not the life which she would never see.

I couldn't get used to the idea that she was never coming back. She'd spent so much time in and out of hospital over the past couple of years that I kept thinking she'd be home again, after a week or two. It was like waiting. I kept thinking of things I wanted to say to her, things about people at school that I'd like to have told her. Jokes. I had known that it was very sad when someone died, but I'd always imagined death as a single event: the moment when someone stops breathing. I hadn't realised how relentless it was; how the person's absence just went on and on and on. Every morning when I woke up I'd feel normal at first, but then I'd remember that her room next to mine was empty now, that I'd never see her again. Every time I remembered it was like my whole tummy was caving in. It was as if I was falling over a cliff. Sometimes, when I was in bed and I couldn't stop thinking about her, I'd get the snout of my toy panda and push it up against my front bottom, as hard as I could. It felt tingly and hot, like a chilblain, only nice. It made me forget about Caitlin again, for a little while.

But even more than missing her I felt guilty. I knew my parents would have preferred it to be me who had died. I knew I had failed them by surviving when Caitlin – the favourite, the special one – was gone. And it was a double failure, because my bone marrow hadn't saved her. It was my fault she hadn't got better. I knew, too, that I had contributed to her dying in other, secret and bad ways. I hadn't asked God to save her often enough and sometimes I'd harboured mean thoughts about her. I'd been jealous of the attention she was getting. There had been times when I'd thought she was putting it on; pretending to feel more ill than she really did, so she could get out of things she didn't want to do. I had hated the way my mum never seemed to notice me any more, after Caitlin got ill.

I didn't even stop being jealous of her after she was gone. In some ways it was worse, because while she was there the fact that she was my sister and the person I played with all the time – and the fact that I loved her – had melted the jealousy. Just being with her lessened it. But after she died she wasn't there to diminish my sense of being left out. It was as though she had become fossilised, frozen into perfection, like Snow White in her see-through coffin. They had photographs of her in frames in the sitting-room and on the chest of drawers in their bedroom. When they talked about her it was always like boasting: how good she had been, how pretty, how brave and sweet. They never mentioned anything naughty or real about her. I wanted to shout at them, to break the spell. I wanted to wave my arms in the air and scream: 'I'm here! Look at me!' I wanted them to recall her as she really was, not as this fairy-tale version that they were inventing. The way they talked about her was rubbing her out, making it hard for me to keep hold of her. It was as if they were making her die a second time. I didn't see why you had to pretend someone was perfect after they'd died.

I moved into her bedroom. It was my idea. Well, it wasn't an idea, exactly; it just happened. A few weeks after she died I was getting ready for bed – brushing my teeth – and instead of going into my room I went into Caitlin's instead. Her bed was made up with the fresh sheets that my mum had put on after she'd gone into hospital for the last time, so I just got into it. I was like one of the three bears, mute and cumbrous, stealing into Goldilocks's girlish chamber. It was dark outside – it was nearly Christmas – but I didn't even put the light on, or draw the curtains across the window to shut out the night. I lay very still with my arms straight down by my sides and held my breath for as long as I could, to try and imagine what it was like being dead. It didn't feel lonely. It actually felt all right. When my mum came up to tuck me in she didn't say anything about me being in Caitlin's room, so after that I stayed. I moved my stuff in there, gradually, over the next few days. My old bedroom had had the evening sun, but the new room got sunlight in the morning, and I preferred that. If I slept with a chink in the curtains, the sun came right on to my face when I woke up. It was like an alarm clock made of light.

They say that time makes everything better, as if time could create a tidy pedestrian precinct of emotion. In some ways it is true: after a few months I only thought about my sister a few times a day, instead of most of the time. Whenever I thought of her it was like being punctured. But in another way time makes it worse, because the longer someone's been gone, the more you miss them. Anyone can put up with a week or two, or even months. When the absence goes on longer than that it starts to weigh on you, literally; it's like carrying a heavy bag up a hill. When I see photographs of myself from when I was ten and eleven, I see how droopy I had begun to look. Even in pictures where I am smiling my sagging shoulders tell another story.

While Caitlin was ill we hadn't been able to go away on holiday because we'd had to be near the hospital all the time, in case anything went wrong with her. And for a couple of years after she died my mum couldn't face sitting around in a bikini pretending to enjoy herself, even though dad tried to persuade her that a break would do her good. Eventually, though, her sister – my aunt Heather who lived near Daventry – insisted that we should all go away with her and her family. They were going to Majorca over Easter; just for the one week. It wouldn't be too hot, she said, at that time of year; warm enough to eat outside, but not blistering. There'd be flowers out. I was excited to be going on an aeroplane. We'd been to France before, on the ferry from Folkestone, but this was different, more exotic. I felt happy to be going abroad. I didn't know that the holiday would ruin everything.

Heather had two sons, who were both younger than me. They were seven and nine and I was nearly thirteen. For the first day I thought they were really childish and annoying, the way they fidgeted and kept doing false burps. But when we went out to lunch at a café on the second day of the holiday and we all wanted chips, they dared me to ask for them in Spanish. Patatas fritas, I had to say. And for some reason this made us laugh and laugh. We couldn't stop saying it. Then we began putting it into other phrases, which made us giggle even more. Patatas fritas which art in heaven; patatas fritas give a dog a bone; Robin Hood and his band of patatas fritas. We went on and on, till we were weak from laughing. After that I liked my cousins and forgot about being too mature for them.

We went on expeditions to look at a glass factory and an old cathedral, but mostly we just stayed in the village and wandered about the tourist shops and sat under the pine trees by the sea wall, eating ice creams. They were different flavours to what we could get at home: choc ices on sticks with bits of almond in the chocolate, and a pineapple-flavoured lolly. Out parents kept having tall glasses of sherry at odd times of the day, when they'd never normally be drinking. They sipped it puckering their lips with what looked like distaste, as if they were sampling it for some very important – perhaps even professional – reason. Every morning they took it in turns to read the day-old English newspaper which my uncle bought. Each time he came back from the shop he complained about the price of the paper: more than a quid, he'd grumble, and it's out of date as well. A strict order was observed: my uncle read it first, then my father, then my mum, then Heather. They all read it from cover to cover, unsmiling, as if it was their bounden duty to acquaint themselves with every word. None of them seemed to be enjoying themselves much. Afterwards, when we got home and the photos came back from the developer's, my mum and dad talked about Majorca as if it was Heaven on God's earth. They told everyone what a great holiday they'd had. But it didn't look it, at the time.

On the last night we went out for a meal in a restaurant. It was a place for visitors, with glossy castanets, like conkers, hung on walls so lavishly plastered that they looked like cake icing. There were replicas of old firearms displayed above the counter and fierce guitar music played. They took a long time to bring our food. The first course was called soup, but it was more like wallpaper paste. The adults had already had two or three bottles of red wine by the time our main courses arrived. My uncle kept saying how good it was for Heather and my mum to be together. 'Honestly, though, Eric,' he spoke to my dad while gazing affectionately at his wife, 'we ought to make it an annual thing. I mean, look at them: sisters. It's good for Heather to see her sister. It's only once a bloody year.' My dad smiled thinly: he was fond of Heather but, secretly, he didn't have a lot of time for his brother-in-law.

Eventually our desserts came: a selection of dark sugary little cakes full of dates and pistachios, and vanilla ice cream with bits of angelica in it. My uncle ordered some sweet wine to go with the desserts. The place had filled up since we'd arrived and there were now holidaymakers, mostly youngish couples without children, at almost every table. I didn't see the gypsy come into the restaurant. It was only when she was at the next table that I noticed her at all, and then it was because my aunt started hissing to her husband. 'Don't let her come over here! They give me the creeps,' she said. I swivelled around to look. The gypsy seemed like a cartoon of a gypsy with her hoop earrings and hooked nose. Everything about her was exaggerated. She was leaning over a woman with bleached hair and bare shoulders. The woman looked nervous, but she might just have been cold.

Then she started over towards us. 'Kenneth!' Heather protested. I don't know what she expected him to do, but whatever it was he didn't do it. 'Leave it, love,' he said. 'It's only a bit of fun.' By now the gypsy was level with my aunt's shoulder and she seemed much older, close-up. She looked almost gnarled. She surveyed us for only a couple of seconds before singling out my mother. It all happened at once: I could feel the dread rising from our table as she bent down to take my mother's hand and then my father sprang up from his chair and pushed the gypsy out of mum's range. One of the waiters came across and started shouting at the woman in Spanish; the holidaymakers' faces were all suddenly turned in our direction. My dad grabbed my hand and pulled back my mother's chair, and then the three of us were outside in the street, walking back to the hotel. I suppose the others must have sorted out the bill. I expect the boys wanted to finish their puddings, and my uncle wouldn't have let the wine go to waste. Anyway, they didn't follow us.

We walked fast, without speaking. My bed was a settee in a little alcove sitting-room off my parents' room, which folded out at night. When we got back to the hotel my mum sat down on the settee with me. Her face looked smudged. My dad said he was going for a shower – I think he wanted to be by himself. I knew mum was going to tell me why dad had shoved the fortune-teller, and I didn't want her to. I thought I knew why. I thought I understood that they had too much at stake: that if a tourist-trap gypsy recognised their tragedy – if she could tell, just by looking at them, that their daughter had died – it would have made a spectacle of their grief, something public and cheap, like a souvenir.

My mum didn't explain that, though. Instead she put her arms around my shoulders and began to rock back and forth. I could feel the warm damp of her breath and tears against my neck. 'I couldn't bear it,' she cried. 'I couldn't bear it if she'd said anything was going to happen to you.' I felt hot with what felt like embarrassment. 'Don't be daft, Mum. I'm all right. It's all all right,' I said. I wanted her to stop crying. After a little while she disentangled herself from me and fished in her bag for a tissue. She blew her nose and then she gave me a watery, pretend-brave smile. 'I can tell you now, Jenny. We've all been through enough. You're my favourite, darling. You've always been the favourite. When your sister was ill I sometimes used to think that I was being punished for loving you more. I don't think I could survive now, to be honest, if anything ever happened to you.' At that, a noise which was half-sob, half-hiccup came out of her throat. Then she looked at me expectantly, as if she was waiting to watch me unwrap a gift.

I couldn't bring myself to meet her in the eye. I saw her as grotesque, with her red blurry eyes and her self-pity and the rim of clear snot around her nostrils, glistening like a snail's trail. I hated her then. If my dad hadn't already occupied the bathroom I would have locked myself in a shower of the hottest water, to scald her words off me.

I sat on the settee and wished that she would leave me alone. I needed to concentrate. I needed to think about Caitlin, to be able to summon her up. I had to take care of her memory. To protect her. I couldn't trust my mother, any more, to safeguard my sister. It was hard, because I was starting to forget things about her; what her voice had sounded like, the texture of her skin before she got sick. Her smell. But I knew that from now on I had to try and remember; try and hold on to her, cherish her. It was up to me.

Paradise Drive

Red Mondeo Turbo, S reg, sunroof, all electric – even the wing mirrors electric. Ace car. Soon as I come out of the magistrates' court, I seen it. Got my name written all over it. Maureen – she's my social worker – she says to me: 'Are you all right, now, Jon? Do you want me to run you home?'

Not in her poxy old Vauxhall I don't. I says:

'No, I'm all right. I'll go on the bus.'

She fishes in her bag, gives me two quid. She's not supposed to give me money, but I know she likes me. She trusts me, reckons the juvenile court's going to have frightened me; she doesn't think I'll do nothing wrong no more. But I'm not going to get no bus, not with that Mondeo sat there. Maureen puts her hand out to shake my hand, then takes it back empty when she remembers she's not supposed to touch me. New rules. She stands there for a minute then she goes:

'Well, I'll see you then, Jon. Take care. I'll see you next week.'

I say, yeah, then she's away.

Wait till Lenny and my uncle Vince see this, I thought. Didn't take me long to get it started. Cheers, Lenny. It was Lenny taught me how to do it: he can get into any motor and be ten miles away in fucking milliseconds. I'm in, got it started up, out the magistrates' car park, then I go to put the radio on. Can you believe it: it's got no sound system! Not even a removable fascia — just nothing. Not even a radio. Who's going to buy a Mondeo Turbo without a sound system, a decent CD player? They deserve to get it pinched.

I'm not going to take it home, no way. My mum don't want to know. I'm going to take it straight to my uncle Vince, at work. He's only in Mitcham. Take me twenty minutes, half an hour max. I know the way, I know all the back roads, how to turn left ahead of the junction, go down the residential streets and miss the lights. I'll tell you what: I'd be a brilliant cabbie. What I know's wasted on me.

Uncle Vince's got off-street parking at his printshop; there's room for four or five cars in there, but it don't look like it from the road, because it's down a narrow entrance. In I go. I could drive through a fucking needle-eye, I could. Jackie — that's the receptionist — sees me out the window. She's all right. She leaves her desk, comes out to see the Mondeo. Ace car.

'Oh, my Lord. Wait till Vincent sees this,' she says, shaking her head like she can't believe it.

'It's a Mondeo. S reg.'

'I can see that, Jon. I can see that,' says Jackie.

My uncle Vince comes out, then. Sees me, sees the car.

'Oh fuck, Jon. What the fuck is this?' he goes.

'It's a Ford Mondeo.'

'Yeah, well, what the fuck is it doing in my yard?'

If you didn't know my uncle like I do, you'd think he was angry. I can tell that Jackie's frightened of him, because she jumps when he talks like that, but it's just his way. I'm used to him. He starts walking around the car, giving it the once-over, swearing at me all the time. He touches the rear left tyre with his foot a couple of times.

'Fuck, I don't know. I don't know what we're going to do with you, Jon. Where d'you get this from anyway?'

'Out the magistrates' car park.'

'What, outside the bloody court? You never.'

'I did.'

'You took it from right under their noses?'

'Yeah.'

Uncle Vince didn't say nothing for a while. He just kept looking at the Mondeo.

'You'll get custodial next time, Jon, if you go on like this. They're not going to let you keep on with probation if you don't pack it in. I don't know. You never fucking learn, do you?' he says. But I can see the pride in his face.

'No, I don't.'

And I know he wouldn't want me to, not really.

★

I should have seen it coming, from the way mum's been acting: taking an interest in my project, saying she'd buy me the shoes I've been after. Like nothing's too much trouble for her. I should have guessed that she was planning another. But she'd made me a promise, after the last time – she'd promised me she wouldn't take another one unless we all agreed about it first, as a family. She said she wouldn't do anything unless we'd talked about it first. So I didn't notice she was planning anything until she'd already got it all fixed up. By the time she told me, it was already arranged. She couldn't have gone back on it by then, even if she'd wanted to. Except she didn't want to.

It's not as if she hasn't got a family of her own. Couples without kids – I can understand that. But mum and dad have got Graham, even if he's not living at home any more; and me. They've got two kids of their own; one boy, one girl. And – this is the strangest part – mum isn't even a very mummyish type of person anyway. She's not the kisses and cuddles and bedtime story kind of mother. She's not the kind who'd tuck you up with a hot-water bottle if you were feeling poorly. She's, like, tough. Probably you have to be quite hard, like her, to want to foster in the first place.

The first one, Tina, wasn't too bad: we had her for nearly a year and a half. She was only ten when she came to us. But Pauline, the last kid we had living here, she was a nightmare from day one. Even dad couldn't handle her. She nicked things (she pinched the aquamarine ring my mum's aunt left her: we never found it), she lied all the time – and she ran up nearly two hundred quid on our phone bill. She was ringing chat lines when none of us were about. She was always going into my room, into my stuff. Mum said that Pauline had been through a very difficult time in her family of origin and that she'd get better, eventually, if she was given clear enough boundaries. My mum talks like that. But she didn't. I reckon she just got worse.

After Pauline, me and dad went on strike, sort of. It was then that we all needed a break. It's brilliant having the house to ourselves, anyway – not having to queue up for the bathroom, or find that the last yoghurt's gone from out of the fridge. Or the biscuit tin's empty, or someone's been and borrowed your CDs and left them lying everywhere, out of their cases. Our house isn't that big; it was just right with the three of us, but it felt crowded when Graham was still at home – and he was family. Is. But mum doesn't like to see his old room sitting empty, when there's kids with no homes out there. That's what she says.

What she doesn't say is that she gets quite a lot of money every week from social services, for a foster placement.

I don't think she really thinks about me. About what I want. If she did she'd never have started fostering in the first place. It's not that I don't feel sorry for the kids, I do. It's not their fault, I know that. But I'm the youngest in our family; I was used to being the baby of the house, the little one: little Ally. When mum started fostering I was thirteen and it took a lot of getting used to, having a younger kid around. They usually have to be the youngest in the house, that's part of the package. She thinks it's just her who does the fostering, but it's not: there's me and dad too. Specially me, because dad's often away with his work. And foster carers have to be fair – they have to treat all the kids in the house the same. It's not easy having to suddenly share your parents with a stranger. They don't have so much time for you any more.

At least this one's a boy. He won't nick my clothes like the other two did, and try and hang around with my friends. He comes from a large single-parent family, but the children's needs weren't being met by the mother – as my mum would say, sounding like a social worker – and he's been truanting a lot, and in trouble with the police. That's all she'll say. Pauline didn't have any contact with her family of origin, but apparently this kid is still going to see his mum and his brothers and sister. I don't know if he's got a dad at all. He's just fifteen – only a year younger than me. He's coming next week. His name's Jon.

★

They've got two cars, they have. The Civic's hers, but I haven't seen his yet, because he's away for his work. He's a pilot, British Caledonian: he's got to have a better car than that Honda. Imagine flying a plane, then driving a fucking Civic! That'd bring you down to earth with a bang, I tell you. About as much acceleration as a shopping trolley. If I was a pilot I'd have an Alfa, at least. Or a BMW 5 series. Something decent. I tell you what – I wouldn't let my wife drive no fucking Honda Civic, not even a new one, like she's got.

It's a bit special round here. The toilet paper's tangerine-coloured, to match the colour of the bathroom suite; and they put mini-placemats on the table for their cups of tea, like beermats in the pub. It's like a show home. And half the time it's not tea at all, because they're drinking coffee. Even the daughter drinks coffee. Alison. Her mum calls her Ally. Ally Pally. Like Alexandra Palace. Makes you think of Crystal Palace. She's sixteen. She don't say much.

Maureen says I'm lucky to be here. I only got here so quick because Jackie – she works for my uncle Vince – she knows them: Jackie's sister-in-law is Mrs Shaw's cousin. Something like that, anyway. And Mrs Shaw's had kids here before, she's registered with social services already, for fostering. Not that I'm being fostered, though. It's all right. Decent-sized TV, fucking coffin-sized freezer full of pizzas and that. Coulsden, near the golf course. It's not far from home.

Not that I'm going to be stopping. My mum's done this before, when I've been in trouble: she's been on to the social services to get me out of the way for a while, give her a rest. Respite care they call it. Spite, more like. But my mum's got enough on her plate already with the kids, the little ones. I shouldn't have never taken that Mondeo. That's what my uncle Vince says. She's had enough. If I keep out of trouble, go to school and that, she'll let me stop at home with her; that's what he reckons. I'm not staying here for long, I'll tell you that. I don't mind it for a week or two, but after that I'm going back to mine.

She won't let me go for long anyway, because I saved my

kid sister's life. I've got the stories about it, out of the newspaper; they've got my picture in, and my name.

When we was in our old place, the flat, there was a fire. Her boyfriend – he was her boyfriend then, Martin – he used to smoke fucking fifty a day. Always had one in his hand. So one night I woke up and the room was thick with it, smoke; you couldn't hardly breathe at all. You couldn't see nothing. My mum and the other two, the little ones, must have all woken up at the same time. Martin had gone, it was the middle of the night. We was all shouting and coughing and the four of us just made it out of the flat and down the stairs before my mum started screaming:

'The baby the baby the baby's in there!'

It was like something on the TV. I didn't even think about it: I just ran up the stairs and back into the flat to get the babbie. She was in her cot, in mum's room. I could feel the fire, then. I could feel the hotness of it, coming from the lounge. When we woke up and went out, the first time, I'd only noticed the smoke; but this time it was the heat. Fucking incredible heat. Burned the inside of your lungs, your eyeballs. The baby was terrified, but I got her, I got her out. It said in the paper that I was a young hero, but I wasn't. I didn't think, see: I just did it without thinking about it. If I'd have thought about it, I probably wouldn't have gone in there. I'd have been too scared, then.

I got a week off school, and when I went in the headmaster stood up in front of everyone at assembly and told them what I'd done. My head was fucking enormous then, to tell you the truth. After I'd had my picture in the paper I thought I was famous. I felt like I was the dog's bollocks. I didn't believe I was a real hero, but I did think I was a bit of a celebrity. I thought I'd never have to worry again, I could get away with murder. But it hit me, a couple of days later, when my mum sent me out to the shops. They'd put us in temporary accommodation then. I went in Kwiksave for some burgers and I was looking around at all the people with their shopping trolleys, and I thought: They think I'm just like them. And I kept looking at them, thinking how special I was, because I'd had my name in the paper; and all of a sudden it was like the air went out of me – like I was winded – because I knew I wasn't no different, not really. No one looked at me, no one pointed me out. I'd had my name in the paper, but I was still just a kid; I wasn't nothing special after all.

★

He drives me nuts. He never listens when you talk to him – if you ask him if he wants a drink you have to say it two or three times before he'll answer you. And at mealtimes it's, like:

'Jon, can you pass the sauce, please.'

Then he doesn't answer, doesn't even look as if he's heard.

'Jon! I said can I have the sauce? Hello, Jon: anybody in?'

And then he'll go: 'Yeah, what?'

'I said, can I have that bottle of sauce in front of you, please?'

And then he'll hand it over, without saying anything; as if you hadn't asked him a million times, as if you were making a fuss about nothing. Drives you bonkers. And he jiggles his leg all the time. Not when he's standing up, but at meals and when we're watching TV. His left leg. It's like he can't keep still.

He's small for his age. He's a head shorter than I am and he's little and wiry. He's got skinny little arms – his skin's ever so pale – but he looks strong, as if he'd come out the better in a fight anyway. He's determined, you can see that. I think he's quite hard, or he'd like to be. He's got L-O-V-E tattooed across his knuckles on one hand and what's meant to be H-A-T-E across the other. But I reckon he did it himself, or got some mate of his to do it – not a proper tattoo shop – because his left hand says H-A-V-E. It's a V instead of a T, and they're the wrong way round as well. So it says HAVE LOVE when it's meant to say LOVE HATE.

He makes this noise, half under his breath, as if he's drumming: it sort of goes 'tv, tv, tv'; like when someone's playing music in another room and you can only hear the bass line without the melody. Or like if you're on the bus sitting next to someone who's playing rap music on a Walkman. We were watching a video the other night and he kept doing it:

'Tv, tt-tt, tv, tt-tt, tv, tv . . .'

I said: 'Jon, can you stop making that noise? I'm trying to watch this.'

'Tt-tt, tt-tv, tt-tt, tv . . .'

'Jon! Are you deaf or something! I'm trying to enjoy this film and you're ruining it, making that noise.'

He didn't answer me, but he stopped doing it. His leg jiggled double time, then. So we sat there, looking at *Robin Hood: Prince of Thieves*, with his leg going on the settee beside me like a dog with a flea. It's like being in a mini-earthquake sitting next to him. About five minutes go by and I'm just starting to forget about the jiggling and relax, enjoy the film, then:

'Tv, tt-tt, tt-tt, ts, tv, tv . . .' he starts up again. I couldn't believe it. I gave up after that, I went up to my room. He's like a cross between a pneumatic drill and a drum machine. That's what he's like.

★

My uncle Vince took me round to see my mum yesterday. I said, 'It's three weeks now, I want to come home.'

But my mum didn't say nothing and my uncle Vince

started talking about his business as if he'd never heard me. I'll have to leave it a bit longer, then. My kid brothers and my sister – she's the baby – they went fucking mental when they saw me. They love me, they do. And the dog does and all.

Mr and Mrs Shaw haven't got a dog; they're not like that, not dog sort of people. They love their carpets too much. Their carpets are all the same colour, through the whole house – sort of biscuit-coloured; but pale biscuit, like a Nice bicky. They all take their shoes off when they come in the house.

Mr Shaw's got a Volvo. Silver-grey, 480 Turbo. It's all right: I'd be happy with it. But he says it's time he traded it in: it's got nearly eighty thousand on the clock. He's thinking of going for another Volvo, or maybe upgrading to a Saab. His work contributes to his car – they pay two-thirds of the lease-hire on it. So he's looking around, he can afford to. Saabs are fucking ace cars. I've never been inside one, but Lenny has – he's told me about them. I didn't tell Mr Shaw he wants to get his wife something better than that poxy Honda while he's at it. That's pathetic, that is.

★

He's making an effort now. It's been a couple of months and we're all settling in a bit better together. Dad likes him, I think. They chat about stuff: cars and sport and that. It's much better than it was when we had girls. Not that he's not annoying, he is. But he's annoying in really, like, obvious ways. You know why you're annoyed with him. Girls are more cunning, more devious. Sometimes, with Tina and Pauline you'd just feel irritated but you couldn't put your finger on why, on what they'd actually done. They just made a bad atmosphere in the house.

Jon and me watch films together. We get a video out once

or twice a week, get some crisps sorted; sometimes we even have popcorn. Mum goes to quite a few meetings: she's on committees for this and that – the new civic centre, various fostering groups – so we get the house to ourselves. Dad's away a fair bit. We don't really talk much, but we have a good evening anyway. We take it in turns to fetch a cup of tea or coffee, or cold drinks. The good thing about him is, he doesn't mind what we watch. He'll watch anything – drama, comedy, even like, romantic stuff. You'd think he'd only enjoy horror films, and action pictures. Car chases and volcanoes and stuff. But he doesn't seem to prefer one kind of film to another. I like most things as well, so it's good. We get a good variety going. It's OK.

*

My mum's got herself a new boyfriend. My uncle Vince didn't tell me about it, he just took me round there and dropped me off. I should have guessed, when he didn't come in the house with me. He just said he'd call back for me at half-six and then he drove off.

He's called Terence. Not Terry. Terence. He's not a big bloke, but he's got a belly on him that makes him look fairly large. He's sat in our lounge, comfortable on the settee, looking at the racing on the television. He didn't say nothing to me and I didn't say nothing to him. When we was in the kitchen, just us two, I asked my mum what he drives. She said he doesn't drive. He hasn't got a car anyway. I asked her why not, and she said she didn't know. She can't be that serious about the bloke if she doesn't even bother to ask him why he's got no wheels.

My little sister went fucking ballistic when she saw me. She went mental. She wouldn't get down off my knee, got her arms round my neck like a bleeding clamp the whole time I was there. She screamed when it was time for me to go: crying and carrying on. 'I want my Jon', she goes. It was horrible. Terence didn't even fucking look up. I waited for mum to tell her not to cry because I'd be back home soon, but she never.

Soon as I got in the car with my uncle Vince to go back to the Shaws' house, I said to him: 'Who's this Terence, then?'

He looked tired.

'He's just some bloke she's met. You don't want to take no notice of him, Jon.'

'He better not fucking touch them kids.'

'Don't worry about it. He's too bleeding fat to get up off his arse. He's not going to touch no one.'

'Well, he better not, that's all.'

Uncle Vince didn't answer. After that, we didn't talk at all, the rest of the way.

★

I don't know what to think about it. It's just so weird. I can't get my head round what's happened, but I can't tell anyone else either – they'd think I was a bit cracked. They'd certainly think Jon was. He probably is, in fact. He's probably not normal.

He's never been in my things before; at least, I don't think he has. One of the things I hated about having Pauline here was the way she was always going into my room, helping herself to my stuff. But what's a lad going to want in my room? I mean, it's just my clothes and posters and that – it's not, like, boy-stuff. Except maybe my CDs, or some of them. And one of the things about Jon, I've noticed all along, is that he's not that interested. He doesn't ask questions – not unless he's talking to my dad about cars or something. He doesn't make personal remarks.

So anyway: I came in from school and mum wasn't there,

because she'd gone into Croydon for something or other. And dad's away this week. It was only half-four, the house was quiet: I didn't reckon Jon was back from his school yet, because it was too early for him. He doesn't usually get in till gone five.

I went to the fridge and got myself a glass of orange juice – I was thirsty because we'd had netball last lesson. Then I went upstairs, to my room, to change. And that's when I saw him in there. Jon.

He must have skived off, because he wasn't in his uniform. He'd only got on a vest on top of his jeans; seeing his whole arms, his shoulders, it was funny. I'd never seen that much of his skin before. He didn't look as scrawny as he does with his shirt on.

So I walk into my room and there he is, sitting on the stool at my dressing table, and I was just about to give him an earful – ask him what he thought he was doing, going in my room – when I saw what he'd done. It gave me such a fright that I couldn't say anything. I just stood there, staring.

He'd only put my make-up on. The lot. When I'd looked at him long enough I saw he'd done a professional job of it, too. So the funny thing was, he didn't look like a pervert, or a bloke in drag or anything. He hadn't just slapped it on any old how. He'd put it on like in a magazine – sort of subtle, like he knew how to show up his best features with it. He'd got two shades of eyeshadow – a mauve and a dusky grey – and blended them across his eyelids; he'd put mascara on his top and bottom lashes. He'd got my powder blusher across his cheekbones, just right. He'd even got on bloody lip-gloss.

I was speechless. I just stood there in the doorway, looking at him. The sight of him made my tummy turn over. He didn't say anything to me, either. He didn't explain what he was doing, and he didn't say he was sorry for being in my room, going in my stuff: I suppose there wasn't anything he could say really. He didn't even look embarrassed. It was as if he was my sister or something; it was almost as if it was normal.

I don't know how long we stayed like that, not saying anything, with him sat there and me standing looking at the make-up – my make-up – on his face. I don't think either of us had said a word before he got up and came over towards me. I thought he was just going to walk out of my room, past me. But he didn't. He came up in front of me and – this is the strangest – we both stopped dead still, staring at each other. In that moment we could nearly have started fighting, or swearing at each other. We were both really tense, I could feel it. And then he started to unbutton my shirt. He undid all the buttons on it, looking down at them, concentrating. He didn't undo my bra. He just slid his hand under it and on to my left breast.

I didn't try and stop him, I didn't do anything. It was like I was paralysed. We were still stood there looking into each other's faces, but I was feeling as if I was going to keel over, then. I thought I was going to collapse, faint or something. My heart was going like an alarm clock, and my neck was all hot. It was like I was melting. When he turned his face up towards mine, I opened my mouth against his, but he didn't put his tongue inside me; he just kissed the corners of my lips, to begin with. I had kissed boys before, anyway. I've kissed Damien from the sixth year more than once, and a boy called Stephen who we met on holiday. But they weren't like this.

When he kissed me he stopped just holding my breast and he took my nipple between his fingers instead and squeezed it, hard. It was like he'd given me an electric shock. It was weird – his mouth was so gentle but his hand wasn't. It made me want him to touch me all over. My insides felt like one of those lava lamps. And he was starting to move his tongue towards the inside of my mouth, then. I couldn't believe the taste of him, it was so totally different from how you'd ever think breath could taste. It was like vanilla. I wanted to go on kissing him for ever. I'd have done anything he said. Anything.

But then he stopped. It was like he was hardly in the room with me at all any more, as if he'd remembered something else he ought to be seeing to. His attention had gone from me completely, as if I didn't exist. It wasn't like he hated me, or as if I was disgusting or anything; it wasn't as though he'd made a decision to stop at all. It felt almost like something outside himself was stopping him. I think I might have made a noise at that point – I didn't say anything, not words, but I wasn't silent any more. I don't know whether he heard, or noticed. He took his hand away from my breast, then, and he didn't even look at me. He just went out of the room and my whole body felt concave and disappointed then, and empty; standing by the open door of my room with my white school shirt all undone and the taste of his mouth in my mouth, still, and the slight tackiness of lip-gloss from his lips on my lips.

*

You never forget the first time. Fucking magic, that's what it was: it's like flying. It's like you own the world – there's nowhere you can't go to after you've done it. It's like you're totally free. In control. No one, nothing, can get at you.

My uncle Vince fixed it for me. He and his mate Lenny and me, we went down to the coast on the train. Lenny's got a garage – he sells used cars, Metros and that mostly – and classic cars are his big hobby. Every year he goes along to the Bromley Pageant. End of June, every year; it's the biggest one-day motor-show in the world, it is. All classic cars: Jaguars, Zephyrs, fucking Ford Anglias, the lot. Lenny takes a car he's been restoring over the past twelve months and shows it off. It was a Rover, the year before.

So it's August and Lenny's brother-in-law who lives in Eastbourne knows some old bird who's selling her old car that she's kept in her garage for years and years, and it's only a fucking 1965 Daimler. Lenny's brother-in-law, he's negotiated with her: he's been round and tinkered with the car, got it started up and ready for the road. He sold her the car she's driving now: some Renault, a Clio, I think it was. French shite. That's how he heard about the Daimler. He's going to meet us off the train and take us to her place, then we're going to drive it back up to town. If the car'll start. That's the plan.

So my uncle Vince and Lenny, they have a few beers on the train and by the time we get off, they're both in a good mood; looking forward to a nice day out. Sunshine, seaside and a classic car waiting for you: life's all right.

That car, it's fucking beautiful. V8. Red leather upholstery, walnut fascia, chrome everywhere. I prefer modern cars myself, but this one's an ace motor. Even I can see that. Lenny and my uncle Vince and Lenny's brother-in-law can't get enough of it. They're all crowding round, admiring the features: the black starter button, the map-light, the gauges. You'd think they'd never seen a car before – they're like a bunch of kids over it. This woman's had this car since it come off the forecourt. One driver! And one lady driver at that. It's too good to be true.

Lenny and his brother-in-law are talking about how V8s have a tendency to overheat in traffic when my uncle Vince says to me: 'I've got a surprise for you coming up, Jon.'

'What's that then?'

'You'll just have to wait and see, won't you? It won't be long, now.'

I couldn't think what it was going to be. I thought it might be going on the pier or something. So we get finished with the woman, get the car started up – there's bluish smoke coming out the back when the engine first comes on, but Lenny says it's normal – and start driving around the town. Cruising. We go all along the seafront, up towards the cliffs. Then right, along these wide streets with great big posh houses and right again, till we get to this big empty street with a golf course on one side and trees sloping down the other. Paradise Drive it's called.

'Here, Lenny, stop a minute,' says my uncle Vince. Lenny usually does what my uncle Vince tells him to do. They've been mates for fucking years.

'I reckon it's time this young man had a go behind a wheel.'

'You what?' says Lenny.

'He's just fourteen. I was fourteen the first time I drove a car,' says my uncle.'

'It's a Daimler, Vincent. It's a Daimler V8,' says Lenny. He's sitting in the driver's seat and he's keeping his hands on the wheel, even though we're stopped still. I can tell he doesn't want to know, but I can feel my ears going all red at the thought of it. I'm scared, but I want a go.

'Tell you what, Len. I'll give you fifty quid, all right?' says my uncle Vince. He's always holding, but you can never tell with him whether he's joking or not. Lenny's looking shifty. My uncle Vince takes a wad out of his trouser pocket and peels off two twenties and a ten.

'Here you go. Now out you get and let's have young Jon up front, shall we?'

It's a dodgy moment. They could start. I've seen them start fighting before. But Lenny does just as he's told and gets out the car, slowly. He doesn't take the money, though.

My uncle Vince shows me what to do. The steering wheel's thin and hard in my hands, like a collar-bone; I have to sit well forward to reach.

'There's no rush, all right, Jon. Just take it steady. And there's no other cars about so you've not got to worry about other drivers. Just keep your eyes on the road. It's like the Dodgems – just a bit bigger. Let the handbrake off, that's it.'

'You'll give me more than fucking fifty if he prangs it, I tell you,' Lenny muttered from the back seat.

'Leave it out, Len. Give the kid a chance. He's going to remember this for the rest of his life.'

'Yeah, all right,' says Lenny.

So we started going along. I didn't know whether I wanted to laugh or scream. I felt like you feel when you fall on the bottom of your backbone – your coccyx, isn't it – and you giggle, but it hurts at the same time. But it got better. By the third time it was fucking fantastic. I was in my stride, I was.

'I tell you what – he's a chip off the old block, this one. Isn't he, Len?'

Lenny didn't say nothing to that.

'He's a natural, he is. Look at the lane discipline on him. Never driven a car before!'

I felt like it was my birthday and the bank holiday and Christmas rolled into one. I could tell my uncle Vince was that proud of me, then.

He was right and all. I'm not never going to forget that day. I ended up driving that car six times along that road – Uncle Vince turned it round for me each end – and by the fourth go I knew I was hooked. Driving a car's like nothing else on this earth. There's not enough words to describe what it feels like. There's just nothing else that can come close.

★

It was Graham's car. My brother Graham's. He'd only got it five weeks ago.

Mum said that Maureen – that's Jon's social worker – had told her that the one kind he'd never bother with was a Vauxhall. She was laughing about it, because she drives one herself and she'd seen how reluctant he was to go in it with her. She was convinced he'd never take one. Apparently he hates Vauxhalls. But Graham's car's a Tigra, so she got it wrong. It seems like everyone got it wrong really.

Dad had a talk with me and said he reckoned it would be better if I didn't go and see him. He doesn't want me upset any more. Jon's still critical, so he probably wouldn't be allowed visitors anyway, that's what I've been trying to say to myself. I don't even know whether his family are allowed to see him.

The car's a write-off. He must have taken the keys out of Graham's jacket, while we were out in the back lighting the barbecue. Apparently Maureen told mum and dad to keep their car keys well hidden while he was with us, but they never told me about it. They didn't think to tell Graham; just forgot. He'd been behaving himself so well that it slipped their minds completely, they said. And I didn't even know he had a thing about cars. No one told me.

He never told me. He never really told me anything. After that time in my room we just went back to normal, never mentioned it. Never did anything like that again. I didn't tell anybody about it, it was just too weird. I thought it was better to forget it had ever even happened. When I thought about it, by myself, it made me feel a bit dizzy. I couldn't really handle what it made me feel about him.

We carried on like before, watching videos together and that. He never looked as if he was that interested in cars. He never pointed them out on the films we saw, or mentioned cars at all.

Dad told me that they reckon he took Graham's car because he was upset: Maureen had had to tell him that his mother didn't want him to come home. Apparently she'd decided that she couldn't cope with him any more, not now his little brothers are growing up. She didn't want them turning out like Jon. And since he was going to be sixteen soon, he'd have been moving out of home anyway. That's what his mother said. It wasn't like putting him up for permanent fostering, or adoption or anything. It was only seven months till his sixteenth birthday, and then he could do what he liked with himself. Except he couldn't go back to her.

They don't know if he'll pull through; apparently his spine was broken in the impact. The other car's a write-off too, but it was parked, there was no one in it. They keep saying, mum and dad keep saying: 'No one else was hurt. That's the main thing.' As if that makes it better, as if it's like it doesn't matter that Jon's lying there in intensive care, so long as no other people are involved. As if that makes it all right. Anyway, people have been hurt, in another way. His mum, his brothers and sister. That uncle who used to come and collect him; they seemed close. And I have been.

There's one more thing they keep saying to each other, especially my mother: 'It was an accident. It wasn't anybody's fault.'

The police came and told us what had happened. It was just like in one of the films we used to watch. My parents were very polite to them both, as if they were out to impress what reasonable people they both are. After they'd gone, I went up to his room, the room that used to be Graham's room. I think I hoped there'd be some sign of him in that room, some smell or something. I don't know. I hadn't gone in there at all while he was with us; you're not supposed to go into foster children's rooms really, and you're not allowed to sit on their bed or anything. They have all these rules.

But there wasn't anything of Jon in there anyway. There weren't any things lying around, no shoes, no bits of paper; nothing. I opened a drawer and his socks and pants were folded in there; vests and a couple of school shirts in the one underneath. Some T-shirts and a hooded sweatshirt. The neatness of them made me feel light-headed. They could have belonged to anybody. It was like Jon had never really existed here.

I lay down on his bed, then, and looked up at the round paper lampshade on the ceiling light. I just lay there for ages, staring above me, not thinking about him; not thinking about anyone or anything. It was like I was floating. And after a while, I went back across to my room, and closed the door.

Bare

'You know Winnie the Pooh, don't you?'

Stella was talking across the table to Lizzie, all her attention beamed on to the child, dazzling her to stillness like the headlamps of a car fixing a young animal in their light. Lizzie's mother Bea had been studying the menu for several minutes – although she'd decided at once what she was going to order – and appeared not to be listening; Bernard, the father, was watching his daughter's face as she watched Stella.

'Well, I call Bernard Eeyore sometimes, because he's a bit gloomy, especially in the mornings,' said Stella. 'I tease him all the time,' she added in a lower, between-you-and-me voice, as if only she and Lizzie were present, conspirators together.

Stella, with her mop of dark curls and her large round eyes, had the fragile prettiness of Elizabeth Barrett Browning. Or a spaniel; she looked so lovable. Lizzie was hooked.

'How old are you?' she asked.

'Oh, I'm about a thousand years older than Bernard. I'm a bit of a cradle-snatcher, me.'

'What's a cradle-snatcher?' asked Lizzie.

'Someone who goes out with someone younger than they

are. You know, as if they'd pinched them from out of their pram.'

'How old are you, then?'

'I'm thirty-three,' said Stella.

'But Daddy's thirty-one, isn't he? Thirty-one today? That's not much younger than you.'

'No, it's not; not really. I'm just being silly. Now, poppet, what are you going to have?'

Bea sensed Bernard glancing in her direction. Her face had become hot. She kept her eyes fixed on the laminated card in her hands and read the phrase 'al arrabiatta' over and over until the words blurred. Bea – it had always been a sore point – was seven years older than Bernard: they'd met during his first year at the university, when she was already a post-graduate researcher and teaching part-time. She hadn't actually taught him, although they had been in the same faculty. The affair had gone on for three years, then; throughout his time at college. But Lizzie hadn't been conceived until some time later, during one of their brief, deliriously hopeless reunions. Bernard had been working in Edinburgh, where he'd met Stella, but recently he'd taken a new job in London and now, on his birthday, they had all assembled for the first time, to celebrate.

Before Stella joined them for lunch, Bea and Lizzie had met Bernard at the Natural History Museum. It was Lizzie's first visit. While they waited for him to arrive they studied the floor plan: they'd go to the earthquake room first, then the exhibition of wildlife photographs and, lastly, the blue whale. That was how Bea liked to do things, in an orderly way, following a prescribed arrangement.

'You've got it all mapped out, then, have you? Which way do we go?' Bernard grinned, tacitly acknowledging Bea's love of tactical planning. The wool of his coat smelled of tobacco, with a damp, unfamiliar, slightly sour underlying odour which might have been stale beer, or a mixture of city rain and bus seats.

'We go right here, I think.' Bea felt mildly annoyed, as though she'd been found out in some minor misdemeanour. She began to hang back a pace or two. Up ahead, Lizzie took her father's hand in hers, chattering like a starling. Bea watched their two fair heads incline towards one another.

The earthquake simulation was a narrow, under-lit corridor, mocked up to resemble a Japanese supermarket. Bottles of tamari sauce – like sepia ink – rattled on their thin shelves and the black rubber floor juddered, like a train lurching into a junction. On the wall were typed notices, announcing the sympathy which the Natural History Museum felt for the people of Kobe, many of whom had lost their lives in the real version of the quake. Bernard nodded wryly in their direction.

'So this isn't at all exploitative,' he said.

'No, no,' smiled Bea. 'No Disneyfication here. This is educational.'

'Interactively educational, please,' said Bernard. He pronounced the last 'per-leeze', irony loaded into the first syllable. It was a habit they had picked up years before from imitating the wife of the college bursar. Generally, they no longer used their old catchphrases with each other; Bea avoided them, stepping around the words warily, as though to hear such expressions might trigger an explosion of feeling, the verbal equivalent of landmines. She had assumed, until then, that Bernard had simply forgotten the things they used to say.

They wandered back through labyrinthine passages, to the nature photographs. There were close-ups of iridescent fish and high-gloss images of pouncing predators, anticipatory spittle glistening across their teeth. The sun was shown setting across miles of tundra, behind mountains, into a golden-syrupy sea. A small bright bird perched on the head of an alligator. To Bea's eyes there was something almost banal in so much beauty and colour, but the others were entranced, studying every picture with twin rapture.

'We won't have time for the blue whale, if you don't come now,' she said.

'Come on then, Lizzie. Mum wants to move on,' said Bernard, with a suggestion of a raised eyebrow in his daughter's direction.

'It's not that I want to stop looking at the photos – it's just that we're running out of time. Didn't you say that we were meeting Stella at one o'clock? And Lizzie particularly wanted to see the whales and dolphins. She did say so.' Bea knew that Bernard thought she was being what he called controlling; she knew, too, that he was correct.

While the others dawdled over a large Victorian display of stuffed hummingbirds in the passageway, Bea went ahead to the cetacean room. She had expected the blue whale to look smaller than it had when she had visited as a child, but it didn't. If anything, it seemed even bigger than it had then. The furrows of its vast throat were like the ridges of earth in her grandfather's asparagus beds, and its belly curved away like the hull of a huge ship.

'Look, Lizzie, look! See how big it is? Think of being in a little boat, and seeing one of those in the water!' Bea wanted her daughter to be overwhelmed by the whale, as she was.

'Wow,' said Lizzie, 'that's cool.' Bernard said nothing. His unresponsiveness irked Bea.

In the summer following Bernard's final year at university, he and Bea had gone to the south of Spain for a holiday.

Neither of them had been there before. They'd spent two or three nights in Seville, then driven through the hills to Cordoba. Bernard had worn dark glasses all the time, even when the sky clouded over; Bea had studied the guide book with a noviciate's zeal, planning. But what she'd read did not prepare her for the enchantment of the mosque at Cordoba, where row upon row of alabaster columns receded like an ancient, shady forest fossilised into stone. Bea had never seen a building so beautiful. She walked around and around each pillar, flummoxed by the scale of it all; the grandeur. Bernard, though, was unmoved and they'd rowed about it, later, in their hotel room.

'How can you not like it? I mean, anyone can see that it's one of the most amazing buildings in Europe,' said Bea.

'I just don't. It's too dark.'

'But it wasn't dark, then; not when it was still being used as a mosque. It was the Christians who filled in all the arches and blocked out the light. The sun would have streamed in, then.'

'Yes, but it doesn't now. It's – I don't know – dingy.'

'Dingy! Christ you are thick, sometimes. Haven't you got any visual imagination? Why can't you picture it as it would have looked? It would have had the courtyard with the fountains and orange trees, and then the columns would have looked like an extension of them; so that the wood and stone would have sort of melded. The whole place would have been filled with light.'

'Why does it matter? Why should I like it, just because you do?' said Bernard.

'It's not because I like it. It's because it really is wonderful – objectively – and I can't believe that you can't see that. It's like a kind of arrogance on your part, to refuse to see that. That's what I can't bear.'

'Well, you don't like the Pompidou Centre, and I don't call you arrogant.'

'But the Pompidou Centre is hideous!'

'I don't think so. Lots of people don't think so.'

'I can't believe you can even mention it in the same breath as the mosque. The trouble with you is that you're a fashion victim: you only like the Pompidou because it's new. It's like your awful taste in music. Sometimes I just can't believe you can be so shallow.'

'God, you're predictable. If I disagree with any of your opinions – or what it says in your bloody guide book – you have to start having a go. You always get personal: start putting the boot in. Anyway, it's not new. There are lots of newer buildings.'

Bea was close to tears. 'I don't just like it because of what it says in the book. I like it for myself, because it's beautiful.'

'The trouble with you,' said Bernard, 'is that you enjoy dishing it out, but you can't take it. It's OK for you to start calling me names, but if I even hint that you're being unreasonable, you start crying.'

'No I don't,' Bea sniffled, contradicting herself. Bernard didn't answer, but switched on the TV and lay back against the brashly upholstered headboard of the hotel bed, flicking through the channels, ignoring her. He wore his capacity for languor like a suit of armour.

Watching his face as he looked up at the colossal form of the blue whale, Bea was reminded of their visit to Cordoba, of what she had seen as his obdurate refusal to be moved. In his silence now she perceived the same implacable absence of humility, and the perception made her feel sour to herself, and old. This was how it was, whenever they met. Bernard had become like the looking-glass in the story of *Snow White*: in the beginning he had made her seem almost radiant to herself; now he mirrored only her flaws, her critical nature, the ugliness of her character. She found nothing lovely any more, when she saw herself reflected through his eyes.

It was time to go: Stella was meeting them at South Kensington tube station. Bea had encountered her only a couple of times before, in hasty exchanges of Lizzie. But today – because it was Bernard's birthday – Lizzie had especially asked if they could all have lunch together, and her parents had agreed that it would be right to present a unified front to their daughter. They would be civilised. It had been awkward, for a moment, deciding who would sit where. It would have been easier if the restaurant had had round tables. As it was, the table was a rectangle: Bea and Lizzie sat on one side, with Bernard opposite Bea and Stella facing Lizzie. Bea hoped that Bernard hadn't noticed her noticing – the tell-tale reddening of the tip of her nose – Stella's hand on his, beneath the marble-topped table.

On their way to the museum that morning Bea had bought a listings magazine, thinking she might visit the cinema after lunch, when Bernard had taken Lizzie. She didn't want to go straight home on her own. She'd leafed through it on the bus, while Lizzie read her comic. In the magazine was an article about body decoration. Piercing and tattoos were all the rage among young clubbers, apparently. According to the writer, taking control of your body by making your own skin a personalised artwork could be a potent means of self-empowerment. There were colour photographs, of a young girl with wispy hair and rings through both nipples, and a man with a full-size swan emblazoned across his back. There was a shaven-headed woman with an emerald in her tongue and a spider inked on to the paleness of her navel, her belly button forming its body. And there was a tattooist who'd covered his own body with strange, abstract designs, in black ink, like a Maori. His hands were covered with swirls and triangles, lines and dots. His flesh looked like a palaeolithic rock carving.

Bea read the short interview which accompanied the tattooist's picture. 'I don't like colour, I don't like pictures. I know this looks severe, but I find it interesting,' he said. His motivation was to set himself apart: 'I don't like many people, and half the time I don't even want to be human. Most people aren't very nice. So I don't want to be most people.' His eyes looked sad, Bea thought. His skin was disturbing, strangely beautiful. Bea had always associated tattoos with pictures of crimson hearts and pirates' daggers, or serpents writhing across swelling biceps. Or with words like 'Mother' or 'Shirley for ever'. The idea that tattoos could not represent anything at all − or only a feeling − had never occurred to her before.

The image of the tattooist − his lonely gaze, the harsh geometric marks on his body − came back into Bea's mind as she sat in the restaurant. She hugged it to herself, like a talisman. Lizzie and Stella were talking about Christmas. 'Last year we took a pine cabin, up in the mountains, in Scotland. It was magic, wasn't it, Ber?' said Stella. In her accent the contraction of his name sounded like bear.

Lizzie, by mutual consent, always spent Christmas with her mother. 'I wish we could go to Blackpool for Christmas. They've got the biggest big dipper practically in the world. My friend Imogen went there in the summer holidays, to see the eliminations.'

The adults laughed.

'We went to Blackpool, once,' said Bernard.

'You and mummy?' asked Lizzie.

'Yup. Your mother and me.'

'Was I born? Did I come, too?'

'No, sweetie. It was before you were even thought of,' said Bea. She remembered it vividly: a rainy weekend in October; the empty trams sliding along the wet streets in the dusk, the towering red-brick hotels along the upper esplanade, the ale-coloured sea. They'd stayed in a guesthouse where their narrow bed had had nylon sheets – making love, sparks of static had crackled about their hair, like fleeting haloes. Bea remembered how much she'd loved him, then.

'Seaside towns aren't my thing,' Stella was saying. 'Too suburban. I like my sea to be wild: cliffs and rocks and big waves. This year for Christmas we're going down to north Cornwall; a group of us. We're all going to stay in a little B & B that one of our friends has been to before, right on the coast. So we'll have lots of cliff walks, and hot toddies to warm ourselves up with, after. Play some games, some pool. Should be good.'

'What's pool?' said Lizzie.

'Like billiards, you know? When you have a green felt table with red balls on, and you have to pocket them with a long stick.'

'Oh. I thought you meant swimming pool.'

Bernard had gone quiet. They'd ordered their food some twenty minutes earlier, and Bea recognised his silence, his sudden pallor – his blood sugar level tended to drop, right before meals. Being hungry always made him listless just as it tended to make her irritable. They'd agreed, after their Andalucian holiday, that the tardiness of Spanish mealtimes had been largely responsible for their frequent quarrels during the trip.

'What's happening about our lunch?' Bea demanded. Her voice sounded crosser than she really felt.

'I don't know. They're probably just busy,' said Bernard. 'I'm tempted to go over there and offer to give them a hand in the kitchen, if they take much longer. I'm starving.'

'Mum!' Lizzie sounded alarmed, indignant. She was old enough, now, to be embarrassed by her mother.

'Let Stella go. She's good at being scary,' said Bernard proudly.

'So's mummy,' Lizzie announced. 'Once we went for a walk and we had to park the car on the edge of this field to get across to the woods, and this man came out and told mummy to move her car and she said the "f" word to him; and he said she still had to move her car, and she said' – at this, Lizzie began to laugh – 'that he should go in and put trousers on if he was going to talk to her like that. She said he shouldn't come up and boss her about when he was half naked. Because he had tiny shorts on. And after that he just walked off, and she left the car where it was.'

'That was ages ago. I'm surprised you still remember,' said Bea.

'Well, Stella's pretty good at getting her own way, too,' said Bernard.

'Shall I?' Not for the first time, Stella's reddened mouth formed a determined moue. Despite her good intentions, Bea could not help noticing the thinness of the top lip which the little pout attempted to disguise. Stella stood up and went to speak to the waiter. No one said a word while she was absent. Soon after she'd returned to their table, the lunch arrived.

'You must be brilliant at being scary,' said Lizzie, as she cut into her pizza.

'I am. I can be really fierce when I want to be.' Stella giggled becomingly, her hair partly obscuring her face. Bernard grinned.

They ate their food. Stella had only a small green salad.

'Is that all you're having?' asked Lizzie.

'She doesn't eat. She's got an appetite like a bird,' said Bernard.

'Lucky you,' said Bea, 'I get so hungry that I'm always overeating.'

'Me and mummy like fairy cakes.'

'It's true,' said Bea, mock rueful. 'And chocolate fingers.'

'We tend to go more for savouries, don't we, Ber?' said Stella.

'She makes these gorgeous crostini things,' said Bernard.

'What's that?' asked Lizzie.

'Tapenade – you know, olive paste – or anchovies with a bit of tomato and garlic, toasted on French bread. Stuff like that,' said Stella.

'Yuk. I hate anchovies. And olives. I love cheese on toast, though.'

'You could have toasted cheese tonight, with us,' suggested Stella.

'She's already had pizza for lunch. She ought to have something a bit more for supper; some vegetables,' said Bea. 'I mean, if that's all right with you.'

'Yes, no problem,' said Stella brightly. 'We can all go shopping together, this afternoon.'

'And mummy?' said Lizzie.

'No, not mummy,' Bea said hastily. 'Mummy's got things to do.'

'Oh! We never do anything, all of us together,' Lizzie complained.

'We're all here now, though, aren't we?' said Bernard.

'And you'll have a lovely time tonight, with daddy,' said Bea.

'And Stella,' Bernard added.

Bea began to feel slightly panicky, almost vertiginous, as if she was being lowered back in the dentist's chair. The word 'we' pricked and pricked her, like an incompetent nurse attempting to find a vein. We meant them, now, and not us. We was an album with empty pages, waiting to be filled with sunny images of the places they'd visited, the people they'd met, the things they had done together. We was the number of miles on the speedometer of their car. The smells in their bathroom. It was exclusive; a sign saying 'Keep Out'. It meant waving from the shore as the little boat of their mutual happiness bobbed prettily on the water. It meant Bernard and Stella – a couple – compact, sufficient.

'What do you think of London?' Bea turned to Stella. She wanted to like her. It might help if they could speak to each other as individuals, not only as before-and-after adjuncts to Bernard.

'It's OK. The job's more appropriate to my skills-set than my last.'

'She's head of department,' explained Bernard.

'Oh. Brilliant,' said Bea.

'It's quite a difficult outfit, politically,' said Stella. 'It's fine for now – to build on my CV – but I don't think that the promotion prospects are that good. They've got very few women at the level I'll be looking at in a year or so.' She sucked air through her teeth, half proud, half aggrieved; like a football supporter assessing the score at half-time.

'So what do you think you might do, then?'

'We're thinking of moving again. Maybe to Strasbourg. There's room within the organisation of the European Parliament for people with my qualifications. If I could put up with being around politicians all the time. Working at the interface of government like I do, you get wary of them, as a breed. But Ber being flexible around his work shouldn't be a problem, and neither of us want to get stuck in a rut at this stage, so . . .' she tailed off.

Lizzie was looking at her comic again. Bea wondered whether she'd taken in what Stella was saying, and hoped she had not. She had been so happy about her father moving down south, closer to her. Bea knew she'd like to see more of Bernard.

'But, yeah, London's all right for now. This girl Lisa that I was at St Andrew's with, she's living in Clerkenwell; and my brother's here too. They're a nice team, at work. It's good.'

'So you don't miss your family, then?'

Stella smiled. 'Do I miss my family, Bernard?' Bernard didn't answer, except to smile back at her.

'No, it's all right. I have a funny relationship with my mother, as Ber knows. Being a few hundred miles away from her isn't too hard.'

'Me too,' said Bea. Tricky mothers: it wasn't the most compelling thing to have in common, but it was better than nothing. They could roll their eyes in comic unity, at least. Bea waited for Stella to show a cordial interest in her, as she had in Stella. For despite her wide-eyed steady regard, her apparent openness, Bea noticed that Stella hadn't addressed a single question to her, a single remark.

'Shall we get some coffee?' said Stella. 'Lizzie – do you want a dessert? Ice cream?'

'So your mother's difficult, is she?' Bea was clutching at straws.

'Not really. She's OK.' It was clear that the subject – and the chink of friendship it might have opened up – was to be closed. Bea felt deflated. A childish sense of injustice flooded through her. She found herself wishing – absurdly – that Bernard would come to her defence. She wished she could appeal to him for clemency from his new lover; wished that he would stick up for her. But if he had noticed the slight she perceived from Stella, he gave no sign of it. Long accustomed though she was to being separated from him, it was hard to adjust to the notion that his loyalties now lay elsewhere.

The meal over, they put on their coats and went out on to the cold street. Bernard knotted Lizzie's scarf, bending over the child; their two faces studious for a moment. Stella and Bea stood by, watching. There were occasions when Bea longed for her daughter's visits to her father; to have time for herself, alone. But when the moment of parting arrived, she invariably struggled to prevent herself from clutching at the little girl.

'I'll drop her back around teatime tomorrow, then,' said Bernard.

'Fine. Great,' said Bea.

They said their goodbyes. Bernard, who had embraced Bea fervently when they'd met at the museum, now made no gesture in her direction. But Stella took a step towards her and the two women found themselves, almost unwittingly, kissing each other on the cheek. The kiss was brittle, gritty-sweet and hollow, like an overcooked meringue.

Walking away, the possibility of recklessness thrilled through Bea like a current. As a child, staying with her grandparents, she had deliberately grasped the electric fence which circled the field behind the vegetable garden. It looked innocent, almost inviting; a taut length of bright yellow string. But when you put your hand on it, heat and pain shot up your whole arm, like burning needles. The sensation – her voluntary submission to it – had made her feel powerful and brave. It was the same feeling she had, now: she was alone, responsible for no one; she could do anything. Go into the nearest pub and order a double brandy, and then another. And another. Buy a fur coat. Go to a pornographic film. She could catch a train to Paris, if she wanted to. The prospect of her own rashness seemed to offer a release, a way out from the tainted sense she had of being herself.

She turned right into Exhibition Road. The sharpness of the wind hit her as she waited for the traffic on the Cromwell Road to come to a standstill, allowing her to cross. She had no conscious destination. At the top of the road the park with its bare trees stretched into the distance before her. Walking in the park was the sort of thing that Bea generally enjoyed, but she was tired of herself today. Instead she turned left towards Kensington High Street. There was a shop selling cowboy boots and Bea stopped to look in the window. Many years before – the year she and Bernard had first met – she had bought a pair of pale suede cowboy boots with elaborate stitching. Even then they had been too wild for her, and had languished unworn in the back of the cupboard. Through the glass Bea caught sight of the man who ran the shop. He had greying shoulder-length hair, permed into poodle-curls and wide hips encased in denim. He looked as if he had once been the road manager of a rock band. Bea realised with distaste that he was probably about the same age as herself.

Without thinking, she turned into Kensington Market and started up the stairs. She began to wander through the stalls. Rows of stiff leather jackets were slung up like carcasses, giving off a gluey smell. There was cheap silver jewellery and fifties clothing. There were skimpy feather boas and psychedelic nylon bell-bottoms. There were patent-leather platform trainers of the type some of Bea's students wore, and red rubber miniskirts and black T-shirts with death's head motifs. Bea had not been here since the nineteen seventies, and it surprised her to find the place so little altered. The acrid odour of patchouli still haunted the musty corridors. The place was almost empty, apart from a small group of young, giggly Japanese girls. At the end of the aisle she came to a curtained stall, where the tattooed man she'd seen in the magazine was sitting with his feet up on a stool, reading the *Daily Mirror*. He did not look up.

In the flesh, the tattooist was smaller than he had seemed in the photograph. His frame was narrow and his face was thin, almost weaselly. The new growth of hair on his skull looked like fuzzy felt. He had outsized feet, Bea noticed, and his hands were big and pale and bony, with prominent knuckles.

'Hello,' said Bea. She had not intended to speak to him, but his hands suggested a vulnerability which emboldened her. She had no idea what she would say next, if he answered.

'All right?' he replied.

'Yes. Yes, thank you. Actually I was thinking about having a tattoo.' Bea's voice sounded ridiculous in her ears: middle-aged, middle-class, false.

Still he did not put down his newspaper. 'Yeah? Have you had any work done before?'

'Work?'

'Tattoos.'

'Oh. Right. No, I haven't.'

'What were you reckoning on, then?' He looked sceptical.

'Well, I saw the thing about you in the magazine and I really like the way you don't have colour on yours. So I was thinking, I don't know, of a spiral.' She had never thought of a spiral before, least of all permanently inked on to her skin.

He folded the paper with a sudden flourish. 'Powerful symbol, a spiral. It's about the mystery of life and death. Egyptians had them, in their hieroglyphs, whatever.'

'You don't think it would look like a target?'

'No chance. A spiral's a spiral. It's about resurrection and immortality, yeah? Where was you thinking of putting it?'

'I don't know,' Bea felt herself flushing, 'maybe on my bottom?'

He stood. His lankiness was more apparent once he was upright, and he seemed younger than he had while sitting down. 'Could be good. What sort of size, then?'

'I think quite big. About five or six inches across.' Bea wanted to impress him. She wanted him to like her, not to judge her.

'Take a while, that size. Probably cost you thirty quid. Depends how long it takes me.'

They looked at each other. Bea felt almost as if she was intoxicated. It was as if the tattooist was the most important person in the world: the one person she had always been waiting to meet. 'It's about resurrection,' he'd said. It was as though he had been sent, to deliver her.

'OK. That sounds fine.'

'All right? You want to go ahead, then, yeah?'

'Yes. Yes, I do.'

'You want to have a think about whether you want it on the left or the right.' He drew back the curtain, ushered her into the cubicle. A flat couch on aluminium legs occupied most of the available space.

'Do I?'

'Course. Right's the conscious, the reason. You're not a bloke, but your right's like the masculine side, yeah? Left's more the magical side, the lunar and that. The feminine. It's more like your intuition.'

'I don't know. I hadn't thought about that. You seem to know an awful lot about the symbolism of it all.'

'Yeah, well. I'm into ancient history – alchemy, and that.'

'Which side do you think?'

'S'up to you.' The tattooist unwrapped a stick of chewing

gum and put it in his mouth. Bea took off her shoes and pulled off her pants and tights. She got up on to the couch and lay on her front, hoicking her skirt up around her middle.

'I just don't know.'

'Depends which side of yourself you think needs renewal. Spirals are all about growth.'

The tattooist had pulled the stool into the booth, and he sat on it now, tearing a small needle from its sterilised plastic pack.

Bea considered. 'I think the left.'

'Right. And just the black ink, yeah?'

'Yes.'

Bea settled her head along the crook of her arms, facing away from him. Having succumbed to the allure of temerity, she was calm, almost sleepy. Towards the tattooist she felt complete trust. There was a feeling of relief, of having reached the safety of dry land. Even the jolt of the needle piercing and pecking at her flesh did not diminish the sense of refuge. The intensity of the pain brought its own kind of relief, like bloodletting. The tattooist worked without speaking, the buzzing whine of the needle only interrupted when he paused to dab beads of blood from her behind. She lay still and thought about Bernard.

Beyond desire, beyond jealousy, beyond even love itself, there remained the things you knew about a person. That's what was left. All that you knew about them: the sounds they made when they stirred in their sleep, the way they buttoned a coat, the books they'd read. What frightened them, what made them laugh. The map of their body. All this knowledge was imprinted, indelibly. Intimacy stayed lodged in the memory long after it had packed its bags and turned its heel upon your heart. In the end the things you knew about another person became almost instinctive, like finding your way home. Like always knowing the way back to an old house, long after you'd moved away.

But you could know the most private things about someone without having any claim to their loyalty, or affection. Knowledge conferred no position, brought no privilege. You didn't even have to like the other person, any more. Every paradox was possible; you could be intimate strangers. You could be, as she believed Bernard was, wistful and indifferent at the same time. In the museum before lunch, while they paused by a video screen showing a manatee in a murky lagoon, he had put one hand on his daughter's shoulder and the other on Bea's: 'My little family,' he'd said, tenderly. She had smiled thinly and moved on. There was something artificial in his familiarity. And other people could find out all that you knew, but it did not make them amiable, as Stella's hostility had shown. This seemed wrong to Bea; like a form of hypocrisy. A kind of blasphemy. It was as if you had taken communion from the same cup – the brightness of its silver still clouded by the print of the other's lips – and yet continued to pass each other, unsmiling, in the parish.

Perhaps there was no escape from what you knew. But maybe there was a way to evade what they knew about you. You could rescue yourself from the inevitability of that, the imprisonment of it. You didn't have to be as they thought you were – tarnished, reproachful. You could be untrue to their memory; betray it, even. You could cheat. Then you could begin to be redeemed, you could cease to be as they remembered you. You could unclench. You could even fail to be disappointed.

The Bounce

To Eddie Campbell

This is what she told me: that as soon as she saw Togare and his tigers she knew she'd never be able to settle down. She'd mapped out a career in ladies' tailoring for herself – a trade, a respectable trade, that she could rise in – but after she saw the big cats enter the ring she forgot all about that. This was at the beginning of the nineteen thirties. She'd gone to the circus with a gentleman friend, of course. But he didn't get a look-in, once she set eyes on Togare. Togare wore satin harem trousers and a plumed headdress, and he was bare-chested. He was quite a showman – he was well known as such – and handsome, too. The Ivor Novello of the ring, she called him.

'Did you fancy him, then?' I asked her. I think I was jealous of her looking at him.

'Togare? Oh heavens, no.' She could sound scornful, Gloria. 'It wasn't him that got me. It was the animals.'

After that first visit she went to the circus again the next night, and the evening after that. She went on her own. Togare shone a narrow beam of light reflected from the blade of his dagger into the tigers' eyes and the animals responded to the glint of the metal, leaping from their pedestals at its signal. That's what it looked like, anyway. When she knew better she found out that they weren't really responding to the dagger at all, but to the sounds Togare made and the way he moved. But she was impressed. More than impressed. Tigers were so big – much bigger than she'd ever imagined, from seeing pictures of them in geography books at school. And a lion: a lion was almost the same size as a cow. It was altogether remarkable to her that one man could control six of them, all at the same time.

Of course she didn't just up sticks and become a lion-tamer overnight. She visited every circus that toured the Manchester and Liverpool area; she went down to Blackpool, too. She saw all the famous trainers of the day, and the more she saw the more it pulled at her. There was one man who performed with a group of nine lions, four polar bears, a brown bear – a Himalayan – and two Great Danes, all in the ring together, weaving and leaping. Trubka, I remember she said he was called – he was a bit of a legend. When she told me about him she recited a passage in the Bible. She knew it by heart: 'And God said, Let us make man in our image, after our likeness: and let them have dominion over the fish of the sea, and over the fowl of the air, and over the cattle, and over all the earth and over every creeping thing that creepeth upon the earth.' She laughed when she said that part, 'every creeping thing that creepeth upon the earth.' The sound of the words amused her. But she'd learned it by heart because it meant something to her: it was about dominion. Man's sacred dominion. The way she saw it, working with wild animals was not a breach of man's trust with nature, but the very living embodiment of it. For Gloria it was akin to a Calling.

Her father was head porter at a firm of auctioneers in the Wirral. There were six of them living in the house: her mother and father, her two brothers, her grandmother and herself. She shared a bedroom with her grandmother. There was no option; it was a three-bedroomed house. But she didn't like being cooped up; that was one of the main things about her. She never regretted leaving that house, even though her own mother didn't speak to her for several years afterwards. They were respectable people and to have their only daughter join a circus and mix with riff-raff – what they thought of as riff-raff – was terrible to them.

Anyway she joined Maître Columbo's, taking charge of repairs and alterations in the wardrobe wagon and selling programmes at the start of each show. All she wanted, though, was to work with the wild animals and she haunted the big cages like a ghost. She'd watch the trainers practising, and the beast boys going about their jobs; she watched and, gradually, she learned. Everyone in circus families knows that a gift with wild animals is something you can't inherit: the best trainers are made, not born. So she was in with a chance. And she'd already decided on a name for herself. She was going to be called Gloria d'Angelo. She said it was a name she could see in lights. Once she'd made up her mind on it she knew she was going to go far. And it was. Gloria d'Angelo was a wonderful name.

★

He would not have married me if it hadn't been for the farm. I know that. I've always known it, but the fact of it is, it never made any difference to me. Because the farm was a part of who I was, just as much as my face, or the turn of my ankle. Courting is all about finding things attractive in the other person, whether it's their laugh, or the way they move their hands, or their money. I don't see why it shouldn't be money, or land. A working farm is not a trivial thing. People have married for much less. A lot of the girls would've walked up the aisle with him without even knowing him really, just for the looks of him. I knew I was lucky to get him: Matthew Brennan, the handsomest man in all of eastern Ireland. We local girls used to giggle and wonder whether he was a changeling, because old Mr and Mrs Brennan had nothing about them – to call them ordinary-looking would have been a compliment. Mrs Brennan in particular: she had dark moles on her face, with little wiry hairs growing out of them, like the eyes in a flawed potato. But Mattie was more than handsome, even as a boy. He was dazzling. When he smiled it was like the sun coming out, his teeth were so straight and the whites of his eyes so white. He was radiant, like an angel. If you can imagine the better-looking brother of the film star Gary Cooper that'll give you an idea. Matthew was beautiful as a young man.

He could've taken his pick. As well as the looks he was hard-working, good-hearted; everyone liked him. I wasn't the prettiest girl around, I knew that. But my hair was nice – shiny like horse chestnuts – and I had a good pair of legs. I liked dancing. And I was the sensible choice for him, because he had been working over at Desmond's place as a herdsman, and of course my da kept a dairy herd himself; I was accustomed to the hours and I knew a lot about cattle. When da passed on, the farm would go to me, and the livestock with it. Everyone knew that.

I think we were both disappointed, on the wedding night. Not that he was rough at all. It didn't hurt as I'd expected it to, but I can't say I liked the feeling of it, either. It didn't make us intimate with one another; if anything it had the opposite effect, as though we both felt ashamed and had to retreat into ourselves afterwards. And I didn't like the smell it left about me – the faint whiff like the shallows at low tide, like seaweed and buttermilk mixed together – as I pulled on my drawers the next morning. I must admit that I hoped, then, that it wouldn't happen every night. And it did not.

I knew what the town gossips said. I knew people thought he wasn't true to me; that a man so handsome would be certain to stray. People thought that because we hadn't had a child after two years of marriage it meant that I must be dry and unwelcoming, like the cracked mud of a stream-bed in high summer. But people were wrong. I never refused him. And I know that he never went with another woman – I was going to say girl, but of course I was no longer a girl really – until she came to us. And she was no girl, herself. Gloria must have had a good ten years on Mattie, although I don't believe he ever knew her age, exactly. It wouldn't have made any difference, anyway: she could have been a hundred and twenty-five. It wouldn't have made any difference.

★

I'd never seen a woman like her. Everything about her was different to the local women: her walk, her voice, the look of her. It was not that she was beautiful, because she was not. But she had such a glamour about her: she wore jodhpurs, even when she was nowhere near a horse, and lipstick in broad daylight. She must already have been in her mid-thirties then, maybe older. Her skin had been darkened by the sun from working outside, like a man's. You have to remember that this was almost fifty years ago – the women in those days valued a pale complexion. I reckon that Gloria was single-handedly responsible for introducing the notion of a suntan into Ireland.

And she smoked all the time. Player's, her cigarettes were, and she'd tap each one several times against the card of the box before she lit up. There was a picture of a sailor's face on the box, and she'd always aim the unlit cigarette – tap tap tap – at its centre. Then as she smoked she'd raise her fingers to her face from time to time, to take away the tiny strands of tobacco which occasionally stuck at her mouth. Each time she did it the rosy tip of her small tongue would be just visible between her lips – just for an instant – like a cat lapping milk. The sight of it used to make me thirsty.

Later on she told me that the way she had of smoking – 'my famous nonchalance', she called it – had been responsible for her first break in circus. She'd been with Columbo's for six months at the time. The maître himself performed the cigarette trick, but the girl he'd been using had to leave for some reason, so he asked Gloria to try out. She had to wear a sequinned dress, and never flinch. She would stand at one side of the ring with a lit cigarette held high, like the Statue of Liberty with her torch; at the far side, the maître would crack a thirty-five-foot bull whip and extinguish the cigarette with a single flourish. It was dangerous, but Gloria was not afraid. She was indifferent to pain, her own and other people's; she relished danger. That's what made her good at her job.

After that she persuaded the maître to let her try out as a beast girl. She moved slowly among the animals and, crucially, she was patient. She'd found out all about the great trainers – there was Sawade, Rudolph Matthies, Hans Brick – and she was determined to train her animals in the Hagenbeck way, by gentling them. The old meat-and-stick methods didn't interest her. But it wasn't only that she was a natural with the animals, and unafraid. It was that she knew how to make them move. That was her secret.

'If you went to the ballet and it was just a lot of girls in sticking-out skirts standing still in a line you'd ask for your money back,' she said. 'Movement changes things, even the most ordinary things. Look at fountains – they're only water. And fireworks: nothing more than sparks of light. It's the movement which gives people the thrill. Same with wild animals.'

We were lying across the bed at the back of her wagon.

'What the audience want, you see, is to feel frightened. They want to feel the real fear they'd have if they met a lion in the wild, but with the trainer taking all the risks for them. You have to try and give them that fear, but without actually terrifying them; you don't want them all dropping dead of heart attacks. It'd spoil the show. So what I do is create enough movement so that the punters in the ringside seats can feel the flurry. Then their thrill ripples backwards into the crowd.'

She was proud of her skill with her lions; it was certainly the thing she liked best about herself. But the funny thing is I don't know, even now, how much her work was part of her attraction for me. I worked with animals myself – always had – and Aisling was as easy and instinctive with the cows in her father's herd as Gloria was with the wild beasts. Knowing about animals is only remarkable to people who don't know about them. It doesn't make a lot of difference whether they're wild or tame, local or exotic. Once you're acquainted with ferrets and foxes it's not such a leap to understand what makes a lion tick. A dog or a pony is not so different to an elephant.

I think what really got to me about Gloria was the contradictions of her. How slight her voice was – almost like a girl's – but how she swore, just for the hell of it. I'd never heard a woman curse before. She could arm-wrestle with the best of the tent-hands, and hold her drink like a man; but there was a delicacy about her also; something discreet and half-hidden that was not like a man at all. Her arms and thighs were lean and sinewy, but her breasts were soft and pale and there was a slight curve to her belly. Her nipples were small and pink as the pads of a new-born kitten's paws. I used to bury my face in the nape of her neck, in the tangle of her hair, and wish that I could just disappear in her.

★

The Columbo entourage arrived at Dun Laoghaire soon after the outbreak of the war. They told us that British promoters were already cancelling the bigger shows, because they were wary of the risk of wild animals escaping if there were enemy bombing raids. There was a famous circus man called Alfred Court who'd somehow managed to get half a dozen trainers and close to a hundred wild animals out of the country. Columbo took his lead from Court and obtained permission to ship his circus lock, stock and barrel from Liverpool docks to the safety of Irish soil. Old Columbo had friends at Palmer's in Dublin; he was hoping he'd be able to contract some of his acts out to them when the tenting season opened, in the following spring. In the meantime they needed winter quarters, which was how they had fetched up at ours.

My da had bought out our neighbour's place, years before. There was more than sixty acres, as well as a set of buildings. We'd not had much use for the buildings – it was the land we wanted, so we'd have grazing enough to increase our herd. By shifting things about a little, Matthew and I were able to let Columbo's have these buildings to themselves entirely, together with a couple of paddocks and the use of a field or two. They'd buy hay from us, and bedding straw. The arrangement suited us, and them too.

I liked it, at first. I liked hearing the lions roaring across the last of the wild fuchsias in the hedgerows, and the way the sound of them made the cows in the milking parlour lift their heads and blink, and listen. Some of the older children from the town rode out on their bicycles – two to a bike, one on the handlebars, one on the saddle – to see what they could see of the circus. The adults soon followed. It was novel. Quaint. To see a pair of camels being led about the greensward, or to catch a glimpse inside the warm secret interiors of the wagons; to see two Hungarians with lighted roll-ups between their teeth juggling seven apples apiece – it made a spectacle, even without the glitter of the big top.

Matthew or I would walk over the farm to them twice a day. We sold them butter and milk, and the odd stillborn calf as meat for the lions. Leeks. I'd guessed there was a woman, even before I saw him with her, because he began to shave every morning; his cheeks hadn't been as smooth for the six years since he'd courted me. I said nothing – I was his wife, not his jailer. I don't believe there's harm in flirting. It wasn't until I spotted the two of them strolling together across the yard that I realised that he'd been with her. I could tell it at once. I could feel it in my body, the heat spilling across my face and my legs going hollow, so I was half dizzy; if I could have sat down there and then, I would've. I had never seen him so concentrated on another person before, that's how I knew. Mattie never rested his eyes on other people; he never stared. His glance skimmed. It was only when he was checking the herd, or fishing, or looking out across the pasture that his gaze would hold and deepen. And that was how he looked at her, at Gloria. As if he was searching for the barely perceptible movement of a trout in the green shade of a river. As though he was trying to find something he'd lost.

*

She never did love me, I can see that now. I think she was fond of me, but truly it was the attention she liked: when she made me gasp in her bed I think it must have been like a little replica of the response she got from an audience. I think she was missing the eyes of a crowd on her, the power she got from her performance in the ring. She knew I was a married man – she couldn't not, at such proximity – but I suppose she thought she would be no threat to Aisling, that she'd move on sooner or later. Perhaps she thought I would forget all about her.

What she loved were her animals. Hours and hours she was with them every day, practising, talking to them in the low voice she kept only for their ears. She'd have them jump through hoops and create variations of pyramids. The one lioness, Artemis, was so gentle that Gloria used to walk down the lane towards Bray with her on a collar and chain; but it was the other one that was her true pride and joy. Delilah. It was Delilah that she was sure she could train to do the bounce.

No woman had ever staged a bounce before. And hardly any men had, either. She used to say that it was a uniquely English trick; that you couldn't see it done anywhere else on earth. She had first seen it performed on the fairgrounds, and not in a circus at all. A fellow called Black Albert had had an actual lion, but bouncers were generally female animals; Tommy Kayes had used two lionesses in the cage while a lion paced outside the bars, to create extra tension. At the end of the thirties she'd seen Eddie Campbell do a spectacular bounce with a lioness at Wilson's Menagerie in Glasgow. She'd gone back to look at the performance, four days in a row. She'd seen others before, but it was that one which clinched it; that's what made her decide to try it herself.

In those days they still used square cages to present animals – it was before the circular arena cages that they have today were widely in use. And you could only do a bounce with a square cage; that's why it'll never be seen again, now. It takes a pair of animals to do it. They circle the cage furiously, moving upwards; their forms should almost blur from the motion, like riders in a wall of death. The trainer stands in the centre of the cage, taking one step forward, one step back to create the illusion of being at the very eye of a storm of frenzied beasts. The magic of the trick is how dangerous it looks, as if the trainer might really be savaged at any moment. There's a long build up to it. Three-quarters of a bounce consists of the trainer circling the outside of the cage, apparently watching for an opportunity to enter while the raging lionesses are not looking his way. The animals should seem so frantic that the audience will practically beg the trainer not to go in. When Gloria saw the bounce in Glasgow people were calling out 'don't do it' in anguish.

Once he's in – surrounded, his life threatened – the climax of the trick arrives. It has to look as if he may never be able to come out alive, as if he had been insane to go into the cage at all. Then, suddenly, at an imperceptible sign from the man handling the gate, the trainer has to hurl himself into the refuge of the adjacent safety cage. Gloria told me that it's here that the full beauty of the bounce, its crowning moment of wonder and terror, occurs. One of the lionesses will still be on the bars at the far end of the cage, but instead of spilling in an arc to the floor, she will leap through the air, towards the safety gate. The gate should actually be closing when the lioness hits it – if the timing is right it will appear as if a four hundred-pound beast, hurtling through the air, has slammed the gate shut by its impact; only a fraction of a second too late to have savaged the trainer. It will seem as though the trainer has only barely, by a whisker, escaped from the very jaws of death.

This was what Gloria wanted, more than anything else in her life, to achieve. That's what she'd been working towards, practising for, before Columbo's left for Ireland. She hadn't had Delilah for long – she'd only acquired the lioness a few months before she came here – but she knew that the beast had the makings of a bouncer. They either have it or they don't: you can't train an animal with no innate inclination to jump to perform the trick. But Delilah had it, Gloria knew that. She had her name – Gloria d'Angelo – and now she was determined to present a spectacle worthy of it, if worthy of the glory of the angels. The bounce was the one – it would be magnificent, enchanting. No one who saw it would ever forget her.

Before Christmas I noticed that she was jumpy, irritable. She didn't stretch out on her narrow bed in front of me any longer, smiling. She didn't light the lamps in her wagon; she just sat in the fading dusk at the small table, away from me, smoking. There was no invitation about her. I'd watch the lit ends of her cigarettes glow and pulse in the darkness – like the eyes of a fox caught for an instant in the lights of a vehicle – as she put them to her mouth; and I'd feel jealous of her cigarette, then. I didn't know how to talk to her; the desire I felt for her made me dumb, like an animal. I knew something was wrong; perhaps she was missing her family, her country. Perhaps she didn't want me any more. I dreaded to ask her, so I waited for her to tell me what was on her mind. And she did tell me, the day before Christmas Eve.

★

Even when we were alone together – the two of us – in the house, the fact of her was always there with us; like a bad debt. Leaden. As the days grew shorter his absences became more obvious to us both, and his reappearance at the kitchen door in the treacly darkness of the early evenings had us avoiding each other's eyes. I could see he wasn't even enjoying it, not by then. He was in too deep for it to be a source of happiness. The house felt as if no one lived there any more: the linoleum on the bathroom floor, the tap that always dripped against the stone sink in the pantry, the thin plaintive chime of the long-case clock at the foot of the stairs; everything seemed shabby and abandoned and forlorn. We'd sit facing one another across the table, drinking our cooling tea, and we'd lie side by side in our bed at night; and she'd be there with us, unspoken. In his mind all the time. I didn't know what to do. I didn't know how I'd manage the herd, if he left me. And then he told me.

'You'll have known that I've been seeing someone down with the circus people. A woman.'

He was looking down at his hands when he said it. I felt cold with fear, panic.

'Don't, Mattie. Will you not tell me, please?'

'I must. I must, now. It's gone beyond not speaking.'

'I can bear it if you love her. I know you love her. But I cannot bear to hear you say so, Mattie. I cannot bear for you to tell me about her. Please. Please don't do it.'

'Aisling, there's . . .'

I cut him off.

'Carry on with it, if you must. God knows I've turned a blind eye enough already. I've faced Columbo and the rest of them, let them stay on my land – my land I got from my own daddy – when I could have turned them off as soon as I saw what was going on. I've had to endure the pity on their faces, the shifty looks when they see me. You turning away from me in your sleep. How do you think that's been for me? But if we speak of it now we'll be obliged to act on what is said. You'll have to choose, and I don't want to be the one you've not chosen. Please, Mattie. I'm asking you.'

'It's not a matter of choosing. There's going to be a child. She's having a child.'

I felt as if I'd swallowed a stone when he told me that.

'You'll be leaving, then.'

It wasn't a question, but he answered me anyway.

'I don't know what will happen. She's set her heart on this thing with the lions; she's worked for years to come to this point with them. She doesn't want a child of mine. Of anybody's.'

I could feel myself blush, at that. Neither of us said anything for a while then. I could hear a dog barking somewhere, across the fields. I felt a lot of things, but the main thing I felt was pity for him. I stood up and went around to where he was standing with his back to the stove and I put my hand out to touch his face. I hadn't touched him, not deliberately, for months. I suppose he wasn't expecting it, and I certainly wasn't expecting what happened next: I had never seen a man weep before. But that's what he did. He stood there and cried out loud like a widow at a funeral, and even when I put my arms around him he still kept his own arms straight by his sides, stiffly; as if he'd been starched with grief. It was terrible to be of no comfort to him. So I waited till he was quiet and then I went outside and stood alone in the yard in the cold, and wished to God that Gloria had never come to Bray.

We got through Christmas. At Mass I knew we were both praying the same prayer: that an answer to our trouble would present itself. All the little noises in the house were grating to us in those days – the scraping of a chair pulled away from the table, the sudden blast of water filling the kettle, the clinking metal latch of the door. After New Year came I couldn't stand it any longer. I told him to go down and talk to her. He came back and reported what they'd said.

'Someone at Palmer's in Dublin has family the other side of the city; near Drogheda I believe she said it was. They've a few acres. She's going to take the animals up there in a week or two. She wants to keep on with the training of them until the confinement. She'll be leaving.'

'And what about when the baby comes? What then?'

'She's saying that she'll see about having the child adopted, when the time comes. There's a convent nearby where she's going. The nuns could help find a place for the child.'

'Why would she do that, Mattie? Did you not offer to go with her and be a father to the baby?'

'I did.' He coloured as he said it.

'Oh, you did. You did offer, then.' I hated him at that moment.

'She has a husband, Aisling, in England. Not far from Liverpool, they live; he has a business there. She plans to go back to him, when this war's ended. She's only away from him now because of the lions, for their safety. She says he need never know about the child. She has a future with him. She doesn't want him to know.'

'She's married?'

'She is, yes.'

'How long has she been married for?'

'I don't know. I didn't ask.'

'But this husband let her go, for the sake of her lions? You mean to tell me that all this has happened just because of a few mangy circus beasts?'

'Don't, Aisling. There's no use for it.'

'You won't hear ill of her, will you; even now. Is that it?'

'It won't put things back to rights, that's all I'm saying to you.'

'No, Matthew, it won't. There's no words that can do that. Not now.'

'We'll say no more about it, then,' said Matthew.

★

The rest of Columbo's entourage stayed on with us, without Gloria, until the middle of March; but I didn't see so much of them, after the new year came in. I was relieved when the time came for them to go and I knew Aisling was, too. The first signs of spring kept us out working for longer and longer hours, and it was better to be outside; neither of us were comfortable together in the house. The winter had dragged like the feet of a pallbearer at a fat man's funeral. There were many evenings when I thought of leaving, not to be with Gloria for I knew she wouldn't have me, but just to be away from everything that I'd known before. Sometimes it felt as if the only way to be rid of the sorrow would be to erase the past altogether, and start again in another place. I'd wake up in the morning wanting her. I felt the grief of missing her like hunger; it was like being famished. But me and Aisling, we had a farm: we knew all about waiting out the bad seasons, getting through the lean times. We held on.

The summer came – it was a dry summer – and we were occupied with the harvest. And then Aisling told me she was going to visit her auntie, who lived up at Navan. She used to go and see her every year, before the autumn; I thought nothing of it. I was glad, in fact, to be getting a few days to myself. It hadn't been the best of times, for either of us.

I was to go to the railway station for her on the following Tuesday. I was early for the train; I am always early for arrivals and departures. There was a man I knew waiting there, too; I fell in with him and we stood there together on the platform, passing the time of day. Then the train came in and there was my wife, and another traveller had to hand her valise down from the carriage because her arms were full. There wasn't time to think or wonder. If there had been more time I'd have guessed she was holding the child as a courtesy, while its mother stepped down. As it was I was by her side in a moment and she was handing me the bundle.

'This is your daughter,' she said to me. 'We'll be calling her Patricia.' That was the name of her own sister, who'd died as a wean.

Then she went to pick up her own case, to carry herself.

★

Patty never looked anything like her birth mother. Only in her colouring: she has tawny hair and her eyes have hazel flecks in them, like that woman; but she's Matthew's girl. Beautiful. But I believe that her beauty has been like a curse to her. She was always so restless, and I think that's why: her looks have been like a passport to her, making her think that anything could be possible for her. Taking her away from home, from us. She'd already gone to London by the time she was eighteen years of age.

It's as if she can't decide who she is underneath the mask of her beauty. One year she came home and told us she was working as an actress, but the year after she'd decided she wanted to be a theatre designer. Then she got herself involved with a group of women who were all into civil rights and she went to live in America for a time. She cut off her hair. She smoked French cigarettes and hardly ever smiled; when she came to visit she spent all her time writing long letters on crackly blue airmail paper. She never wrote so often to us, when she was away. She brought little bags of rice with her, because she wouldn't eat potatoes at that time; she was into macrosomething. She was as pale as the flesh of a mushroom, then. She left America and spent some time in a Buddhist community in midwest France. She grew her hair again. Began painting. And somewhere in the middle of it all she produced a child. Fern.

She's never told us who the girl's father is; I wonder if

157

she even knows herself. Whoever he was, he can't have been much to look at, because Fern's not lovely like her mother. But she has a charm to her: she's slim, with a boyish frame and great big hands. Got a long straight nose like a queen on a roman coin. She must have been nine years old – maybe ten – when she came to stay with us. Patty was planning to travel across the islands of Indonesia for the winter; even she could see that it was an unsuitable journey for a child to make – the heat, the bugs. And there was her education to consider. So we enrolled her into the high school in Bray, just for the one term. Her mother'd be back for her in April, she said. We all believed it, at the time; Patty probably believed it herself, too.

But she didn't come back. Letters came, explaining the delay; she'd be back for Fern in June, she wrote. Then it was to have been the autumn. She'd met some Dutch people and travelled to Nepal with them; months later word came that a couple of Australians had invited her to join their trip to Singapore. It was with these two that she eventually pitched up in some sort of commune, just outside of Melbourne; it was a small group of craftspeople. She wrote to say that she had begun painting a series of pictures inspired by the Aborigine myths. There was a man. She sounded happy. Fern had been with us for a year, by then. She'd settled, made friends. She loved her mother, but she's like me: she's happier with the routine of life on the farm here, among dependable people. So she stayed on, with us.

★

Patty was six years old – already in school – when Aisling came back from the doctor's and said she was expecting: she was almost five months gone. We'd never done anything to prevent a child from being conceived before then, but it had not happened. I'd grown to accept that it was something about the chemistry of the two of us put together which didn't work; I'd never blamed her for it. I don't know why it should have come about, after all that time. But it did, and Neil was born the year after the war in Europe ended.

He's steady, like his mother. The girl takes after myself, more. Fern. She has a look of Gloria about her, as well. The old farm will go to Neil and his family – he's three children of his own – but Aisling's willing the sixty acres to the girl, with the bungalow. It's her home now after all, and her grandmother thinks the world of her. She's been here with us almost ten years now. After Neil married we converted the old cattle stalls – where Columbo's used to store their hay and animal feed, when the circus was here – into a three-bedroom bungalow. We had the third room for Patty, in case she ever came.

I've never spoken about what happened, not in all the years. It wouldn't have been respectful to Aisling. People who knew the real story of Patty's birth, or guessed it, kept their mouths shut; and I guess people forgot, mostly, in the end. But I have told the girl. I told her at the end of last summer, before she went off to university. It was partly because she's the only person who's ever asked me about the past. Patty's always been so caught up with her own life that it's never occurred to her that anything's ever happened to Aisling and me, and Neil just takes things as he sees them. His children are closer to their mother's side of the family. So there's no one else except Fern who has ever enquired about what it was like, when we were young. And I thought, as well, that it would help her to make sense of her mother if she were to know that flight was in the blood. It was Gloria's legacy to her daughter, the one thing which Patricia inherited from her. The not being able to stay.

★

159

All my life I have prayed, without ever being sure of my faith; without being able to know for sure that my prayers would be heard. My mother used to tell me that there is grace to be found through observation and I have always hoped that what she said was true. I prayed that God would guide me through the dark times and show me the right course. And I confess I did pray selfishly for myself, as well: I asked that Matthew would love me, would grow to love me. I always understood that he wasn't a very imaginative man; not that he was shallow, but that he took things as he saw them. Knowing that made it possible for me to see why he became caught up with that woman. It made me able to forgive him, the understanding why. There was nothing metaphorical about her, if you can say that about a person. She was all glamour and sequins and full of danger: she was so literal. I could see how he'd be dazzled. It took me a while to stop blaming him, but after she'd gone and I'd decided not to part from him; after I'd decided about taking in the baby, I used to pray that he'd start to love me. If we were going to have a life together he might as well love me. And he did. In the end, I know he did.

★

I knew I didn't have to tell the girl not to mention it to Aisling. I knew she wouldn't hurt her grandmother with talk of it. But I did ask her not to go telling Patty when she writes to her mother: it'd only upset her, all that way away. If her mother comes back here after Aisling and me are buried, she can tell her all about it then. Perhaps it'll bring the two of them closer. But it's to be our secret together, for now.

'But did you ever see her again, the circus lady? Did you never speak to her?' she asked me, one day.

'No. She never got in touch, not after she moved away.'

'So we'll never know whether she did the trick, the bounce. Or what happened to her.'

'She did do it. That much I do know. She did the bounce in Blackpool over in England, at the end of the nineteen forties. Caused quite a stir, apparently. She was the first woman to achieve it. The only woman, probably.'

'How do you know? How do you know that, if you never saw her?' She doesn't miss anything, that Fern.

So then I told her about Chipperfield's Irish tour.

When Neil was a lad – he must have been thirteen or so at the time – he'd come home from school begging to be taken to the show. There were bills posted all over town, that's how he knew about the circus. Everyone had heard of Chipperfield's – the name was like a legend in itself. But his mother wouldn't hear of it: Neil was not to go, even if all his schoolmates did. She didn't want him mixing with circus rabble. The answer was no, and there was an end to it. But I went. It was the only lie I ever told her, after Patty's birth. I told Aisling I was going down to Wicklow to see about a bull. Of course I went to the afternoon show and afterwards I walked around the far side of the big top, to the wagons. I could smell the animals before I saw them. It's a smell I like – like untreated wool and dung and new leather and fresh hay all mixed up together. It reminded me of Gloria, but I didn't mention that to the girl. The smell of the animals brought back a powerful memory of her: her strong wrists, the lovely colour of her skin.

There was a man near the tiger cages, mixing up what looked like feed for the horses. When I first saw him I took him for a lad – his frame was so slight – but as I neared I saw he had the face of a man in his fifties. He looked like an old ventriloquist's dummy. An old ventriloquist's dummy that's had too many whiskies.

'Public entrance is round the other side, chum. You're not allowed around here.' The man didn't even look up.

'I was wanting to enquire after someone I was thinking you might know. She used to train lions for Maître Columbo; it'd be going on for forty years ago. Gloria d'Angelo. The name was Gloria d'Angelo.'

The man stood straight. 'Who's asking?'

I didn't like his manner at all. 'I'm a friend of hers. I was. It's nothing to do with money, if that's what you mean.'

'Old Gloria d'Angelo. Now there's a name I haven't heard for a year or two. Gloria the loin-tamer, that's what we used to call her.'

I could feel myself colour at that.

'Whoops! Have I said wrong? 'Scuse I, sir! No, she was was all right, was Gloria. One of the best. She wasn't scared of anything − except spiders. Did the bounce at Blackpool, after the war, put on a marvellous display with it. Got offers from all the big-name troupes after that, she did. European tours, Mexico; the lot. She could have gone anywhere with that act. She was good. Nothing ruffled her.'

'Is she still working in the business?'

'I doubt it. That I doubt very much. She got mauled − must have been in '51 or '52 − and lost the use of her right arm altogether. There was a lion, it'd done the rounds; been sold on from one place to another. Nobody could do much with it − it was a mean-tempered bugger. Big. Anyway, Paul Gowing − he was the manager of Columbo's at the time − he bet her she wouldn't be able to quieten this lion down. She should've known better, of course. Hagenbeck's Golden Rule: if an animal shows any sign of becoming dangerous, exclude it from the show. She of all people would have known that, but if you remember Gloria you'll know what she was like. She couldn't resist a challenge. She bit off more than she could chew there, to coin a phrase.'

'Was she badly hurt?'

'Like I say, it was her arm. The rest of her was all right. Didn't touch her face, which was lucky. I believe she met a man from overseas a while after it happened – South African, I think he was – and emigrated out there, with him. He wasn't a circus bloke.'

'What about her husband, the man she'd been married to before the war?'

'There wasn't no husband! She wasn't one to be tied down, not Gloria. No, she was never married – I don't know where you got that idea from. She was never the family type. Well, you'd know that, seeing as you were friendly with her. I'll tell you what, though; old Mario – he's in charge of the big cats – he might know more about her. They were pally, for a while. I'll go and give him a shout, if you like.'

'No, don't trouble yourself. I was just asking, is all.'

'No bother. Mario might even have an address for her, you never know. At least he'd be able to remember if it was South Africa; it might have been Rhodesia, now that I come to think of it. Stop here, look, and I'll go and fetch him from his trailer. Two ticks.'

The man scuttled off before I could stop him. I didn't want to wait to hear any more. For a moment I just stayed where I was, then I turned back towards the field where the cars were parked and walked off as fast as I could. When I got to the van and started driving home there was nothing in my head except the road in front of me. At Enniskerry – less than a mile from the farm – I pulled over on to the verge for a while. I wanted to try and think about what he'd said; I wanted to digest the lie she'd told me. I didn't tell the girl this part, of course. I just told her about meeting the man and that he'd said Gloria'd done the bounce. I left out about the not being married, I don't know why.

It was coming towards the end of the day. The sky was all glowing, with only thin lines of its paleness showing through the colour, like the marbling of fat through a side of beef. I didn't get out of the van, I just sat there thinking and looking at the sky. I tried to feel something. I knew I should be angry about the deception; hurt, too. I should have hated Gloria, then, for rejecting her child without any reason except her own ambition. But I did not. Visiting Chipperfield's, that had brought her back – but it was only a memory, a reminder of the past. I could remember how it had been to desire her, more than forty years ago. I could almost taste her, still, in my memory. But to have felt something more about her now, in the present, would have been like saying that my life – all of our lives – since that time have not been worth anything. It would have meant that she still mattered more than the rest. And that's not so. I've had a family, a farm, Aisling; I've been all right. And she got her moment of glory, there, with the bounce; whatever happened to her afterwards, she had that. Perhaps, in the end, you just have to trust that the life you've lived is the right one for you. I think you do.

Indian Summer

I didn't mind being fat. Everyone else seemed to expect me to be embarrassed by my weight – I mean my mother and my Aunt Rose – but it didn't really bother me. To be honest, I even quite liked it. Watching telly on the settee after I got home from school in the afternoons, I could scrunch whole inches of my own flesh between my fingers, or squidge bits together and encase my fingers in between. I could run my thumbs down the descending folds of my tummy; they were like a solid waterfall of skin. It actually felt quite nice. In bed at night I'd put my hands under my pyjamas and feel how the temperature of me altered from one part to another. The thin bits, like my forearms and chest, were hot; but the fat parts – especially my lower abdomen – always felt cold to my touch. I don't know why this was, but it made my skin feel interesting. People always think that fat people are warm, but they're not; not necessarily. Not all fat is the same. Some bits are soft and cushiony – how thin people imagine fat would be. My tummy is like that. But other parts, at the tops of my legs and arms for instance, feel hard and tight; more like a full suitcase.

Everyone else in my family was thin. Everyone except my father's mother, who never got up from her chair and spent all her time drinking little glasses of sweet sherry and talking on the telephone. My fat wasn't like hers. I walked home from school every afternoon and I went swimming twice a week; once with the school and once on my own, at the weekend. I wasn't fat from lack of exercise. I think I was just fat because I ate too much food.

I didn't especially enjoy eating. It was never at the top of the list of things I liked to do. I preferred reading, or watching telly, or even doing nothing. Thinking. I liked just sitting in my room. I didn't get fat because I loved food or anything; it was more that I seemed to need a lot of it. Floury things most: biscuits and toast and bowls of cereal. Lots of bowls of cereal.

Every now and again my mother would decide that she was going to be a perfect mother, smiling over the stove like the woman in the Bisto advertisement. Then she'd cook a proper meal for us both. She'd go out and buy loads of vegetables and a joint of meat and she'd make a huge roast dinner. In her enthusiasm for her new role she'd make much too much food for just the two of us: enough roast potatoes for six; a great dish of soapy Yorkshire pudding. If she cooked enough for a big family, she thought she could create the atmosphere of one: the warmth, the conversation, the friendly bickering. But there weren't enough people to eat up all the food she'd prepared and she and I couldn't make enough talk to go round, either. We'd sit there with dishes of only a quarter-eaten food going cold around us and not be able to think of anything much to say to each other.

These meals occurred every few weeks. The rest of the time my mother didn't really go in for cooking at all. She wasn't very interested in things like housework; she had too much else on her mind, she said. There'd be a baked potato for supper, or tinned spaghetti on toast. Sometimes sausages.

But most of the time I'd just make myself a snack when I got in from school, and then have something before bed. I think that's how I began to put the weight on. I didn't know about calories or anything – I was twelve or thirteen. I just wanted not to feel empty.

She did her best. It wasn't her fault that she wasn't like everybody else's mothers and in some ways she was preferable to other mums, anyway. When she was in the mood, she was more fun, more daring. She wasn't strict or anything; you could do pretty much whatever you liked and she didn't really notice. She never told me off, not as such, although she could be sharp-tongued. She didn't make me go to bed at a certain time every evening, or remind me to brush my teeth or say my prayers. She never even asked if I had home-work to do. All that was up to me. I could have stayed up till midnight every single night and she wouldn't have turned a hair. Lots of kids would have envied a mother like that. A lot of boys would have thought I was lucky.

But she wasn't always happy-go-lucky. Sometimes she didn't seem to notice when I spoke to her and she wouldn't answer properly. After her mother died and my dad left home, she went to the doctor for her nerves and he gave her these little blue pills; I think it was partly to do with them that she got a bit absent-minded, especially in the evenings after a drink or two. She liked to sit in the kitchen, then, and play patience with the pack of cards spread out on the table in front of her. She'd frown as she leaned over the upturned cards and sometimes, if I came in to get a drink or a biscuit, I'd see her as if she wasn't my mother at all, but a stranger, and I'd remember how pretty she still was. I didn't really like seeing her in that way, because it made me feel sorry for her, and helpless. And I didn't enjoy being in the same room as my mother, because there was always something a little bit unsettled about her. Restless. It was as if she was always waiting for something, or someone. It felt like sitting in the waiting room at a railway station, or the dentist's. It gave you the kind of feeling that made you want to keep clearing your throat.

Quite recently, when I talked to him about that time, Mr Richards said it struck him that although my mother and I had been living under the same roof together, we'd both been very isolated. He wondered whether we might each have retreated into our separate worlds because of all the loss we'd both had. I wasn't sure about that theory, although of course I didn't want to be rude and contradict him. It was kind of him to take an interest. But I'd always liked being on my own.

The thing about my mother – it was actually true of both my parents, this – was that she was unpredictable. She didn't stick to a routine, or have any kind of timetable for her life. She did things at unexpected times. Like the time she took me to the lido.

Up until then she hadn't shown any sign of even noticing that I liked swimming, although by the time I was thirteen I was going to the baths three times a week, sometimes four. I loved it because my weight didn't make any difference, not in the water. It was an advantage, actually. Whales and dolphins have thick layers of blubber, after all; it felt right to be fat when I was swimming. It was as if I was in correct balance with the water, matching its density. It was as if I was in my true element.

In the last week of September that year there was a bit of a heatwave. The first couple of weeks had been rainy and quite cold, but then it seemed as if the summer had come back again; the sky was so blue and the air was warm and light on your skin and the pavements smelled like the thick brown paper you used for wrapping up parcels from having the sun on them. I'd started back at school ten days before and I was glad, really, to be back into my routine; the holidays had dragged on a bit. I was going to be starting my O-level coursework and I felt busy and excited and purposeful, like you do at the start of something new.

One night my mother woke me up by coming into my room and shaking me by the shoulder. She did that, sometimes. Usually she'd say nothing; she'd just sit on my bed for a little while in the dark and then go back to her own room. I could hear her breathing. I don't know whether she wanted anything, but I don't think she did. Anyway we never referred, either of us, to her occasional night visits. But this time she spoke.

'Francis! Francis, wake up,' she was hissing, as if she was trying not to wake anyone else in the house, although of course there were only the two of us there.

I rolled over. 'Mum, what's the matter? Are you OK?'

'Of course I'm all right. Come on, wake up: we're going swimming.'

'Oh, Mum, I'm tired. What time is it?'

'Never mind about that,' she was giggling. 'It's a beautiful night and we're going to the lido. There might never be another night like it. I've got the towels. Grab your trunks and we can get going. It's an adventure.'

She kept laughing. I was yawning, still in my bed. She could tell I didn't really want to get up, in the quick and unexpected way that she was always able to sense things after she'd been drinking.

'Oh for God's sake, Francis. Where's your sense of fun? Come on! If you don't come, I'll go without you.'

I couldn't let her go alone. She might have drowned; anything could have happened to her. So I got my swimming things – my trunks and goggles – and pulled on some trousers and a T-shirt and put on my gym shoes without any socks, and followed her out of the house and on to the pavement. The street lights were the same colour as the transparent paper which Lucozade bottles came wrapped in. I thought I heard a train in the distance, but there was no other noise in the empty street. Mum had bare feet. She was fumbling with the car key, repeatedly failing to get it into the narrow lock of the driver's door.

'Come on, bugger you!'

'Mum!'

'Not you, darling. I'm talking to the bloody key. There. Hang on, I'll unlock your door from the inside.'

Actually I liked going in the car with my mother. She was a surprisingly good driver – at least it always impressed me how zippy she was behind the wheel, and how she concentrated. And she always seemed happy when she was driving; more confident, younger than when she was on her feet.

It was a few miles to the lido, mostly through residential streets. In the daytime it took about twenty minutes to drive there; but at this time of night there was no one about; we only passed a couple of other cars. I wondered where the people in them were going. Now that I'd woken up properly, I was excited about our expedition. I was thinking that because it was the middle of the night (my watch said half-past two) we'd have the whole pool to ourselves. We'd have to climb over the railings into the park, and then over the fence into the lido area itself. We might get caught. We could be prosecuted. It was probably against the law to go there at night, when the place was unattended. Maybe they had guard dogs patrolling the park. I'd heard that guard dogs were kept hungry to make them fiercer, and some of them were even trained not to bark before they rushed at you and attacked. There might be Alsatians, or even Dobermann pinschers. A boy in my class had a younger brother who had been savaged by a Dobermann, a family pet. His dad hadn't wanted to have the dog destroyed, even after his son had had more than forty stitches on his shoulder and arm. But his mum had taken the dog to the vet while her husband was at work. The boy in my class told us that she hadn't stayed to hold the dog while it was given its injection. She told him that she didn't want to touch that animal, ever again. You'd think it would have put them off dogs altogether, something like that, but it didn't. They still kept their other dog, the little one. I think it was a small schnauzer.

My mother was singing half under her breath as she drove along. When she was in a good mood she often sang snatches of the songs from old musicals. I think they reminded her of when she was young, and she especially liked the ones from Fred Astaire films.

> Must you dance every dance
> with the same, fortunate man?
> You have danced with him
> since the music began
> Won't you change partners
> and dance with me?

When she sang she sounded like a girl; her singing voice didn't have any cigarettes or disappointment in it, not like when she spoke. Most kids feel embarrassed when their mothers sing – I know that from when we had parents' assembly at school, and all the other boys went pink and fidgety as the hymns started up. But I didn't. I felt proud of her, singing and driving at the same time. It was like nothing could get her down.

When we got to the park we climbed the railings and then ran across the closely mown grass to the wooden fence which gave on to the pool area. I'd expected the lido to seem enormous with no one else there, but it didn't. If anything it looked a bit smaller than on sunny days when it was crowded with families, like rooms do without furniture. The water seemed black, thick almost, in the darkness. Like oil. It seemed a pity to disturb its smooth surface by swimming in it – just to see the water, still and silent beneath the night sky, would have been enough. But we'd come out especially for this, so I dived in anyway. My mother stood at the side – the deckchairs got stored away at closing time – holding the towels. I saw her face glow for an instant, as she lit a cigarette. She had brought a towel for herself, but I knew she wouldn't swim. She never went into the water, not even the sea.

I swam up and down, doing my best crawl. I don't know how well she could have seen me, but I wanted her to notice the neatness of my stroke; how smoothly I could cut through the water. I didn't splash at all. Deft. I was deft in the water.

Sometimes, at home, when I was having a bowl of cereal in front of the telly, my mother would come into the room and I'd catch her looking at me in a funny way; as if she'd mislaid something very important and she was sorry that I didn't know where to find it for her. Maybe it wasn't really anything to do with me, but when she looked at me like that it made me feel ashamed of myself. And in the empty lido that night I suddenly wanted her to see me in a different way: to see how well I could swim, how unencumbered I was. I could do a whole length under water, but of course she wouldn't have been able to see that, not at night. So I concentrated on my stroke instead, pacing my breaths to each third under-arm, not allowing my torso too much roll, keeping my knees slightly bent. It was a nice, even stroke; supple and fairly fast. I would have liked her to have been proud of my swimming.

I don't think she noticed, though. The thing about my mother was that her mood could change very suddenly, when you didn't expect it. This was one of the reasons I preferred not to have school friends round to tea – in case she turned funny without any warning and gave them a fright. And that's what happened next, at the lido.

'All right, that's it. That's enough. Out you get.'

'Oh, Mum! Just one more length, please?'

'Francis. I said that's enough. Now get out. Now.'

I didn't argue with her when she spoke in that voice. I didn't even swim back to the steps, but put my hands flat on the smooth concrete edging and lifted myself out of the water. She came up and thrust a towel at me.

'Here. Dry yourself with that, if you can get it round you. I'm going back to the car. Don't be long.'

There was no mistaking her tone. It was hard and stinging, like a slap on my wet skin.

I did as she said, pulling my T-shirt over my still damp arms, my trousers resisting against the moisture on my legs. It was always better to do as she said; that way there was a fair chance of avoiding any more words. If I kept quiet and did as she said – at home I just kept out of her way – she might lose the thread of her anger. But if I snagged against her at all, it created a domino effect; one little source of rage knocking against another until all her furies were clacking down. She sometimes said awful things, then: that she wished she'd never met dad, wished she'd never had a child. Me. She'd say that she wished she could be rid of me and be free from responsibility; free to live her own life. She never said what living her own life would be like – perhaps she didn't know herself. I tried not to let it hurt my feelings, because I guessed she didn't mean it, not really. She never went on like that in the daytime. If I went to my room before she'd had too many drinks I could usually avoid her altogether, by the time she got like it. But now I had to sit next to her for the drive home. I could feel the dread in my tummy as I climbed over the railings to go back to the car.

It turned out all right though, because as soon as she saw me she began to laugh. Because I'd been anxious to catch up with her, I'd forgotten to take off my goggles, or dry myself much. So I suppose I must have made a funny sight: a fat boy with wet hair plastered low over his forehead, emerging from the darkened shrubbery in a pair of goggles. A lot of people find something comical about overweight people hurrying, I know that. People have often laughed at me when I run, and I was running then. So by the time I got into the car she was in a good mood again, as if laughter had nudged the needle along the gramophone record which was playing inside her head, and on to a more cheerful song.

We didn't say much on the way home, and she didn't sing this time. Every now and again she chuckled and told me I was a funny boy; I looked out of the window. It was beginning to get light. There were streaks of pink raised against the whiteness of the sky, like bramble scratches on the pale skin of a child. The back of my T-shirt was damp against my shoulders from where my hair was dripping on to it; I could smell the tang of chlorine from the water.

My mother never offered to take me swimming again after that, and I never asked her to.

My Aunt Rose had moved away not long after my grandmother – her and my mother's mother – had passed on. She'd gone to act as housekeeper to a priest, Father Penrose, whose parish was in Gateshead, just over the river from Newcastle upon Tyne. I used to go and stay with them in the school holidays, once or twice a year, throughout my teens. My mother had mixed feelings about her only sister – I had sensed that by then, or at least by the time I was fifteen or so – but wanting a break, time to herself, overrode her ambivalence to Rose. Anyway I was glad to go, because Rose and I had always been special friends.

Father Penrose had a lot of energy and if he kept still at all he made strange noises under his breath, as if motionlessness required a great, almost physical, effort. He was supposed to be very brainy. He had taken his A levels when he was only sixteen and he'd got a scholarship to Cambridge, and then a first in theology. He'd been the cleverest novice at the seminary. But he seemed to find it difficult to meet people in the eye, and his glance would slide over you like ice cream melting down the side of a bowl. I wasn't sure about him at first. I was embarrassed by the odd sounds he made – it was nearly like grunting. When we sat down together at meals I'd cough falsely or talk in a loud voice to try and cover it up. I'd glance at Rose to see if she'd heard him, but she never seemed to take any notice, and in the end I got used to his snuffling and didn't try to disguise it for him any more.

He didn't make a noise when he went to the pictures, though. Father Penrose loved the cinema and when I stayed with them he and Rose took me to a matinée every Saturday. There was a kind of ice lolly that you could only get in cinemas: raspberry-ripple ice cream in the middle, with peach water ice round the outside – like a Mivvi or a Split, only much, much nicer. We would all three have one, sitting in a row in the dark. I used to sit in-between them, as if we were a family; if he hadn't been wearing a dog collar people might have taken us for mother, father and son. I noticed then that priests and fat people have something in common: if they eat in public it makes other people uncomfortable. It's rude to stare, but people think it's all right to stare at you if you're overweight; especially if you're having a bite of something. They look at you accusingly, as if to try and rebuke you out of what they think is your being greedy. But of course fat people have to eat, just like anybody else, and so do priests. It's only that other people don't get stared at while they're eating.

What with being so clever, Father Penrose had thought he'd be some sort of theologian, not work as a parish priest. He was a bit funny – I mean funny peculiar, not funny ha ha. He didn't seem to be very easy with people, very natural. Not that he was a bad community priest; people seemed to like and respect him, and the fact that he'd grown up in the area made a difference. He knew about the local problems that some of his parishioners were facing: redundancies, unemployment. I think he was a good listener; certainly people came calling to see him.

The third time I went up there my aunt told me about Father Penrose's mother. When he was a little boy of about eight or nine, his mother had taken him for a picnic lunch to the seaside at Craster, which was quite near where they lived up the coast from Newcastle. There was a ruined castle just along the headland, that you could only reach on foot. The Penroses went there once or twice a year, usually in August when the wind from the North Sea was quieter than at other times. They had a blue tartan picnic rug with fringes, and they always took cold sausages to eat, which Mrs Penrose cooked the night before. Mrs Penrose used to tuck her skirt into the sides of her knickers and paddle in the cold water at the shoreline.

Father Penrose – young Matthew, as he was then – was making a sandcastle. He was trying to make a copy of the ruined Dunstanburgh Castle, so he sat on the beach with his back to the sea, looking up at it; concentrating. But when he'd finished he realised that his mother wasn't near him any more. He got up and ran up to the ruins, looking for her and calling. He didn't know what to do, but he'd always been told to stay in the same place if he lost his mother, so she'd know where to find him. So he went back down to his sandcastle and waited. Hours went by – anyway it felt like hours. Eventually – it was well into the evening – an elderly couple with a dog came along and found him, and took him back to their cottage in the village. They telephoned his house and his father came to collect him. His mother didn't come back that night because she was in hospital: a fisherman had pulled her out of the North Sea into his boat and brought her back.

She made a full recovery. She came home and no one ever talked about what had happened: it had been an accident. Years went by. They still visited Craster at least once each summer, still took the same rug with the smell of hardboiled eggshells embedded in its wool. Sometimes, in later years, they had salami instead of sausages. Their lives went on as normal. The summer that Father Penrose finished at university was especially hot. He left Cambridge and went home as usual; they went off to Dunstanburgh for a day out. After he and his mother had finished their food they both lay stretched out on the sand with their eyes shut, sheltered by the dunes. He told Rose that he recalled being able to see swirling motes of sunlit dust, like particles of light itself, even after his eyes were closed. He could see them floating and shimmering against the inside of his eyelids. It was like looking into infinity.

He didn't know how long he'd been asleep, but when he woke up his mother wasn't there. It didn't even cross his mind that anything was wrong. Eventually he strolled back towards Craster and went to the pub to wait for her. He had half a pint, then another. Then he had a bowl of crab soup. Then he walked back to the ruins. Then he walked back to the village again and got change for the phone box and rang home to see if she'd somehow made it back there without him; and he was startled because his father shouted at him to get the coastguard, the police, the lifeboat. But they didn't find her, not for three days, until her body was washed up a few miles up the coast.

I don't usually dislike people: I don't feel it's up to me to judge others. But what Rose told me made me feel that I didn't like Mrs Penrose.

'She could have done it while he was still away at college,' I said. 'Why did she have to wait until she'd got him there? It's as if she did it on purpose to make him extra miserable.'

'It might have been an accident,' said Rose.

'Do you think it was?'

'No. I don't know.'

'But did she hate Father Penrose? Is that why she waited 'til she'd got him with her?'

'I think she loved him. I think he must have been the one person she did love. I think she needed him there, so she could be brave enough.'

I found this too difficult to understand. None of it made sense, whichever way you looked at it. Up until then I'd always thought that every mother did her best to look after her child, to do what was best for them: that's what being a mother was. I knew that they didn't always get it right, but at least they tried. I thought they did. But the story of Mrs Penrose raised questions which didn't seem to have any answers.

'Do you think she wanted to kill herself the first time, when he was small?'

'I suppose she must have.'

'Why do you think she waited so long, then, to try again?'

'I don't know, Francis. Maybe she made a pact with herself to wait until Matthew was grown. But we'll never know what was on her mind.'

'What about Mr Penrose, I mean Father Penrose's father?'

Rose shrugged.

'Well, I think it was a terrible thing to do to Father Penrose. He'll never feel safe to go on a picnic again.' Even as I said it, I knew I was being silly. Picnics were the least part of it.

'It's been very hard for him; a dreadful burden. It's the not knowing why. It's because of his mother, you know, that the Bishop decided that Matthew should work in a parish, among people. The Bishop thought that life at the heart of a community of people would help him; and that his experience of the mystery of suffering would help the people, too. He couldn't have done that in a library.' Aunt Rose stopped speaking and looked at the back of her hands. 'So there it is.'

I didn't say anything. There didn't seem to be anything else to say.

'But, Francis – you won't let Father Penrose know what I've told you? He wouldn't want you to be worried by what I've said.'

I promised I would not.

Eventually it was Rose who suggested that it was time I saw a doctor about my weight. Up until then it had been accepted that I was just plump: it was puppy fat. But by the time I was fifteen I was over eleven stone and it wasn't really possible to go on pretending that my weight wasn't a problem. I knew that I had grown wiry hair around my genitals because I could feel it, as well as observing it in the mirror when I got out of the bath. But I couldn't see it, not if I looked down, because my stomach was in the way. I got out of breath when I went swimming. And I was having trouble sleeping; starting awake lots of times every night, feeling as if I was suffocating.

Usually I caught the train from Newcastle when I went home after visiting Matthew and Rose, but this time Rose drove me all the way down south, so she could talk to mum about my health. She didn't say that was what she was planning – she said she hadn't seen her sister for ages, a visit was long overdue – but I could tell. Once Rose decided on something there was no dissuading her. The first night they played cards together and Rose even drank some gin and they laughed a lot about stupid things they both remembered. But on the second night of her visit I heard them quarrelling together in hiss–whispers, like kettles coming to the boil. I stayed in my room, crouched in the doorway, straining to hear snatches of what they were saying.

'. . . just can't ignore it any longer.'

'How would you bloody know? You've never had a child.'

'He's not a child. He's practically sixteen. If you didn't drink so much you'd have noticed. It's not good for him.'

'So of course you know best: you know what's bloody good for him, just like you knew what was good for his father.'

'That's got nothing to do with it. This is about Francis, not about you and me.'

'It's got a lot to do with it. Everything's to do with it. Look at us! Do you think we'd be like this if his father hadn't gone? Do you? You come here trying to blame me, but it's you who's to blame. You. You're the one who broke up this family.'

'Oh for God's sake . . .'

'You've already taken my husband: now you want to take my son as well. You've always taken everything that was mine, even when we were little.'

'I've already practically gone into exile for you – what more do you want? Do you think I wasn't lonely enough up there, with no family, no friends? I did it for you, to get out of your way so you could patch the marriage up. What more could I have done?'

'You could have left him alone, in the first place. You could have bloody . . .'

At this point one of them shut the door. My heart was fluttering and I felt a bit sick. I dreaded to think what else they might say to each other; I wished I hadn't listened to them. I went to bed and turned on my transistor, just to make sure I wouldn't be able to overhear anything more. But the next day they seemed to be the best of friends again, and Rose telephoned to make a doctor's appointment for me. So she had won.

Dr Mansfield wasn't exactly slender himself. He wore a brown corduroy suit and he behaved as if he'd never thought of hurrying in his life. He weighed me and took my blood pressure, then he told me to go away and make a note of everything I ate for the next week. Everything – even if it was only an apple. I wasn't to try and cut down; just to record it all, every last mouthful.

The following week he looked at my notes for a long time.

'There's a lot of sugar, here. A lot of refined foods and carbohydrate,' he said. 'Do you know about the different food groups?'

I said I did, sort of.

'Well, the general idea is to get a balance between them, so that you're having the correct amount of each group: fat, protein and complex carbohydrate. Baked beans on wholemeal toast, followed by a piece of fruit; that's a well-balanced meal.' He pulled out some paper from a drawer in his desk. 'I'll give you a diet sheet to take a look at and then pass on to your mother. She'll need to make sure that you're eating the right things. Then you can come back and see me – say, in a month's time? All right, Francis?'

I said yes. But I didn't want to cause my mother any extra trouble. She couldn't be doing with too much cooking, or thinking about mixing up the food groups, or whatever; so I thought I'd just try to sort it out for myself. Not eat so many crisps and biscuits. And I thought I was doing well – cutting down – but when I went back to Dr Mansfield a few weeks later I found out I hadn't lost any weight at all. He didn't seem too fussed, not the first time; but when we discovered I'd gained a further six pounds over the next few months, he started questioning me more closely. I told him the truth, then: that I'd been trying my best, but that I didn't want to burden my mum with a special diet for me. So then we talked a bit about home, and that's when Dr Mansfield suggested I could go and see Mr Richards.

After that I went to see Mr Richards once a month. At first we just went over what home had been like when I was small, before my dad left. We talked about that a lot. To begin with he would ask me questions – how did that feel? how did you feel when your grandmother died? – that sort of thing. After about six months he began to make sugges-tions, as well as just asking questions and listening to what I said. He didn't always get things right. He said that perhaps I was overweight partly because I felt, deep down, that my mother didn't like men very much: that being fat was a way of not becoming a real man. He wondered whether my mother had a part of her that didn't want me to be sexual, and whether I might, unconsciously, be responding to that wish in her. He made me sound like some kind of eunuch. I could feel myself going red with shame on his behalf. That didn't sound like my life at all. Mr Richards was always trying to bring the conversation around to sex. He seemed much more interested in sex than ordinary people are. I didn't know anything about sex. I was still a virgin and the thought of it was acutely embarrassing to me. But I didn't believe, as he seemed to, that everything people feel is to do with sex. I still don't believe that.

But some of what he said did make sense. He suggested that it must have been hard for my mother, because she had never been anybody's favourite. All her life, he said, people seemed to have loved her sister better than they loved her: first her own mother, then her husband and finally even her son. Me. I had never thought of that before. My mother was the pretty one; the one who could sing and be funny. Rose was very nice and sensible and kind, but she wasn't glamorous at all, not like mum. Mr Richards said that, because of the fact of everyone loving Rose more, my mother was probably very angry on the inside and that made her not be very good at loving other people, or taking care of them. She might find it hard to be a nurturing mother, those were his words. He said he thought that this might have made me feel that something was missing – that I might have started to eat immoderately as a result. To try and fill myself up. He said that my mother felt a gap, too; but she used alcohol to try and fill hers. He thought that both of us – my mother and me – felt empty on the inside. I think he was right about that.

Father Penrose and my aunt had been suggesting that I

should try for Durham University, when I left school. That way I'd be only twenty minutes or so away from them; I'd be able to spend weekends at their house in Gateshead so I wouldn't be lonely, starting out at college. Father Penrose was involved in a number of youth projects within the parish, and I'd met quite a few people of my own age up there, over the years. There was someone I liked especially, a girl, Bridget. I knew Rose thought it would do me good to get away from home; and Dr Mansfield thought so too. I don't know what Mr Richards really thought, because he tended not to give that sort of advice: he was interested in feelings, not practical solutions.

I was tempted, I really was. It wasn't getting any easier, at home. Sometimes I had to lift mum into bed at nights because she just zonked out in her chair. I'd take her shoes off and put them together, half under the bed, but I always left her clothes on, and then she'd usually wear them the next day, all crumpled. Quite often she went whole days without leaving the house; it didn't much matter to her if her skirt was creased, or her blouse was grubby. And it didn't really matter to me, either. Just because I didn't like mum drinking didn't give me the right to make her change. I mean, I was sorry to see her looking so dishevelled, and I was quite worried about her; but it wasn't as if it made any real difference to my life; not really. I still did my studying, went swimming, all that. What people do in the privacy of their own homes, that's their business. Some people would have thought it was sinful that Aunt Rose shared a bed with Father Penrose – I knew because I had often heard her creep along the passage to his room, in the night – but I didn't believe that. The fact that he had someone who loved him like that probably even made him a better priest, because he didn't have to be lonely. Or regretful.

It was what Mr Richards said that made me come to my decision. Because I thought about it, afterwards; and I thought about my mother and I realised that it wasn't true about not loving her best, not for me. Maybe it was so with the others, with my granny and my father. And it was true that I did feel easier with Rose than I did with mum and that things went more smoothly in my aunt's ambit. Shirts got ironed and the table got laid and the marmalade didn't run out and the TV licence didn't get forgotten. She kept a diary with a sharp little pencil in its spine, and a clean handkerchief folded in her handbag. She remembered people's birthdays and whether they took one spoonful of sugar or two in their tea. Rose – so reliable, always such a faithful Believer – wanted more than anything to be good; but I think she knew that she hadn't really succeeded in that wish. Whereas my mother just wanted to be loved; and like her sister, she hadn't had much luck in getting what she wanted, either. But I did. I did love her.

Anyway, I decided to stay. I thought about Matthew Penrose's mother and how he'd believed she was all right, all those years and I realised I wouldn't leave mum. Not now. And once I'd made up my mind to stay, I felt much better: I even started to lose a few pounds. Sometimes when you make choices you have to go for the option which isn't going to be the happiest for yourself. But doing something for someone else doesn't necessarily constrain you. That could even be what trying to do the right thing is for. I don't know. But what I thought was: I've got my whole life in front of me. I've got time.

EDWIN DEREK

THE
AVENGERS
OF
SAN PEDRO

Complete and Unabridged

LINFORD
Leicester

First published in Great Britain in 2008 by
Robert Hale Limited
London

First Linford Edition
published 2010
by arrangement with
Robert Hale Limited
London

British Library CIP Data

Derek, Edwin.
    The avengers of San Pedro. - -
(Linford western library)
1. Western stories.
2. Large type books.
I. Title II. Series
823.9′14–dc22

ISBN 978–1–84782–963–4

Published by
F. A. Thorpe (Publishing)
Anstey, Leicestershire

Set by Words & Graphics Ltd.
Anstey, Leicestershire
Printed and bound in Great Britain by
T. J. International Ltd., Padstow, Cornwall

This book is printed on acid-free paper

1

The sky was as black as ink although it was at least an hour until sunset. Stinging hail, driven by the storm-force wind, lashed down. Brad's horse whinnied nervously as thunder echoed ominously in the nearby hills. Lightning briefly lit up the sky, but thankfully, the centre of the storm was still some distance away.

Driven by the howling wind, the hail cut into his face. Thankfully, it soon turned to torrential rain. But within a few seconds, Brad was soaking wet and shivering with cold. This was the first time he had ridden so far West and the ferocity of the storm had caught him completely unprepared.

Brad was on the trail of a gang of renegades who had killed almost everybody in a small and isolated settlement called San Pedro. Its people, mainly Mexican, were unarmed because they were under the protection of the nearby Double M, one of the largest ranches in Texas.

Unfortunately, a serious outbreak of rustling on the opposite side of the ranch to the San Pedro settlement meant that it had been left unprotected. And that was when the renegades struck.

Strangely, the renegades had left a young Mexican girl alive to identify the gang and relate her terrible ordeal. Three renegades had raped her in front of her mortally wounded husband, a young American called Seth Madden. As they performed their vile act, their leader repeatedly called out their names and incited them to further acts of bestiality. The three gang members involved were Frank Tucker, 'Reb' Rosin and a gunman called Spite. They were known to be part of Nate Killner's outlaw gang wanted for robbery and murder in Kansas and Texas.

Although he was only twenty-one

years old, Seth Madden had already featured on several wanted posters. Like many before him, he had drifted into bad company and hit the outlaw trail. Yet, once freed from their influence, he was a decent enough lad and had tried to go straight. Perhaps it was the love of a beautiful woman that had made him want to settle down. So the Double M had decided to give him that chance and had given him a job as wrangler in spite of a $500 dollar reward for his capture, dead or alive.

However, Brad could not believe that the reward had been the renegades' motive for killing Seth. Not only had they ridden off without trying to claim it, they had also killed many innocent and unarmed Mexicans.

The renegades' motive for attacking San Pedro was a complete mystery. Robbery could not have been the reason. The Mexican inhabitants were either poor dirt farmers or worked as dollar-a-day cowboys on Double M. But how did the renegades know the settlement was undefended and why had they left the girl alive to tell the world who had raped her and carried out the massacre? To find the answers to these riddles and to avenge the good folk of San Pedro, Brad had taken leave of absence from the Double M and followed the trail left by the outlaws.

One of the renegades' horses had a curious v-shaped grove in its front right hoof. Surprisingly, its owner had not changed the horse or had it reshod. In fact, the renegades had made little attempt to hide their trail, so Brad was able to follow them as they rode out of Texas into New Mexico.

That had been some time ago. Now, the violence of the storm had washed away the renegades' trail. In fact, Brad was lost. He could only guess he was somewhere near the Arizona border. But if that was so, neither the heavily wooded landscape nor the inclement weather was anything like the arid semi-desert his fellow Texans had told him to expect.

There was no way Brad could outrun the storm. His horse, Prince, had thrown a shoe. Indeed, if it had not been for the thunder and lightning, Brad would have dismounted and led the stallion, cavalry style, towards any shelter he could find. But Prince was too spooked to be held by his reins. So there was no alternative, he had to ride on. However, he guessed that Killner's gang would seek shelter from the storm, so with every limping stride of his gallant horse, he was gaining on them.

Brad knew the renegades were headed to Blackwater. With the aid of the v-groove, Brad had been able to track them to a small settlement near El Capitan Mountain. Surprisingly, they had not been shy in disclosing their names when they bought fresh supplies. Indeed, they had even told the store-keeper they were headed for a town called Blackwater. It almost seemed as if they wanted to be followed.

As the rain became even stronger, the

two full canteens of water Brad had been advised to carry seemed a mite superfluous. Again lightning flashed across the sky, but this time it was nearer and the thunder was even louder. He could almost feel the panic in his horse.

Prince had reason to be scared. Brad was only too aware that lightning seemed to be strangely attracted to a solitary rider unfortunate enough to be caught out in the vast open expanses of the West. So he had to find shelter before the lightning found him.

Another bolt lit up the indigo sky, and struck the ground with a frightening roar. This time, it was near enough to cause the panic-stricken horse to rear and Brad had to keep the beast under control. But at least the lightning temporarily lit up what was left of the trail and Brad could see it split into two.

The rain had washed out all signs of tracks on the main trail but he could still detect some signs on the side-trail. These had been made by the wheels of a heavily laden wagon. One track wobbled badly, indicating the rear, left-hand side wheel was dangerously loose, so loose that it was clear that the wagon could not have travelled much further. Therefore, he guessed that there might be a ranch or homestead not too far down the side trail.

There was. The wobbly wagon tracks led directly to a small ranch house, or was it a larger than usual homestead? Whichever, Brad reached it just in time. The worst of the violent storm was now almost directly overhead, scaring Prince out of the few wits he possessed.

Smoke coming from the chimney of the ranch house indicated that it was occupied, although there was no other sign of life. Brad looked around for somewhere to stable Prince, but the fence of the ranch's empty corral was broken, rendering it useless. Fortunately, there was a barn nearby and its door had been left ajar. On closer inspection, the door was also in need of repair and could not be fully closed.

But any port in a storm, thought Brad, as he led Prince into the barn's gloomy interior.

They were met by the frightened neigh of a terrified horse. Much to Brad's dismay, the huge beast was still harnessed to an ancient wagon laden with rough-sawn timber. Presumably the timber was to rebuild the corral and repair the barn door, but the load had proved too much for the old wagon. Although its back wheel was still attached, it slanted outwards at a crazy angle, accounting for the wobbly tracks he had followed. Timber must have come from a sawmill. So was there a town nearby? Was it Blackwater? Even if it wasn't, the renegades might have stopped to shelter there. Brad decided to ride on as soon as the storm had died down and find out.

Providing, of course, Prince could carry him. Unfortunately, the interior of the barn was far too dark to examine Prince's leg. So, instead, Brad unharnessed the terrified carthorse from its wagon and tethered it to a hitching rail which, unusually, had been built inside the barn.

Brad looked round the barn's gloomy interior. Apart from the wagon, several lengths of rope, a few cans of paint and a small quantity of hay, it was surprisingly empty. However, as he looked upwards into the murky gloom of the barn's roof, he spied a wagon wheel lashed to the rafters.

Brad could not close the broken barn door unaided, so he hitched the still terror stricken Prince next to the other horse. However, as both horses were in a state of panic, he picked up a length of rope and expertly formed it into what the Easterners called a lasso, a term seldom used by true Texas cowboys who confusingly called the lasso a rope. He used it to hobble the forelegs of Prince and then used a separate rope to hobble the other horse. He didn't want either of them to rear in panic and smash their forelegs into each other.

Both horses needed rubbing down, but the likelihood of the horses being spooked by lightning or thunder made the job too dangerous. Besides, Brad was wet and cold and the smoke coming from the ranch-house chimney indicated that there was a warm fire underneath it. The code of the West meant that if he paid a call, he should be invited into the ranch-house.

After careful deliberation, Brad decided to leave his Winchester carbine in the barn. He did not want to provoke or scare the occupants of the ranch house into a rash shot. As events were to turn out, this seemingly unimportant decision was destined to set into motion a series of events which were to change the rest of Brad's life.

As he hurried across the courtyard to the little ranch house, his star-shaped work-spurs jangled over the noise of the storm. But he was drenched again by the time he reached the ranch-house door because the reinforced arches and tall heels of his cowboy boots were made for riding, not running.

Lightning flashed overhead, but this time there was no thunder. Instead, the roaring wind reached little short of hurricane strength and almost blew him over. Ice-cold rain lashed brutally into his face making him wish he was back in the comparative safety of his Texas home.

He rapped on the door. After what seemed an age, it was unbolted. Framed by the flickering flames of a welcoming fire was a young woman. But she didn't seem friendly for she held a cocked six-gun, pointed at Brad's chest.

2

The six-gun remained steady. It was a Navy Colt, but at such close range its small .38 calibre bullet could be as deadly as the .45 fired by Brad's new Peacemaker.

'Ma'am, my horse is lame, so I need shelter.' Brad had to shout to be heard over the raging storm.

The woman beckoned Brad into a surprisingly large and well-kept room. All of its oak window-shutters were closed and secured firmly by stout bars. The room was lit by a single oil lamp augmented by the flames of a log fire, and altogether the room gave out a warm and friendly feeling. The feeling was heightened by the delightful aroma of cooking emanating from the kitchen. Its delicious smell reminded him he had not eaten that day.

'Close the door and bolt it,' ordered

the woman, keeping her old six-gun pointed straight at Brad.

He complied with her orders without protest. But his clothes were so wet, his slightest movement sent streams of water cascading on to the polished oak floor. However, the woman seemed unconcerned at his plight.

'Unbuckle your gunbelt,' she ordered. 'You can stay for the duration of the storm, even if you are one of Jed Hawker's new gunmen. But one false move and I will shoot to kill!'

'Understood, ma'am, but you've nothing to fear from me. You have my word as a Texan. I was just riding through when my horse went lame, so I got caught in the storm.'

As he spoke, Brad slowly unbuckled his gunbelt and gently lowered it to the floor. Although she had not so instructed, he kicked it over to her. Even so, she was still not satisfied.

'If you're riding through, where's your horse?'

'Took the liberty of putting him in

your barn, ma'am, before coming to the house. Although Prince is lame, he's too skittish to rub down; I guess he doesn't like this storm any more than I do.'

'What about my horse?' she asked sharply.

'Took another liberty there, ma'am, and unharnessed him. He and my horse Prince are both tethered and safely hobbled.'

The woman smiled briefly, but her attitude remained unchanged it seemed. As Brad stood in front of the now bolted front door, water from his saturated clothes still continued to pour on to the floor to form an ever growing pool. He felt like a drowned rat.

'I thank you for unharnessing my horse. Normally the big fellow is as quiet as a mouse, but I guess the storm got to him and made him wild. Unfortunately, I'm not that experienced with horses and he was too lively for me to handle.'

'No trouble, ma'am,' said Brad

beginning to relax. As he did so he slightly lowered his hands.

'Keep your hands raised,' the woman snapped. 'If you lower them another inch, I'll fill you full of holes. Do you understand?'

'Yes, ma'am. I won't move. But you've nothing to fear from me. I swear that I've never heard of this Jed Hawker you just mentioned.'

The rain must have turned back to hail for Brad could hear the wind driving it into the shutters. Then, much to his surprise, the woman suddenly retreated into the kitchen. However, she was only gone for an instant. She returned carrying a large pink towel in her left hand and threw it on to the floor by his feet. However, she still held a six-gun in her other hand and continued to point it at Brad.

'Strip off your boots and clothes, then dry yourself,' she ordered.

'But, ma'am!'

Brad began to protest but it was no use. She had the gun and it was still cocked. His struggle to keep his body hidden behind the towel as he stripped caused her much merriment. But, in spite of his embarrassment, Brad found the sound of her gentle laughter quite pleasant.

She bent down, picked up his gunbelt, and then took it into the kitchen. This time when she returned she carried a fluffy, pink dressing-gown. Much to Brad's further embarrassment, she made him put it on. Again, he could not argue, for her Navy Colt was still pointing at him. She then picked up his clothes and again retreated back into the kitchen. This time, when she returned, she carried a bowl of hot stew instead of the old six-gun.

'You don't look quite so ornery just wearing your hat and my dressing-gown,' she said, smiling. She put the stew on the table and beckoned Brad to sit down.

Her face lit up as she did so, softening her appearance, made to look unnecessarily severe by the tight bun at the back of her head into which her hair had been curled.

While he was eating, Brad studied her face. She was not a classic beauty. Her chin was a little too determined and her cheeks just a little too broad for that. Nevertheless, there was something about her that instantly set her aside from any other woman he had ever met. Although she wore a simple cornflower blue gingham dress, it could not hide the near perfection of her body. Indeed, in the flickering light of the oil lamp, she looked nothing like his image of a homesteader's wife. Then he noticed she was not wearing a ring.

'Finished looking me over?' she asked sharply.

He hadn't realized he had been staring.

'Sorry, ma'am. No offence meant. You don't fit my idea of a homesteader.'

'This is a ranch not a homestead, and dressed in my old pink dressing-gown, you don't fit my idea of a gunman,' she said drily. 'But do stop calling me ma'am: my name is Jane Latham.'

'I'm Bradley Miller. My friends call me Brad, Miss Latham.'

'Well, you're hardly dressed for formality, but I shall call you Mr Miller until you call me Jane.'

'Yes, ma'am, I mean, Jane. Thanks for the stew, it was delicious. It sure warmed me up.'

'Just rabbit and a few vegetables and herbs,' she said modestly. 'I'm afraid I'm a bit short of provisions at the moment.'

'I noticed your barn is almost empty, but surely you're not here in this wilderness on your own?' asked Brad remembering she had said the big carthorse was too spooked for her to unharness.

A look of apprehension passed across her face, telling him he had guessed correctly. He spoke quietly to reassure her.

'I know I'm a stranger to you, but I gave you my word, so you are quite safe.'

'I begin to believe that I may be, but I'm not usually alone, something or somebody has driven my men and my Indians into the hills.'

'Your Indians?' replied Brad in surprise. 'I thought this part of the world was home to the Comanche.'

'Apache not Comanche. But in any case, they haven't bothered me since I settled here,' Jane replied. 'No, my Indians are the Yampai. They are very timid and primitive people, nothing like the Apache.'

'Yampai? I don't think I've ever heard of that tribe,' said Brad.

'Nor had I until I came here,' replied Jane.

Brad found talking to her was surprisingly easy and gradually began to feel at ease, in spite of the garment he was wearing. He learnt that she had been born in New England where she had been a schoolteacher. Unfortunately, her father had contracted consumption; ironically, he had been a doctor. They had chosen to come West in the belief that the warmer and drier climate would help him recover.

Although the climate, especially in winter, had been much warmer than in New England, this part of New Mexico hadn't been quite as dry as they had expected. Nevertheless, initially all had gone well and they settled in what was then the quiet little town of Blackwater. But soon after they had moved in, silver had been discovered in the nearby hills.

Jane said that at first the discovery of silver was good news. The sudden influx of miners led to an urgent need for a doctor, first in the mining camp and then in Blackwater. But the miners kept on arriving and with them came gunmen and gamblers. Unfortunately, the once quiet little town rapidly became a lawless den of iniquity.

And yet this did not deter the arrival of more and more miners. Soon there were too many for Blackwater to accommodate. So the company which had appeared out of nowhere and taken control of the mine, established a permanent camp within easy walking distance from the mine entrance and a little over two hours' ride from Blackwater.

At first, most of the miners stayed put, only visiting the town at weekends and they contented themselves with getting drunk. However, trouble flared between them and the local cowboys, and the miners usually fared worse. Although patching up the injured miners provided more work for Jane's father, the trouble had serious repercussions; the mining company began to hire gunmen to protect their men.

The tables were turned on the cowboys until the Bar Zero, by far the largest and most powerful ranch in the area, also began to employ gunmen. Unfortunately, the situation worsened as several more saloons opened in Blackwater. In them, prostitutes vied with gamblers to relieve the miners and cowboys of their hard-earned money.

Apart from the shootings in Blackwater's saloons, accidents at the silver mine were frequent. So her father was all too often called out. As a result, his health began to decline. However, the miners paid well and he was soon able to purchase a small but unprofitable ranch. For that reason, it had been called the Little Use.

Sadly, the decline in Jane's father's health continued apace. The New Mexican climate, instead of curing him, merely postponed the inevitable and he died from consumption before he could move into the ranch.

Typically, just before died, Dr Latham befriended and treated for free, several local Indians from the Yampai tribe. He even travelled into the nearby hills to deliver the baby of the chief's wife. So, when Jane eventually moved into the ranch, a few of them began to do chores for her. She also changed the name of the ranch to the Little U, which was a rough translation of the name given to the baby of the Yampai chief.

Jane kept the next part of her life story to herself. The ranch which was in poor condition, deteriorated still further before she could move in. Unfortunately, her father, never good with money, had spent most of his earnings and the salary she earned as a schoolteacher was only just enough to live on.

However, there had been and still was a huge demand for saloon girls, especially as pretty as Jane. Few of the miners or cowhands who patronized the Lucky Strike cared that Jane's singing voice was less than perfect. Quite the opposite, for to compensate, her dresses were so revealing, the former school-teacher soon became the toast of Blackwater. In less than a year, she made enough money to begin to rebuild the Little U and hire a couple of hands to help run it.

But Jane didn't tell Brad how she had raised the money. Instead, she told him how her hired help had departed although the work was barely half done. Since then, she had been unable to hire anybody else.

But she had already paid for the timber to rebuild the barn door and the corral, so with the help of several miners who remembered her daring performances at the Lucky Strike Saloon, the timber was loaded onto her old wagon. The load had almost been too heavy for it and she only just made it back to her barn. That had been just as the storm broke, barely an hour before Brad had knocked on the ranch-house door.

As she talked, time seemed to fly by, even if the storm did not. When she retired, it was almost midnight and still raining as hard as ever. Brad bunked down on the large couch in the main room.

3

Brad slept soundly. After weeks on the trail, sleeping rough, the couch was a luxury not a hardship. He awoke to find that his boots had been cleaned and were on the floor beside him. However, there was no sign of the rest of his clothes, or his new Colt Peacemaker.

Dawn was just beginning to break. It seemed the storm had abated. Brad put on his boots and, clad only in the pink dressing-gown and his hat, quietly slipped outside. Everywhere was covered in deep puddles but the rising sun revealed a cloudless sky. Although the wind had died down to a whisper, it was still surprisingly cold.

Brad made his way to the barn, hoping he did not look as ridiculous as he felt. Luckily, it seemed that Jane's Indians had not returned for there was nobody about. As he reached the barn, he was greeted by welcoming neighs from Prince and Jane's cart-horse. Now that the storm had passed, they were both back to normal, so Brad removed the hobbling ropes from their forelegs.

Next, Brad hurried to his saddle-bags and pulled out the spare set of clothes he always carried and quickly put them on. Then, he carefully examined Prince. The horse had cast a shoe and there was severe bruising above the unshod hoof. But it didn't look too serious. After a few days' rest in the barn, Prince should be fine. However, that meant the trip into Blackwater and a visit to its blacksmith would have to be delayed.

Using some of the hay stacked in the corner of the barn, Brad fed the horses. Whilst they were greedily feeding, he examined the wagon. The rear wheel was damaged beyond repair. However, with a little bit of ingenuity, it could be replaced by the one lashed to the rafters. But first, he would have to unload the timber.

Before he could remove the broken wheel, he would have to connect one end of his rope to the rear axle of the wagon and then run the rope over the block and pulley fixed to one of the main roof beams. The other end of the rope would have to be attached to the cart-horse. As it walked out of the barn, the rope would tighten and lift the rear of the wagon off the ground and that would allow him to remove the damaged wheel and replace it with the spare. Finally, the cart-horse would walk back to the wagon, thus releasing the tension on the rope. The wagon should then drop back to the floor, almost as good as new.

But first, the horses had to be groomed. As his thoughts turned to getting the wagon wheel down, the sound of approaching riders interrupted his deliberations. At first, Brad thought it was none of his business and continued to groom Prince. However, when he heard Jane's voice raised in anger, he decided it was time to make it his business. Reaching for the Winchester carbine he had left in the barn the night before, he slipped silently outside. Two riders had dismounted and one of them was giving Jane a hard time.

'My boss, Mr Hawker, thinks it ain't fitting for a single lady to live out here on her own. He says he has had a long chat with your mangy Indians, so is certain that they will not be back to keep you company.'

Apart from the pearl-handles of his two six-guns, the speaker was dressed completely in black. However, he was not wearing chaps, essential leg protection for any cowboy or drover, so Brad concluded the man was a professional gunslinger.

The second man was wearing chaps and his clothes looked trail-worn. Although his gun-rig also had two holsters, they were entirely different in style. Only the left-hand one, cut down for a quicker draw, revealed a six-gun. Strangely, its frame appeared to be almost yellow in the early morning light.

The one for the rider's right-hand looked like an old cavalry-style holster complete with a flap on top of it. As the flap was firmly tied down, Brad could not detect what sort of six-gun made it bulge out, but wrongly assumed it must be an old Dragoon Colt, perhaps the largest handgun made by Sam Colt's men. To complete his armament, the rider also carried a Bowie knife in a shoulder rig.

'Miss Jane,' said the second rider politely, 'changing the name of your ranch from the Little Use to the Little U won't make it any more successful. As a ranch, it is really too small to be much good, so I'm afraid it's still of *little use*!'

Both gunmen were so busy laughing at the play on words, neither noticed Brad approach. For the moment, he paused and listened, as the flashily dressed gunslinger continued to talk to Jane.

'My new friend from Texas is right,' said the flashily dressed gunman. 'So why not be sensible and sell? My boss, Mr Hawker, will pay enough for you to go back East and still have enough to start teaching again. Why, for your safety, he might arrange for me or my friend to ride guard on your stage-coach!'

'Miss Jane, this country is too wild and dangerous for a woman on her own,' said the second rider, 'I'd sure hate for you to have an accident out here.'

'So would I,' said Brad, carbine in hand. He had stopped, quite deliberately, about thirty-five paces away from them. 'Are these men bothering you, ma'am?'

'Who the hell are you?' asked the gunman dressed in black before Jane could reply.

'The man with a Winchester,' replied Brad quietly. 'Now if you've had your say, there's nothing to keep you here, so I'll bid you good day.'

Had he taken the carbine to the house instead of leaving it in the barn, Jane would have undoubtedly taken possession of it last night. Consequently, this morning, he would have been unable to make the intervention which was to affect the rest of his life.

But at that moment there was nothing to suggest this, nor was there anything threatening in Brad's words. It was just that he was standing just too far away from the gunmen for them to get an accurate shot from their six-guns. However, for a Winchester carbine, thirty-five or so paces was point-blank range.

'Stranger, I don't take kindly to you interfering in matters that don't concern you,' said the gunslinger dressed in black.

'You just made them my business and, as you can see, I've the carbine to finish it here and now, if you've the mind,' replied Brad.

At that, there was the merest flicker of recognition in the second gunman's eyes and he smiled as he spoke.

'Easy there, friend. Ain't no need for gun-play; the lady might get hit. We're just errand boys delivering a message. So now that's done, we will be on our way. But Mr Hawker will expect a reply. No offence intended, Miss Jane.'

So saying, he doffed his white Stetson and then mounted his palomino horse which had an unusual white flash its right flank. This mark was well known to most law officers of Texas. So, as an occasional deputy, Brad should have recognized it, but he did not. As the owner of the strangely marked horse rode away, he turned and smiled. However, the gunslinger dressed in black was not so friendly.

'Like you say, stranger,' he said to Brad, 'you have the Winchester. Enjoy your advantage. But you won't catch me out again. Better leave today, because if we meet again, I'll kill you.'

Jane paled at the venom the gunslinger put into his words. But before she could speak, he too mounted his horse and then rode furiously after his fellow gunman. Jane turned to Brad.

'I thank you for your help, Brad, but that was Chad Dorrell. I'm afraid you've made a bad enemy there. He has a mean and ugly temper and a fast draw to back it up. They say he's outdrawn at least six men. So I guess you might want to take his advice and ride out after breakfast.'

'Ma'am, I'm not going to let words of any flashily dressed gunslinger worry me. But something about his friend does bother me. I think he might prove to be a far more dangerous man to cross. I don't suppose you know anything about him?'

She didn't. All she knew was that he had arrived in the area a few days ago and it had been rumoured he had been hired by the Blackwash Mining Corporation. Since he was riding with Dorrell who was one of the mine's top gunmen, it seemed that the rumour might be true.

However, according to Jane, the

Blackwash silver mine had another, even more notorious gunman on its payroll. Yet he wore a badge. It was common knowledge that there was a lot of rivalry between them since they both claimed to be the fastest gunman in New Mexico.

So why would Hawker need a third fast gun? Apart from the expense, surely that would only add to the already existing rivalry? Brad pondered the puzzle, but not for long. The pangs of hunger turned his thoughts to breakfast.

A woman-cooked breakfast was a rare treat for a man who had lived on the trail since leaving Texas, so it was not surprising that Brad enjoyed every mouthful. However, there was something he had to get sorted out. Although there was plenty of money stashed away in his saddle-bags, he felt any offer of payment would be taken as an insult by his hostess. Instead, using his horse's lameness as an excuse, he made an offer he hoped Jane would find difficult to refuse.

'Ma'am, as it's going to be a few days before my horse is fit to ride, if you want, I could earn my keep working around your ranch until he's recovered.'

'Please don't keep calling me ma'am,' replied Jane. 'I guess if you're in no hurry to leave, the wagon needs fixing; the corral has to be rebuilt and the barn door needs mending. Then, if you don't mind doing even more mundane work, the house and barn could use a coat of paint. But I'm afraid I couldn't afford to pay you much.'

'Money's not necessary. A few breakfasts like the one I've just eaten and a bite to eat in the evening will be payment enough. I'll stay at least until my horse is fit to ride again. First, I'll fix the barn door so I can bed down in there tonight.'

'That will be fine,' replied Jane. 'It should be safe for you to stay at least a week. The Blackwash Mining Corporation have asked me three times to sell my ranch. Each time they have waited several days before returning for my answer.'

Brad didn't tell her he had no intention of leaving the Little U until he had discovered the whereabouts of Killner's gang. Besides, no true son of the Lone Star State would leave a woman alone in this wilderness, especially after she had been threatened.

But Jane had another problem.

'Before you decide to stay, I think I should tell you that Blackwash aren't the only ones who want my ranch. But the Little U is my home and is not for sale to anyone at any price.'

'That won't be the answer those gunmen or anybody else will want to hear.'

'No,' agreed Jane, 'but then it's not your fight.'

'Perhaps not,' agreed Brad, but in spite of his overwhelming desire to track down Killner and his gang, something told him that it had a good chance of becoming so.

4

It was late afternoon and hot; all traces of the spring storm had gone. From his seat on the porch in front of Blackwater's jail, Marshal Len Ward commanded a view southward down Main Street. The buildings were nearly all saloons, the largest and oldest of which was the Lucky Strike.

The Overland Stage depot straddled the southern end of Main street. It consisted of a combined ticket office and waiting-room, at the back of which was a large warehouse. Facing these, on the opposite side of Main Street, were Overland's large stable and smithy.

Some way beyond the Overland's buildings was a tall post, which marked the beginning of Blackwash County and the southernmost end of the town of Blackwater. The post also denoted the official limit of Marshal Ward's jurisdiction.

It was normally time for the marshal to make his rounds. But not today. Instead, he continued sitting on his porch waiting for the delivery of a very special parcel. The weekly Overland stagecoach had already arrived but he did not want to draw attention to the parcel by collecting it himself.

Fortunately, it was mid-week, so there were no miners or cowboys in Blackwater to cause any trouble. Therefore, he was surprised to see Sheriff Dent of Blackwash County ride into Blackwater.

For all his swagger, Dent had no legal jurisdiction in Blackwater. He was just an appointee of the Blackwash mine. But not only did the mine do a great deal of business in Blackwater, their miners spent most of their pay in the town's saloons. So Blackwater's town council had come to an arrangement with the mine. No objection to Dent's appointment would be raised so long as he only operated within Blackwash County.

But there was a major flaw in the scheme. Dent's fast and deadly draw meant few opposed him. So he went where he wanted, because the few who had disputed his right so to do, were now permanent residents of Blackwater's ever growing Boot Hill.

For that reason, Marshal Ward had backed away from a show-down with Dent for he knew he was no match for the county sheriff. So, once again, he pretended to look the other way as Dent dismounted and entered the main store.

Another depot marked the north end of Main Street. This one belonged to the New Mexico Territories Stage & Freight Company. Locally known as the New-Mexican, it was little more than a local freight line serving the large encampment at the Blackwash silver mine. It also owned several prairie-schooners specially adapted to carry miners to and from Blackwater.

However, the New-Mexican's prized possession was a heavily armoured coach which, when escorted by Hawker's gunmen, was used to ship the silver-ore back East. Like the mine, the New-Mexican was owned by Jed Hawker.

The afternoon peace was further disturbed by Jane Latham as she drove her old and battered wagon into town. It had seen much better days, so its brand new back wheel looked strangely out of place. Seated next to Jane was a stranger and beside the old wagon was a fine sorrel stallion with a chestnut-coloured mane. Oddly, whilst its forelegs were walking, its back legs seemed to be trotting. However, the sorrel was limping badly on its right foreleg. Despite this, Jane drove straight past the New-Mexican depot which, like the Overland Stage, boasted a blacksmith.

As the wagon rolled slowly past the jail, the stranger dismounted. The sorrel seemed unwilling to follow the wagon, so the stranger hitched it to the jailhouse rail and then approached the still seated sheriff.

'Afternoon, Marshal. I'm Brad Miller. Used to work on the Double M back in Texas. I'm just a cowhand on my way to Arizona but I got caught in the storm and was offered shelter at the Little U. As I'm going to be working there for a while, I thought I'd better introduce myself.'

'I'm obliged,' replied the marshal.

It was something of a tradition in the West that a new arrival in any town should introduce himself to its lawman, especially if that new arrival was a gunslinger. Marshal Ward noted that, in spite of his claim to be only a cowboy, the stranger's six-gun was slung low across his right hip in a way few real cowboys would do since it might impede roping a steer, or be accidentally fired whilst still in its holster.

Then, there was the matter of the stranger's fine horse. The sorrel was clearly several rungs in the price ladder above the feisty mustangs normally used by Texas cowboys. Moreover, the stallion's magnificent saddle must have cost well over a hundred dollars.

Then, last but not least, word of the stranger's run-in with Chad Dowell was all over Blackwater. Few ordinary cowboys would risk incurring the wrath of such a notorious gunslinger. Indeed there were many who claimed Dowell was even faster than Dent. So the sheriff guessed the stranger standing in front of him was one of the Double M's gunmen.

The Double M was one of the biggest and best known ranches in Texas. It was noted for sending two herds per year to the rail-head towns such as Abilene and more recently Dodge. It was also notorious for employing gunslingers to ensure their herds arrived safely. As a result, even in New Mexico, there were few lawmen west of the Pecos who had not heard of the Double M or its redoubtable owner, Abe Mitchell. Since the end of the Civil

War, he had not only defied the carpet-baggers, but had made the Double M into one of the wealthiest ranches in Texas.

But the code of the West dictated that a man was entitled to keep his past a secret. Moreover, handbills for Wanted men issued in Texas carried little weight in Blackwater since New Mexico was a territory and not a federal state. So all that concerned Marshal Ward was that the stranger stayed within the little law he was able to enforce.

'That's a fine-looking stallion you have,' he said. 'But I've never seen a horse move like that.'

'It's called a fox-trot. All his line move like that. Originally, they were bred in the Ozark region of Missouri, hence their name, Missouri Fox-Trotters. If you're on the trail all day, they are just about the most comfortable horse you could ride.'

'But not when they are lame,' laughed the marshal.

'He's only thrown a shoe,' replied

Brad, 'but I had to ride him a mite too long before I could find shelter from the storm.'

'Hell, that was no storm, just a little Blackwater dew,' replied the marshal. 'If you're aiming to stick around, you might just get to see what a storm is really like.'

'Ain't got much choice at the moment,' replied Brad pointing at his horse.

'We've got two blacksmiths in town, but the Overland Stage's man is the best in this part of New Mexico. I could send word to have him fix up your horse if you like.'

'Be obliged, Marshal.'

'Will!' Len called loudly.

Will Langer came scurrying out of the jail. Much to Brad's surprise Will, who didn't look much more than seventeen, was wearing a star. His clothes were more appropriate for a sodbuster than a deputy. Although he carried a shotgun, he wasn't toting a six-gun.

'Will, take Mr Miller's horse down to the Overland and tell Max I'd like it reshod as soon as possible.'

It was clear that young Will had a way with horses. Although he did nothing more than speak to the horse briefly, Prince eagerly followed him to the Overland smithy.

'Two blacksmiths and two stagecoach lines, that's a mite unusual isn't it?' asked Brad.

'Guess so, but their rivalry isn't the main problem round here. There's a large silver mine about two hours' ride from Blackwater. Their land begins about twenty miles south of the Cactus Hills and they form the southern boundary of the Little U. It's common knowledge the mine owner, Jed Hawker, wants to buy the Little U. But even if Miss Jane wants to sell, he won't get it without one hell of a fight.'

'Why's that?' asked Brad.

'Because the land to the north of the Little U belongs to the Barr Zero ranch. Old man Barr was killed about six months ago in what was supposed to be a riding accident. His daughter, Kayleigh, claims he was beaten up by a bunch of the mine's gunmen, then left to die. But she couldn't prove it. In any case, they found his body in the wastelands between the Cactus Hills and the mine. My jurisdiction only covers Blackwater.'

'So who runs the Barr Zero, now?' asked Brad.

'Kayleigh.'

'Another woman ranch owner?'

'Yep. But never underestimate Kayleigh Barr. She ain't much more than a kid, but in spite of her looks, she's got a mean temper and she's every bit as tough as her pa used to be. She hates the Blackwash Silver Mine and ain't about to let it take over the Little U.'

'How could she stop the mine buying the Little U if my new boss wanted to sell?' asked Brad.

'The Barr Zero ain't just any old ranch. It's fifty times the size of the Little U and employs almost as many cowhands as the Double M.'

'So, the Little U is a buffer between them,' said Brad.

'Yep. As long as Miss Jane doesn't try to sell.'

'From what she says, I don't think she will,' replied Brad.

'Good. But that don't mean I ain't got trouble coming,' said the marshal pointing at Sheriff Dent as he came out of the store which Jane had just entered.

Dent mounted his horse and then road slowly past the jailhouse. He barely acknowledged Ward. It was clear to Brad that the sheriff from Blackwash County was no friend of the town marshal of Blackwater.

'Dent treats his star as a licence to kill anyone who opposes Hawker, but he is only authorized to operate within the limits of the mining camp. However, that doesn't stop him. As he's much faster than me with a six-gun, he does as he pleases.'

'Is he that fast?' asked Brad.

'Yes, some say as fast as Dorrell.'

'Any idea what brings him to Blackwater?' asked Brad.

'I guess he's looking for miners who have gone absent from the silver mine,' replied the sheriff.

'How come?' asked Brad.

Marshal Ward paused for a second before answering. This stranger seemed to be asking a lot of questions. On the other hand, he was working on the Little U and was entitled to know what he was getting into.

'I have an arrangement with the owner of the Blackwash Mining Corporation, Jed Hawker. His miners only come into Blackwater on pay-days and that is usually the twenty-first of each month. The miners stay until they are broke, which mostly takes no more than a couple of days. Then, Hawker uses his New-Mexican wagons to take them back to the mine. But some hide out. There's free travel on the Overland stage to Tombstone for any miner prepared to work there.'

'What about the hands from the Barr Zero?' asked Brad.

'I have a similar arrangement with the ranch. As the ranch pays out on the first weekend of the month, the miners are long gone before the cowboys arrive in town.'

'Sounds as if you've had some trouble between them in the past,' said Brad.

'Yep. Sometimes more than I can handle,' admitted Len.

'Well, if you ever need any help, just say the word. It wouldn't be the first time I've been a temporary deputy,' said Brad.

'I hope I don't have to take up your offer, but if I get to know you better, I may not have any choice. Apart from the usual problems, there's too many strangers around for my liking.'

Brad's interest heightened. Could any of these strangers be part of Killner's gang? But for all he knew, the marshal might be in league with them, so he refrained from asking any questions on the subject.

'I guess I'm another stranger to add to your list,' he said instead.

'Maybe not,' replied the marshal. 'Jane Latham is mighty particular who she hires, so if she is prepared to take you on, that's recommendation enough for me. Besides, your run-in with Chad Dorrell is all over town and he's no friend of mine.'

'Nor mine,' said Brad.

'Says he told you to get out of the territory and been bragging he will call you out, next time he sees you.'

'Sorry to hear that,' said Brad calmly, 'but I'm not going to leave until I'm good and ready.'

'Guessed that was going to be your decision,' said the marshal.

'Blackwater also seems to have more than its fair share of saloons,' said Brad, as he looked down Main Street.

'Five so far. The Lucky Strike was built years ago when the Spanish used Blackwater as a stopping post *en route* to California. The rest have sprung up since the silver mining started. But these days we get a good many folks passing through to Tombstone, so even when the miners and Barr Zero hands are working, most of them get pretty busy in the evening.'

Could any of the folks passing through have been the renegades? From his own experiences at the end of each cattle drive, Brad knew saloon girls could be a good source of local news. So they might be his best bet to find out whether Killner's gang had been in Blackwater. But which saloon would the renegades have used?

'Which saloon would you recommend?' he asked.

'Clem Mullet at the Lucky Strike has the best beer and prettiest girls in town. But take care if you like to gamble because I believe their tables are rigged even though I haven't been able to prove it yet.'

'Thanks, Marshal, but gambling isn't one of my vices,' said Brad.

'Well in that case, as I said, they have

the best-looking girls in town. Alice Albright looks after them, but she doesn't live in the saloon like most of the girls. She has her own little spread, just out of town. She's a good friend of mine, so if you want a more private place to meet any of her girls, I could arrange it for you.'

'After I've caught up on the backlog of work on the Little U, I'll take you up on that offer,' replied Brad.

Alice Albright might be the best person to question about the comings and goings in Blackwater. However, the sound of the old wagon rumbling across the street heralded Jane's return and ended the discussion. But it was barely half full of provisions. She was not slow in relating the cause.

'The store would only let me have what I had the cash to pay for,' she said indignantly.

'So that's why Dent went into the store. Seems like Hawker is going to stop at nothing to get the Little U,' said Marshal Ward who never called his rival by his appointed title.

'Is there nothing you can do?' asked Brad.

'Well, it ain't a crime to refuse credit,' said Len, 'but I'll call in on the store and find out what Dent has been up to.'

But before he could do so, his young deputy returned from the Overland depot. In his hands was the special parcel the marshal had been waiting for. However, there was no sign of Prince.

Will explained that the blacksmith, Max Gillard, thought it best for the stallion to rest up for a few days before he reshod it. Until then, the blacksmith had offered to keep Prince in the Overland's stable.

After the marshal's glowing testimonial, Brad could hardly refuse the offer. So the arrangements were confirmed and Brad left Blackwater as he arrived, a passenger in Jane's old wagon.

Few words were spoken during the trip back to the Little U. Jane was still furious about the general store's refusal to give her credit; Brad had other things to think about. Although he had picked up some useful information in Blackwater, he was no nearer to locating Killner and his gang.

5

The following day, as Brad was repairing the corral fence, several riders approached the Little U. However, they were not from the Blackwash silver mine and although their leader wore men's clothes and rode on the distinctive, Texas style, cowboy's saddle, it was clear, even from a distance, the rider was a woman.

As she halted her men in front of the ranch house, it was also evident she was a woman of outstanding beauty. However, Brad soon discovered her temper was as short as her black hair was long.

'Fetch Jane Latham,' she ordered. 'I'm here to do business, not chat to the hired help.'

'I only take orders from Miss Latham,' said Brad quietly.

'Do you know who I am?' she said angrily.

'No, but I have no objection to you telling me.'

'I'm Kayleigh Barr, owner of the Barr Zero ranch.'

'Am I supposed to be impressed?' asked Brad.

Infuriated by his reply, Kayleigh savagely spurred her horse. The startled beast reared up, directly in front of Brad, as she had intended. In the same instant, she lashed out at him with her whip. To control the rearing mare using only one hand was an amazing feat. However, it was what happened next which drew gasps of astonishment from the assembled riders.

It was over so quickly, none of the watching riders could describe exactly how it happened. Somehow, Brad managed to side-step the rearing horse and, at the same time, catch hold of the whip in mid-air as it snaked out towards him. Before any of the riders could react, the whip was in Brad's hand.

Jane had been busily baking and

preparing the evening meal when she heard the riders approaching. That she was content to let Brad deal with them was an indication of how much she had grown to trust the Texan during the few days he had been working for her. However, when she heard the familiar voice of Kayleigh Barr, she quickly made her way outside.

'Good morning, Miss Barr, would you like to dismount and come inside?' Jane asked, ignoring the commotion caused by Brad's actions.

'No. I've come to buy your little ranch, not to socialize. The Barr Zero's offer is twenty cents per acre for all your ranch, including the hill land, paid in cash.'

'It's a fair offer, Miss Barr, and better than that of Jed Hawker. Even so, my answer is the same: my home is not for sale.'

'You may be holding out for another offer from Hawker, but if you try to sell to the Blackwash mine, you won't live to spend it,' said one of the riders.

Apart from Kayleigh Barr there were five other horsemen, but that did not deter Brad as his hand hovered over his Peacemaker.

'The lady has said she is not selling, so I don't take kindly to your threats,' he said coldly.

'My, you're the sassy one,' said Kayleigh, seemingly not in the least put out by having her whip taken from her, 'but there's no need for violence. We are happy to have the Little U as a neighbour, so long as it's under your ownership, Miss Latham.'

'That's mighty nice of you,' said Jane sarcastically.

'But nothing happens in the town of Blackwater or Blackwash County without our permission,' continued Kayleigh, seemingly unaware of Jane's sarcasm. 'So, if you ever change your mind, you must sell to us or face the consequences.'

'Which are?' asked Jane, her voice icily calm.

'Seeing your ranch house burnt to

the ground and your range absorbed into the Barr Zero. Don't doubt that we will do it before any deal you strike with Hawker could be completed. So be warned. Sell out to Hawker and we will ensure that the Little U will disappear without trace leaving you with nothing!'

After issuing her threat to Jane, Kayleigh Barr gave Brad a long, deliberate look. She appeared to be not entirely displeased with what she saw and smiled as she spoke to him.

'We are behind in completing our round-up. There's long term work with regular wages at the Barr Zero. If you're interested, look me up.'

However, before Brad could reply, she wheeled her horse around and galloped rapidly away. The other riders followed quickly after her.

'Must be nice to have such friendly neighbours,' said Brad, attempting to match Jane's earlier sarcasm.

'Of one thing you can be sure,' replied Jane, 'the Barr Zero will back up their threat. Their bite is much worse than their bark! But as I said before, it's not your fight.'

Brad did not reply but over dinner that evening, he voiced the questions that had been bothering him since his arrival at the Little U.

'Is there anything special about your ranch which makes Hawker and the Barr Zero so determined to buy it?'

'Nothing as far as I know. My ranch is tiny compared with the Barr Zero. It has about four thousand acres of decent pasture. Beyond that, about three thousand acres of hilly scrubland which leads to what the old-timers call the Cactus Hills,' replied Jane.

'Cactus Hills? That's a strange name.'

'Yes,' agreed Jane. 'The ground up there is covered by a special cactus which only grows in New Mexico. In springtime, its flowers give off a scent like a lemon. But the ground is worthless. The Yampai live in the hills, but not in the caves. They believe the spirits of their ancestors dwell in caves in the hills and only their medicine man is permitted to enter the caves to seek advice from them.'

'The Barr Zero's offer is worth a lot of money,' said Brad.

'Yes. But this ranch was my father's dream, so it's not for sale at any price!'

'I guess I feel the same about the Double M,' said Brad.

'Did you work there long?' asked Jane, but the question was not as innocent as it seemed.

'I grew up there,' replied Brad, a little too proudly.

'And yet you left it to come to New Mexico,' said Jane shrewdly.

'But one day, I intend to go back,' replied Brad hastily.

The conversation had taken an awkward twist. Brad realized he was in danger of revealing too much about himself and the real reason for staying on at the Little U. So he changed the subject.

'Of course, what the Yampai believe about the caves is nothing more than superstition, but has anything unusual happened lately in the Cactus Hills?'

'Yes, Brad. A few days before storm, two prospectors went into the hills and have disappeared without trace.'

'Strange. Could they have passed through the hills and then got lost on the other side?'

'Not likely. Beyond the Cactus Hills, the ground becomes an open, semi-desert. It continues like that right up to the mining camp. Except for paydays there are usually over a hundred miners in the camp which is guarded by regular patrols. I doubt the prospectors or anyone else could get past them without being seen,' replied Jane.

'Well, their disappearance makes two mysteries,' said Brad.

'What's the other one?' asked Jane.

'I can understand the Barr Zero wanting to stop the Blackwash Mining Corporation from getting a foothold on their boundary line, but why on earth should Hawker be interested in taking over the Little U?'

'I don't know,' confessed Jane.

Brad thought for a moment. Could Killner and his gang be hiding out in the Cactus Hills? Perhaps the prospectors had run into them? If so, the renegades would have had no qualms about killing them. But then again, surely someone at the mining camp would have heard the shooting. However, the outlaws might have only stayed for a few nights and then ridden on to Arizona. There was only one way to find out. However, he was not ready to tell Jane the real reason he wanted to search her hills.

'After Prince has recovered, and if you agree, perhaps I might take a look at your Cactus Hills? Maybe I can find a clue to the whereabouts of the prospectors or even turn up something which might explain the reason why so many different parties want to buy your ranch.'

'Well it couldn't do any harm to have a look round,' said Jane, who was unaware that Killner might be holed up in her hills. 'In fact, to save time, I think I'll come with you. I could take you straight to the caves and act as your interpreter if we run into any of the Yampai.'

There was no way Brad was going to risk taking Jane into the Cactus Hills, even if a small part of them did belong to her ranch. Yet to refuse her offer outright meant he would have to tell her about the San Pedro massacre. He thought she had enough worries without adding to them, so swiftly changed the subject.

'You understand the Yampai dialect?'

'Just enough to get by on,' said Jane modestly.

Jane was unusually quiet for the rest of that night. Was it because he had shown no intention of leaving before the return of Hawker's gunmen? Or perhaps, she had something else on her mind?

However, he was too tired to care. Fixing the heavy barn door and mending the corral fences had been hard work. Once he could have taken the work in his stride, but in recent years, he had become unused to manual labour. As a result, he was exhausted and so decided to turn in. The hay in the barn's loft made for a warm and comfortable bed and he immediately fell into a deep sleep.

Next day was uneventful. Jane and Brad painted the ranch house. It took them all day but it was worth it. Brad was surprised what a difference a coat of white paint made to the appearance of the small ranch house. But the painting chores were far from over and the following morning found them painting the barn.

However, their work was interrupted by Deputy Will Langer. In spite of the dangers of the open range, or perhaps because of them, Marshal Ward had insisted that the young deputy was unarmed, except for his shotgun. Even in this lawless part of New Mexico, the sheriff believed that nobody would draw on a man not carrying a six-gun. Unfortunately, events were to prove the marshal wrong.

The reason for Will's visit was the return of Brad's horse. Prince had been reshod and had fully recovered from his ordeal in the storm. Indeed, the beast was back to his cantankerous self. Nevertheless, the boy controlled him with ease, never having to raise his voice above a whisper.

Brad was impressed. Once the Killner gang had been dealt with, he resolved to take the boy back to Texas with him. Since the murder of Seth Madden, the Double M was in need of a good wrangler.

The young deputy stayed for a leisurely lunch. Brad was glad of the diversion. Manual labour had long made forgotten parts of him remind him of their existence by inflicting considerable amounts of pain.

After lunch, Will headed back for Blackwater. It was the last time anybody saw him alive, except of course for the person or persons who shot him.

Chad Dorrell's fussily dressed companion found the body of the young deputy. The gunslinger claimed to have come across the corpse near the Cactus Hills. The deputy had been shot in the back.

However, the gunslinger strenuously denied shooting young Will, and he had actually taken the deputy's body back to Blackwater. After a long and private discussion with Marshal Ward, the gunslinger left. Since the crime had been committed in Blackwash County there was little Blackwater's town marshal could do.

Nevertheless, the marshal was puzzled. The Cactus Hills were not on the trail between the Little U and Blackwater. In fact, they lay in almost the opposite direction. So why had the young deputy ridden there?

To try to find out, Marshal Ward rode out to the scene of the crime and briefly searched it. Although there were tracks of several horses leading away from the murder scene and into the Cactus Hills, he decided against following them. Instead, he rode on to the Little U to inform Jane and Brad of the tragedy.

Brad took the news badly. Had he not left Prince in Blackwater and agreed to Will returning the horse to the Little U, the young deputy might have remained in the relative safety of the town.

As soon as the marshal left, Brad also rode to the scene of the murder. As he had almost expected, amongst the many horse tracks, he discovered one which had a familiar v-notch in it. That, together with the cold-bloodedness of the crime, told a grim story to Brad, one the Texan thought best to keep to himself for the time being.

6

It was mid-morning and blazing hot. The late spring sun beat down with an intensity it usually reserved for mid-summer. In fact, part of the range beyond the stream was already turning into a dust bowl. Yet it was home to Jane's many hens. She had already clipped all their wings to prevent them from flying away, so now they roamed freely. But, perversely, they preferred to lay their eggs on the far side of the stream, out of sight of the ranch house. In spite of the heat, Jane was busily collecting them to sell in Blackwater the following day.

As Brad was finishing painting the barn, a lone rider approached the Little U. Brad recognized the rider's horse instantly. It was the palomino with the strange white flash on its flank. Its rider was the gunslinger who had accompanied Chad Dorrell when he had tried to persuade Jane to sell her little ranch.

At the time, he had seemed more friendly than Dorrell. However, had he been biding his time, waiting for the right moment to pay back Brad for their confrontation? Or was he merely calling to see whether Jane had changed her mind about selling her little ranch?

Brad was not about to guess the answer, so hurried into the barn. Seconds later he reappeared carrying his Winchester, fully loaded, cocked and ready to fire. But, surprisingly, the rider reined in his horse while the palomino was still well out of six-gun range. Nevertheless, the range was easily within Brad's Winchester. Once again the Texan held the advantage.

'Be obliged if I could set down a spell,' the gunslinger asked politely.

'So long as you keep your gun hand where I can see it and remember I have the Winchester, you're welcome,' replied Brad curtly.

The unusual white flash on its flank again stirred a distant memory. But

Brad could not quite bring it into focus since most of his attention was focused on the right-hand of the gunslinger as he rode the palomino across to the water-trough before dismounting.

'That's far enough,' said Brad, as he raised his Winchester to his shoulder. 'You can say what you want to say from there.'

'Fair enough,' replied the gunslinger. 'Is the lady of the house about?'

'No, but I can tell you her answer is still the same. You can tell your boss she has no intention of selling.'

'I guessed as much. Dorrell is busy at the mine, cooking up some plan with Hawker, so I volunteered to come alone to get Miss Jane's answer. But that's not the real reason for my visit.'

'In that case, why are you here?' asked Brad curtly.

'For the same reason as you,' came the surprising reply.

'I doubt that,' said Brad, still pointing his Winchester at the gunslinger.

'Seth Madden was kin of mine and a

long time ago, I used to ride with your pa,' the gunslinger said quietly.

Brad swore quietly under his breath as he remembered. Almost two years ago Brad had been a temporary deputy and the gunslinger's description and that of the unusual flash on the palomino's flank had been on a Wanted poster. There was no doubt, the man standing in front of him was one of the most notorious and deadly gunmen Texas had ever known.

'I guess that must make you Ethan Madden,' replied Brad, still pointing his Winchester at the gunslinger. 'My pa often talked about you, but the last thing I heard was you had been shot-up during a bank raid and arrested.'

'That's what people were intended to hear,' said the gunslinger mysteriously.

But Brad was in no mood to add another mystery to the ones he already had.

'So why are you here?' he asked again, this time a little more sharply.

'I need your help,' came the surprising reply.

'Why should I help an outlaw?'

'The raid you spoke of was about eighteen months ago. I just happened to be in Somerville when the gang struck. Its sheriff and me were old friends, so I tried to help him. But I got shot for my pains. For saving the bank's money, Governor Coke offered me parole. Then, after I recovered, he arranged for me to become a Texas Ranger.'

'I heard that the Rangers were back in operation again, but it's the first time I've heard them called the Texas Rangers!'

The one time outlaw carefully pulled open his jacket. Pinned to his shirt was a large silver star enclosed in a silver ring which bore the inscription, Texas Ranger on it.

'Texas was added to the title of Rangers when Governor Coke got funds from the state legislature to reinstate them. But only a few rangers wear a star and there are several different versions,' admitted the lawman.

Brad lowered his Winchester and smiled.

'Before they were disbanded, the rangers were always welcome at the Double M. But I seemed to be forgetting my manners. Care to get out of the sun and come in for coffee?'

'Sure would,' said Ethan and followed Brad into the ranch house. 'Frankly, nobody was more surprised than me when I was offered the pardon and the badge. But whilst Miss Jane is not here, I want to talk about the Killner gang. I take it you haven't told her you're after them.'

'Too right! I've only told her that I worked for the Double M and I'd appreciate you telling her the same.'

'If that's the way you want it, then that's fine by me. Me and your pa go way back, but I was the one who used to kick over the traces,' replied the ranger.

'So he said. But although I've only

been here a short time, that's long enough to see that the Little U has more than enough troubles of its own. It seems that everyone round here wants to buy it and won't take no for an answer.'

'I'm guessing there must be something special about this spread we don't yet know.'

'You said you needed my help,' interrupted Brad.

'Yes. I think there's a fair chance Killner's gang is based in the Cactus Hills.'

'I'd come to the same conclusion,' agreed Brad.

However, he kept the details of the v-shaped horse track to himself. Ethan Madden had arrived at the silver mine some days before Killner's gang. So how had he known where to look for them? Brad had seen no proof other than a tin star to back up the former outlaw's story. And Madden was quite fast enough to have outdrawn almost any lawman he encountered. If he had done so, he could have then taken the star from the dead man's body and that man could have been a ranger.

'Have you ridden into the Cactus Hills?' asked Ethan, interrupting Brad's train of thought.

'Not yet. But Jane said there was a system of caves in the centre of them. For what it's worth, I think there's something very strange going on in the Cactus Hills, but it may not be connected with Killner's gang.'

'If it's not, what are the outlaws doing there?'

'I've no idea. Nor why they left a trail across New Mexico an Easterner could follow!'

'There are a lot of things about this which don't add up. But you're right; the first thing we need to do is to find out if the gang are really using the caves in the Cactus Hills for their hideout. Until I've checked that out, I don't think we should mention our chat to Miss Jane. But, for what its worth, I don't think it's in her best interest to sell the Little U — '

'Why would one of Hawker's hired gun-hands not want me to sell out to the Blackwash Mining Corporation and what's all this about a gang of gunmen on my ranch?' asked Jane from the doorway.

Brad had been listening so intently to Ethan he had failed to hear her return.

'Firstly, ma'am, I'm not one of Hawker's men, though I don't blame you for thinking so,' replied Ethan as he again displayed his star. 'I'm afraid it's probable that a gang of renegades has recently established a hideout in your hills.'

'But you are not absolutely sure?' asked Jane.

'No. Back in Texas, when I was working undercover, I discovered the gang had a new hideout somewhere near Blackwater. The mining camp seemed a likely place, so I've been there with Chad Dorrell in the hope they might contact him, but until the killing of the young deputy, I hadn't found any trace of them.'

'But, even if they had contacted Dorrell, why would he tell you?' asked Jane.

'I used to be an outlaw and for a short time rode with Killner. So, if Killner had a hideout in New Mexico, what could be more natural for me than to want to join them there?'

'You figure Dorrell is connected to the renegades?' asked Brad.

'Yes,' replied the ranger. 'If they are hiding out in the Cactus Hills, some-body in the mining camp must be supplying them with food. But whether Dorrell is secretly part of their gang, or they are all on Hawker's payroll, is anybody's guess.'

Jane was not convinced and voiced her doubts.

'Either way, what can you do? Surely a Texas Ranger has no jurisdiction in New Mexico?'

'Quite right, ma'am. But I intend to use my six-gun to persuade them to return to Texas and stand trial. But first I have to locate them. Then, I was hoping to borrow your man to help me take them back to Texas.'

'He's not my man,' Jane retorted rather too abruptly. 'In any case, you will also need a guide to get you round the hills. Someone who knows the back-trails and location of the caves. Otherwise you might blunder into them and find yourself outnumbered.'

'Do you have anybody in mind?' asked Brad.

'Me. It's still my land, so I'm coming with you,' said Jane.

'No, ma'am, it's far too dangerous,' said the ranger.

'If you knew just some of the terrible things these renegades have done, you would know the ranger was right,' said Brad bitterly, thinking about the San Pedro massacre.

'Nevertheless, I'm coming with you,' she said very firmly.

Brad's words made Jane look at him sharply. The suspicion that Brad had not been entirely open with her began to grow in her mind. Certainly, he seemed to know a lot more about the gang than he was letting on. Of course, it might have been a coincidence, but it seemed that if Killner and his men really were in the Cactus Hills, then Brad might be following them. If so, he was probably a bounty hunter and not the cowboy he claimed to be.

She found the possibility that Brad might have deceived her oddly upsetting. For some reason, the notion made her even more determined to ride with them. She had never met a bounty hunter, but some of the newspapers her father used to buy when they lived in New England regularly featured their activities and gloried in their often brutal killings. Yet somehow, she could not imagine Brad as a brutal man-hunter.

Brad tried a different approach.

'Even if we agreed, you can't ride that great carthorse,' he said.

'Then I'll borrow a pony from a

friend who lives in Blackwater,' she retorted.

Brad tried again.

'Even if the Killner gang are in your hills, they won't be easy to find. So we might have to stay overnight.'

'And that means sleeping rough,' added the ranger.

'In that case we will need a pack mule to carry provisions and blankets,' she replied.

Brad's elder sister had been just as stubborn as Jane, so he knew he was beaten. He glanced ruefully at the ranger who reluctantly nodded his agreement.

7

Two days later, the trio set out, but not until Jane had cooked a huge breakfast. Jane was mounted on a docile pinto pony which she had borrowed from her friend, Alice Albright. While she had been making the arrangements with Alice, Brad had bought a pack mule from Matt Gillard, the blacksmith at the Overland Stage depot.

It would have been a relatively short trip to the Cactus Hills had the trio ridden directly to them. But the relatively flat ranges of the Little U offered little cover, so they would have been easily detected by any lookouts posted by the renegades. Guided by Jane, the trio rode parallel to the hills until they reached the end of them. Then she turned south and continued until they reached the arid scrubland on the other side of the Cactus Hills.

These scrublands, known as the wastelands, stretched for miles and separated the Cactus Hills from the area owned by the Blackwash Mining Corporation. Although he had no legal title, Hawker regarded the area as part of his domain. So, several times per day, he sent out bugle blowing, cavalry-like patrols to back up his claim.

However, Jane had chosen this route because the wastelands was the home of a forest of giant cacti. Although tall cacti were not uncommon in the Texas Panhandle, Brad had seen nothing as remotely as big as these. Each one of them was as tall as a fully gown tree and many grew close together, forming perfect cover for any horseman.

As a result, the trio and pack mule were able to approach the hills safe from detection from either Hawker's patrols or Killner's band of oulaws. In spite of her companion's original doubts, Jane had begun to prove her worth as a guide.

The wastelands contained dozens of

trails which criss-crossed each other as they circled individual hills or plunged into deep-sided ravines many of which were nothing more than blind or box-canyons which Jane expertly avoided. However, as dusk approached, she led them into a massive box-canyon, which also appeared to come to a dead end. But this one hid a secret known only to her and the Yampai Indians.

At first, it looked like any other canyon. However, long ago, there had been an avalanche which had deposited a huge pile of rocks in front of the sheer cliff face. Jane led them beyond these rocks and continued right up to the canyon's towering cliff face. Only then did Brad see that there was a narrow track, far too narrow to be called a trail, between the rock pile and the cliff face. Although it appeared to lead to another dead end, Jane led them into it. They had to ride in single file because the track was so narrow.

In the gathering gloom, the uneven-ness of the ground caused Brad to rein in Prince and reduce his speed to barely walking pace. The ranger, following behind Brad and struggling to control the pack mule, was obliged to do the same.

No so Jane. In spite of riding side-saddle, she continued to ride her pinto at a steady trot. Consequently, by the time she reached the end of the passageway, she was a fair distance in front of the men. Then, to Brad's amazement, she and the pinto turned sideways and disappeared into the cliff face.

Risking all, Brad spurred Prince into a gallop. Unable to see what had happened, Ethan was taken by surprise and was left behind. In any case, the pack mule was proving to be less than enthusiastic about travelling along the narrow track and the ranger had to drag the stubborn beast behind him. He turned to rebuke the mule. When he turned to face forward again, Brad had also disappeared.

Yet the answer was simple. About

twenty paces before the end of the passageway, there was a narrow split, barely wide enough to ride through. But owing to the peculiar configuration of the cliff face, it was not possible to see the split until you reached it.

Although it was almost pitch black, Ethan urged his reluctant palomino into the split and, leading the even more reluctant pack mule, gingerly edged forward. It took only a few minutes before he emerged into the gloomy light of an oval-shaped arena, but it seemed a lot longer.

The arena was totally enclosed by towering cliffs which contained several caves. By the time the ranger had emerged with the reluctant pack mule still safely in tow, Jane and Brad had already dismounted in front of one of them.

'Damn near got my head bashed in following you and Jane,' grumbled the ranger as he rode over to them.

'Sorry,' apologized Brad, 'but I didn't know what had happened to Jane.'

'Chancing after a pretty woman is likely to get you into a lot of trouble,' chuckled Ethan as he dismounted.

'Damn right! And I guess they don't come much prettier than Jane,' replied Brad, whose tongue had suddenly taken control of his mind. So the compliment was out before he could suppress it.

Jane said nothing but could not prevent herself from blushing deeply. But the men didn't notice. Evening approached and the sunlight barely reached halfway down one of the cliff sides and the floor was plunged into eerie darkness.

'Unsaddle the horses, while I check things out,' Jane ordered, as she tried to compose herself. Then she disappeared into the inky darkness of the cave before either man could object.

Without a word, they carried out Jane's order and also unloaded the mule. Then they turned the beasts loose to graze on tufts of wiry grass which were dotted about. The only way out was the way by which they had entered and neither horses nor mule would voluntarily enter that dark tunnel.

They had barely finished their chores when the pitch-black interior of the cave was suddenly lit up, revealing that it was nothing more than another small tunnel, even narrower than the one they had just ridden through. In the centre of it stood Jane, carrying an oil lamp. Without a word, she turned round and started to walk back down the tunnel. Brad followed with Ethan again bringing up the rear.

The floor fell steeply before leading into a surprisingly large cavern. An ice-cold breeze blowing in Brad's face made him shiver, but it suggested there might be another way out of the cavern.

The dim light of the oil lamp also revealed an enormous pile of tinder-dry wood, enough to last several weeks. There was also a large stack of cans of beans, several bags of flour, sugar and coffee beans. There were also two boxes of ammunition. Brad examined one of them and found that the ammunition matched that of his Winchester. Was this the outlaws' hideout? Jane swiftly dashed that idea.

'This cavern was used by the wife of the Yampai chief when she gave birth. But as she and her baby almost died, their medicine man said it contained evil spirits and forbad the Yampai to use it again. When Papa knew he was going to buy the Little U, he brought me here. It was his wish that the cavern should always be stocked with provisions in case the Little U was attacked by the Apache.'

'If nobody else knows of the cavern's existence, it would make an ideal base for us,' said Ethan.

'I'm glad you think so,' said Jane, smiling rather too smugly. 'As far as I know, apart from the Yampai and Papa, we are the only ones ever to set foot down here. So tell me, would you have found it without me?'

'It doesn't seem likely,' Ethan was forced to admit.

'Well, wait until tomorrow, you haven't

seen anything yet,' retorted Jane.

Knowing when he was well and truly beaten, Ethan retreated back up the tunnel and began to bring in the fresh food carried by the mule. Brad busied himself making a fire. The wood was so dry it blazed fiercely without emitting any smoke and the cavern soon began to loose its chill. Jane made a stew and they built up the fire for the night.

Unused to cave dwelling, Brad slept fitfully, twice rising to build up the fire. Yet, without the light of the rising sun to wake him, he slept through the unseen dawn. He was eventually roused by the smell and sound of bacon rashers sizzling and there were eggs from Jane's hens to go with them. Although he worried about the dangers they might yet encounter, even Brad had to admit that she had become indispensable.

But Jane had another surprise in store for them, but not until Ethan had watered the horses and pack mule. He did this by emptying his canteen into his hat and letting the animals drink from it.

As soon as he returned to the cavern, Jane picked up the oil lamp and led both men into yet another tunnel. This one was situated at the back at the furthermost point from where they had first entered.

After a sharp descent, they passed a small stream which cascaded down a crevice, making it a simple task to refill their canteens. Then the tunnel levelled out and widened enough for the trio to walk abreast. But as the tunnel began to rise steeply, its roof became lower until they had to crawl on their hands and knees.

Eventually, the tunnel burst out in the daylight. Brad found himself on a high, craggy ledge sheltered by an outcrop of rocks easily large enough to hide the presence of the trio. This ledge overlooked a deep, green and surprisingly fertile valley. At the bottom of the valley, which sloped steeply in a southerly direction, was a fast flowing river, still swollen by the violent storm which had caught Brad so unawares.

Along the river-bank was a large herd of cattle engaged in prolonged bouts of drinking. In doing so, they completely ignored the lush alfalfa all around them. There was not a cactus to be seen in this green and pleasant place.

'Jane, didn't you say the Cactus Hills were completely barren?' asked Brad.

'They are, apart from this valley. But the Yampai told me that the river dries up by mid-summer.'

While Brad and Jane were talking, the ranger extracted a pair of field-glasses from his saddlebags, then studied the cattle very carefully.

'Miss Jane, is this valley on your range?' he asked.

'Yes. Officially the Little U boundary extends just beyond here.'

'I see. Care to have a look through my field-glasses?'

Jane took them and quickly scanned the herd. She instantly recognized the brand they were all carrying.

'All Barr Zero stock!' she exclaimed in amazement. 'But why would Kayleigh Barr put one of her herds on my land, especially as this part of it is quite near the Blackwash mine?'

'May I look?' asked Brad.

The frown on his face deepened as he carefully studied the herd through the field-glasses. Brad was an experienced cattleman and noticed the sides of the newly branded steers were bathed in sweat and lather. It suggested to Brad the herd had been spooked and stampeded last night.

'What do you make of it?' asked Ethan.

'That Kayleigh Barr and her men had nothing to do with driving the herd into your valley.'

'I don't understand,' replied Jane.

'Of course not, but if you had been brought up on a big ranch, like me, you might. Take another look through the glasses and tell me what you see.'

Jane did as she was bid, but shook her head as she saw nothing new, then returned the field-glasses to Ethan.

'But you can see the lather on their flanks,' said Brad patiently.

'Yes, of course.'

'So they must have been driven very hard or, more likely, deliberately stampeded. In either case, that's something the Barr Zero hands would have been desperate to avoid.'

'Why?' asked Jane.

'Because cattle are sold by weight on the hoof. Now on a trail drive, they will lose weight, so they are fattened up before starting on the drive. Then at least some of the excess fat should be converted into meat during the drive, thus reducing weight loss. Unfortunately, during a prolonged stampede, cattle will burn off a great deal of that fat and so lose more weight during the actual drive.'

'But couldn't the stampede have started accidentally?' asked Jane.

'Panic-stricken cattle may run wildly but they usually tire quite quickly and then it's much easier to turn the leaders and stop the rest of the herd.'

'But judging by their sweaty condition, they didn't tire quickly this time,' said the ranger.

'I guess they were repeatedly spooked to keep them stampeding,' replied Brad.

'But who would do such a thing?' asked Jane.

'The outlaws, and I guess they ain't too far away,' said the ranger grimly.

8

Safely hidden by the outcrop of rocks, the trio kept watch from the ridge high above the valley floor. They had been watching for almost two hours, hoping that at least some of the rustlers would return. But none did. However, Jane thought she saw someone moving about in the rocks on the opposite side of the valley. But when Brad took over the field-glasses, all he could see were jack-rabbits and so concluded it was a false alarm.

He was wrong. But then as many a vexed trooper would verify, there are none better than the Apache at keeping out of sight.

Whilst they kept surveillance, a discussion about the rustlers took place. Brad thought they could only be Killner's gang, but the ranger expressed his doubts.

'Well, I guess it don't take much more than a few gunshots and a lot of yelling to spook a herd during the night, but what would Killner do with them?'

'You have a point. No rancher would buy Barr Zero stock unless the seller had a certified bill of sale,' agreed Brad.

'But don't rustlers usually rebrand the cattle they steal?' asked Jane.

'It's been known,' replied the ranger ruefully.

'Believe me, branding cattle is very hard work and takes a fair amount of experience, not to mention skill,' said Brad.

'I'm not proud of it, but as I said before, just before I left the outlaw trail, I rode with Killner's gang,' said the ranger. 'But I couldn't stomach the things they did. Even so, I got to know the regulars in the gang. None of them has handled cattle. In fact, they were the scum of the earth who would do anything for money except work for it.'

'So could the rustlers have come

from the mining camp?' asked Brad.

'Although I remember meeting several Irishmen, most of Hawker's miners were Swedish, Dutch or Chinese immigrants. I don't recall meeting any former trail hands,' said Jane.

Brad looked taken aback at her revelation and Jane realized she had nearly said too much. For some reason she could not yet understand, she found herself wanting to keep the details of her past life at the Lucky Strike Saloon away from him.

'Sometimes, I used to go to the mining camp with Papa,' she added hastily.

'Now you mention it, I didn't see any cowhands in the mining camp,' said the ranger.

Much to Jane's relief, the discussion was interrupted by the appearance of a rider, dressed entirely in black in the valley far below them and Brad didn't need the field-glasses to recognize him: it was Chad Dorrell.

The gunslinger dismounted by the

river and allowed his horse to drink. To those far above him, it seemed as if he was waiting for someone, since he showed no interest in the cattle all around him.

Ten minutes later, the suspicions of the watchers on the ridge were proved to be correct. Two more riders appeared, riding at a leisurely canter. However, even using the field-glasses, Brad did not recognize them, but the ranger did.

'The first rider is Nate Killner and the other is his number two, Reb Rosin. He's meaner than a rattler and twice as deadly. They call him Reb because he never stops boasting about the time he rode for Anderson's guerrillas and in his head, he is still fighting the Civil War.'

Brad felt nothing but hatred and revulsion as he saw the architects of the San Pedro massacre. Unaware of his presence, they made an easy target. But he had left his Winchester in the cavern, otherwise the two renegades would now be dead.

Unfortunately, the ridge was too far above the riders to hear their conversation, but it was quite clear that a heated debate was taking place between Killner and Dorrell. Rosin stood idly to one side, seemingly taking no part in the debate which lasted about twenty minutes. Then, all three mounted and rode up the valley. The ranger watched them closely through his field-glasses. It seemed that the two men were following Dorrell back to Blackwash mine.

The three on the ridge waited for another hour to see if any more outlaws came to tend the herd. None did. So, led by Jane, the trio made their way back down the tunnel and into the cavern. It was a surprisingly difficult descent. Brad found it much harder to crawl on all fours going downhill than he had crawling upwards. He was not the only one.

'One thing, for sure, I'm not cut out to be a miner,' grumbled the ranger as he clambered to his feet and entered the cavern.

Brad relit the fire and Jane cooked the rest of their provisions, leaving those already in the cavern largely untouched. Over the meal, they discussed what to do next. Jane was all for going straight to the Barr Zero ranch and telling Kayleigh Barr what they had just witnessed, but Brad disagreed.

'From what I've seen of Kayleigh Barr, that young lady acts first and thinks afterwards. She is quite capable of ordering her men to attack the mining camp. Even if we are right about Hawker, a lot of innocent miners could get killed.'

'Then I think I should go back to the mining camp,' said Ethan. 'If Killner and his side-kick are there, we will know for certain that Hawker is involved. If there's no sign of them, I'll poke around and find out if they, or any other strangers, have been seen.'

'Somebody ought to keep an eye on the herd in case Killner or any of his men return,' said Brad.

'Seeing they ain't real cattlemen, I

doubt they will. Might be better if you both continued to look for their hideout,' the ranger suggested.

'Might be at that, but I can't risk taking Jane with me. You know what Killner's gang are capable of doing to a pretty girl.'

It was the second time Brad had indirectly paid Jane a compliment and she again blushed with pleasure. The ranger noticed, but made no comment. Instead, he kept talking to Brad.

'Yes, you're right. Miss Jane had better stay here and keep an eye on the herd. As long as she is sensible, the rocks on the ridge should provide plenty of cover, so she's not likely to be seen from the river. I think she would be far safer here than in her own home with nobody to protect her.'

'Seems the best plan,' agreed Brad.

'When you two have quite finished talking about me as if I'm not here,' said Jane, having recovered her composure, 'I will tell you one thing: this is my land, so I will make the decisions. The first one being that I'm not skulking on the ridge, or hiding in the cavern, while you pair risk your lives!'

'But Jane, I'm just thinking of your safety,' protested Brad.

'You wouldn't have found the two members of this gang you seem to think is so terrible if I hadn't brought you here. And you still need my help to locate their hideout.'

'No, Jane, I won't risk your life,' said Brad firmly.

'Miss Jane has a point,' said Ethan. 'So, children, instead of arguing, why don't you both go back to the ranch house and collect the old wagon? You could fill it with supplies and bring it back here. If we do end up in here for any length of time, eating only beans and sourdough will soon get mighty tiresome.'

'We would have to go into Blackwater to get the supplies, but I doubt the general store would let me have them on credit.'

'No problem, I've got enough cash to

pay for anything we need,' said Brad.

'So that's settled,' said Ethan. 'I don't want to alarm you, Miss Jane, but the Little U could be sitting in the middle of a range war. Common sense says we can't defend the ranch house by ourselves. But there's plenty of water in the cavern. As long as we got food and ammunition, we can hold it against a Yankee army, even if it was led by Grant himself.'

'Right then,' replied Brad. 'We can drive Jane's old wagon into Blackwater and I'll buy enough supplies and ammunition to last us a month.'

Jane looked in disbelief at Brad. Supplies in Blackwater were far from cheap. The silver strike and the influx of miners and new saloons had seen to that. Brad had already purchased the pack mule, which was far more expensive than an ordinary horse, so how could a dollar-a-day cowboy still have enough money left to buy supplies?

'Fine,' said Ethan, interrupting her

train of thought. 'I would sure like to stick around until you two find out, but I've got to get back to the mining camp. I'll take the mule to explain why I've been away so long.'

'Find out what?' asked Jane.

'You will know *what* when the time is right, and my guess is that time ain't so far away,' he replied chuckling mysteriously.

'Ethan!' exclaimed Jane in exasperation. But he ignored her entreaties, picked up his saddle and, carrying it over his shoulder, walked awkwardly down the narrow tunnel towards the arena.

Jane looked questioningly at Brad, but he, too, had no idea what Ethan meant.

While Jane put out the fire and tidied up the cavern, Brad saddled up Prince and then commenced to saddle up Jane's pony. However, her European type of side-saddle had been designed to take a short stirrup. Not only did that make the task of controlling the

105

horse more difficult, it made tightening the saddle correctly absolutely essential. Yet Brad managed the tricky job with ease, unaware that Jane having completed her chores was watching him.

'It looks as if you've done this before. Does your wife ride side-saddle?' she asked, with much feigned indifference. For some reason, her heart was racing as she waited for his answer.

'I'm not married, but I've had years of practice with these side-saddles.'

'How come?' she said, desperately trying not to look too pleased about the first part of his answer.

'Pa is a bit old-fashioned in some ways. He insisted that all his girls rode side-saddle, even after the accident. Always said anything else was not lady-like.'

'Accident?' asked Jane.

'To my half-sister, Emma. She was some years older than me and always liked her ponies to be lively. One day, her favourite threw her as she was trying to jump across one of the streams on the Double M. Unfortunately, Emma was dead when the cowhands found her. They said the straps to her side-saddle had not been fastened correctly. I was only a boy when it happened, but from then on, I always made it my business to saddle-up my younger sisters' ponies.'

It was the first time Brad had talked about his family. Jane wanted to hear more, but there was work to be done. Reluctantly, she mounted her pinto, then led the way through the main tunnel and down to the passage way. As Brad deemed speed to be essential, she took the most direct route out of the Cactus Hills.

As they did so, the ranger reached the mining camp. He explained his prolonged absence by saying he had been trying to persuade Jane Latham to sell the Little U but she had again refused. Then, on his way back to the camp, he had found the pack mule. So he had decided to scout the cactus wastelands for its owner, but had found nobody.

Although Hawker was not convinced by Ethan's story, he had more important problems on his mind. Tomorrow was pay-day at the mine and seeing the miners got the right pay and then transporting them to Blackwater took a lot of organizing.

But that was the least of his problems. The mine was no longer as profitable as he had led its investors to believe. In fact, this month, there was only just enough money to pay the miners and next month promised to be even worse. The truth was, the mine was almost played out. Although New Mexico was only a Territory and law enforcement rudimentary, Hawker knew that the irate investors he had defrauded would find a way to ensure he faced several years in a penitentiary.

But Hawker had developed a ruthless plan which would rid him of the failing mine and make him one of the richest and most powerful men in New Mexico. After much preparation, all the players were now in place, so he decided it was time to make his first move. In spite of his doubts about Ethan Madden, tomorrow morning he would send him back to the Little U to run Jane Latham and her big-mouthed hand off the ranch. Dorrell could go with him to ensure Madden got the job done.

9

Brad and Jane reached the Little U just as night was falling. While Jane went to the kitchen to cook the evening meal, Brad led the horses and pack mule into the barn. They were greeted by a welcoming neigh from the cart-horse. Brad fed the great beast and ensured he had plenty of fresh water. Then he unsaddled and rubbed down Prince and Jane's pinto. He had just finished his chores when Jane called out that dinner was ready.

Not only had Jane cooked a superb meal, she had found the time to change into the one almost respectable dress she had kept from her saloon days. Nevertheless, its neckline was daringly low. Her hair was no longer tightly curled into a bun but hung loose and just touched her bare shoulders.

Brad was so astonished by the

transformation, he could hardly speak. However, much to Jane's amusement and pleasure, he eventually managed to splutter out a few incoherent compliments.

After the meal, there were several questions Jane wanted to ask Brad about his life at the Double M. Unfortunately, for her, he was extremely guarded about his private life and she learnt little that she did not already know. Soon afterwards, he retired to the barn where he fell into a deep sleep.

Not so Jane. Although she had the comfort of her own bed, thoughts of Brad kept her awake. She could not deny that she had begun to care for him. Why else would she have put on her best dress? But doubts about who he really was, plagued her mind. Whilst it was obvious he knew a great deal about cattle ranching, he had already spent far too much money to be an ordinary cowboy. Then, his words to the ranger came back to haunt her.

'*You know what Killner's gang are*

capable of doing to a pretty girl.' Brad's words to Ethan suddenly came back to haunt her. She was pleased that Brad thought her pretty, but how did he know so much about the Killner gang? She refused to believe he was an outlaw. Yet, if he was a bounty hunter, why had he gone out of his way to help her? She eventually fell asleep still trying to work that out.

Early next morning, they set out for Blackwater. Jane drove the supply wagon; her pinto trotting passively behind it. The cart-horse was not made for speed but the empty wagon proved little challenge to the great beast, so they made relatively good time. As usual, Brad was mounted on his Missouri Fox-Trotter, Prince.

A little over an hour after they had left the Little U, Dorrell and Ethan arrived at the deserted ranch. Dorrell's highly inflated ego soon led him to believe Brad had left the territory rather than face him and that had finally persuaded Jane to quit the Little U. As

Dorrell was eager to break the news to Hawker, they left immediately.

As soon as Jane and Brad reached Blackwater, they made for the store. However, still acting under instructions from Hawker, the storekeeper refused Jane credit. As he had promised, Brad paid in cash. The storekeeper reluctantly accepted Brad's money, but refused to help load the wagon. But help came from an unlikely source.

Acting on the instructions of Jed Hawker, Dent had ridden to Blackwater to prevent any trouble between his miners and any Barr Zero cowhands. Not that the sheriff expected any. Marshal Ward had so far managed to keep the miners and cowboys apart. However, Dent had another, far more profitable reason for riding into town.

But for the moment, his business would have to wait. Dent noticed the Little U's wagon outside the hardware store. Indeed, he could hardly miss the great cart-horse standing patiently before it. So he rode over to the store and decided to investigate.

'Morning, Miss Latham. Need any help toting your supplies to your wagon?' he asked, as he entered the store.

Jane was so taken aback by the offer, she could only nod her head in agreement. However, loading the wagon enabled Dent to check out the kind of provisions Jane and Brad had been buying. After examining them, the sheriff correctly guessed they were intended to provide meals on the trail rather than the relative comfort of the Little U's kitchen.

Of course, Dent was unaware of their true destination, so like Dorrell, concluded Jane had finally decided to leave her ranch. His suspicions seemed to be confirmed when, instead of turning the wagon round and driving back to the Little U, Jane drove out of Blackwater in the opposite direction and took the border trail to Arizona.

Hawker would want to be sure the pair were actually leaving the territory.

Before he could follow them, Dent had some very private arrangements to make. However, his business shouldn't take long, so he anticipated no difficulty in catching up with the slowly moving wagon.

Because of the unwanted attentions of Marshal Ward, the Lucky Strike's gaming tables were set fairly while the Barr Zero hands were in town. As Hawker didn't want the Blackwash mine's straightlaced shareholders to know he owned the Lucky Strike saloon, he kept well away from it, so had no idea that the gaming tables were rigged when the miners paid their monthly visit to his saloon. The chief beneficiary from the ill-gotten gains was Dent, although the bartender, Clem Mullet, received a sizeable cut.

But Dent realized that the crooked tables could not go undetected for much longer. So while Hawker was still absorbed with his master plan, Dent decided the time was right to make one last financial kill and walked over to the

Lucky Strike to make the arrangements.

Apart from a few saloon girls, the bar was almost deserted. Dent arranged with Mullet for the Lucky Strike's girls to serve as much free beer as it took to get most of the miners too drunk to notice that the tables had been rigged. Only then was the gambling started.

For those miners who were not drunk, Dent arranged another distraction. Those saloon girls prepared to put their charms up for sale were given leave to do so openly. As he had already bribed the mining-camp's pay-clerk to tell the miners of the treats in store for them at the Lucky Strike, they collected their pay and hurried to the covered wagons waiting to take them to Blackwater. If the clerks short changed them, they never knew.

By the time Dent concluded his business in the saloon, the first prairie schooner was almost due. So the bar had become full of saloon girls. Amongst them were some who had only just arrived in Blackwater and so not yet under the watchful eye of Alice Albright. Mullet offered the services of any of the new girls to Dent.

The sheriff of Blackwash Mining Corporation was eager to sample the delights of the prettiest new girl. As a result, it was some time before he hit the trail and headed after Jane's wagon. By that time, Jane had turned the wagon off the border trail. Brad had carefully erased the wagon tracks, so Dent missed their turning place and continued along the trail, unaware that the wagon was safely on its way to the hidden cavern in the Cactus Hills.

However, after a little while, Dent also turned off and headed towards the mining camp. Indeed, he actually rode along the edge of the wastelands and passed within a mile of Jane's wagon. But hidden among the giant cacti, even the wagon's dust trail was impossible to detect.

By the time the sheriff reached the mining camp, Dowell had already informed everyone still left there, that the Little U had been abandoned. Dent's somewhat abridged version of the day's events in Blackwater only confirmed Dorrell's story.

Jed Hawker was delighted with this news. But he was less impressed with the news that his latest acquisition had been questioning the miners about any new arrivals. But then, he believed that Ethan was an outlaw and a man on the run might reasonably be expected to ask such questions. So he let the matter rest and sent the undercover ranger on the evening patrol.

Hawker then dispatched Dorrell to Killner's hideout with instructions for the gang leader's next move. The time for action had arrived. Not content with taking over the Little U and thus provoking the Barr Zero into range war in which his own hired guns would make him the victor, Hawker then planned to take control of Blackwater. He intended to accomplish this by unleashing the renegades against the town. So now, maintaining the peace in Blackwater by keeping his miners and the Barr Zero cowhands apart was the last thing Hawker wanted.

'Time for you to deal with Marshal Ward,' he said to the delighted Dent. 'Then, when things have settled down a bit, I'll see to it that you become the next marshal of Blackwater.'

10

The ranger had confirmed beyond doubt the link between Hawker and the outlaws. So as they rode into the wastelands, Ethan looked for a way to slip away from the patrol.

He planned to rejoin Brad and Miss Jane who, by now, should have returned to the hidden cavern. But with two riders behind him and two in front, even in the growing gloom of dusk, there was little opportunity to get away. Indeed, the unusual formation of the patrol suggested to Ethan that he was under suspicion. But that belief made him even more determined.

His chance to escape came in the most unexpected and alarming manner. Bugle-blowing patrols had ridden unchallenged through the wastelands since the departure of hostile Indians. But an arrow in the chest of one of the leading riders announced they were back. Suddenly, the patrol was beset on all sides as braves leapt out of the ground, seemingly from nowhere. Luckily for the ranger, apart from the dead leading rider, it was the two riders behind him who took the brunt of the attack.

In spite of the speed at which the patrol was galloping, the last two men were dragged bodily from their horses. At first, they put up a good fight. But they were soon overwhelmed. Tomahawks glinted in the dying rays of the sun and both men ceased to struggle.

As an arrow whizzed past his shoulder, Ethan savagely spurred his horse forward and the palomino responded instantly. The ranger desperately tried to follow the rider in front of him, but the man rode straight into a trap. More arrows sped through the air as another group of Indians suddenly appeared ahead of them.

The rider crashed to the ground, two arrows protruding from his chest. The palomino hurdled the fallen gunman who was still alive. But not for long. However, the Indians concentrated their attack on the downed man, enabling Ethan to gallop away. Spurring the palomino to even greater effort, he reached the safety of a large cluster of tree-high cacti and disappeared behind them.

Nevertheless, Ethan kept his horse at full gallop until it was almost exhausted. Only then did he stop and turned round. But the Indians had not followed him and that made him believe they were not on horseback.

The ranger had been too busy escaping to identify the Indians, but in this wild and desolate country, even on foot, almost any Apache could outrun a man on horseback. Therefore, the ranger reluctantly left his horse for the Indians but not his saddle.

He put on the moccasins he always carried in his saddle-bag then tied his boots together and strung them round his neck. Also strung round his neck was his water canteen. With his heavy

Texas-style saddle perched precariously on one shoulder and his saddle-bag on the other, he toted a heavy load. The task was made harder as he also had to carry his Winchester.

Fortunately, there seemed to be little need to hurry. By the time the Apaches had dealt with Hawker's men and found his horse, it would be dark. Even if they had no alcohol with which to celebrate their victory, the ranger's experience told him the Indians would rest until dawn, by which time he intended to be near the hidden cavern.

The ground was so hard, Ethan guessed even the most experienced Indian would find his trail hard to follow. In any case, he hoped any signs left by his Indian moccasins would confuse his trackers and throw them off the scent.

It was hard going, even for a ranger, and the heavy load slowed him down more than he expected. As a result, it was dawn before he reached the blind box-canyon. He paused to drink the last drop of the water in his canteen. Then he checked that he was not being followed. When he was sure that he wasn't, he ventured into the canyon.

His main worry now was the old supply wagon. It was far too big to be taken down the passageway or to be concealed at the blind end of the canyon. But he need not have worried: there was no trace of it to be seen.

But did that mean that something had gone wrong and Jane and Brad had not yet arrived? There was only one way to find out. So he proceeded down the narrow passageway as fast as his heavy and awkward load would permit. It seemed to take an age before he reached the schism in the cliff face. Then he turned into its inky darkness and inch by inch, groped his way into the arena.

Daylight had not quite reached the floor, although the top of its near vertical sides were bathed in the early morning sunlight. The cart-horse neighed its usual greeting. Jane's pony and Prince were too busy eating hay to acknowledge Ethan's arrival.

Thankfully, he dropped the heavy saddle and the saddle-bags. Then he made his way slowly down the cavern tunnel. Once again, he was immersed in almost total darkness. However, he had not gone far before he saw the flicker of light from the actual cavern. His voice echoed eerily as he called out.

'Hello, don't shoot; it's just your tired and hungry ranger paying a social call.'

'Well, come on in and help yourself to breakfast,' Jane replied. Strangely, there was much less echo when she responded.

'Where's the wagon?' Ethan asked as he sat down by the fire and helped himself to coffee and bacon.

'This is not the only hidden cavern in this canyon. It's riddled with passage-ways and secret caves. The wagon is hidden away in one of them. It's quite safe. You could ride right by the entrance, yet not see the wagon,' replied Jane.

Over breakfast, Ethan recounted his adventures. In spite of his narrow escape, he did not seem to be concerned. But Jane was shocked to hear about the attack by the Indians.

'In spite of what Hawker's men claimed, a war party of Indians might explain why my Yampai Indians have disappeared,' said Jane.

'Possibly; except I think it was a scouting party of young bucks,' Ethan replied.

'What makes you say that?' asked Jane.

'They made a poor job of the ambush, otherwise I wouldn't be alive to tell the tale. Nor did they have horses or guns. In my experience, Apache war-parties usually carry plenty of both.'

'So you don't think they were Apaches?' asked Brad.

'Didn't get much chance to get on speaking terms with them, so I don't really know,' said Ethan, drily.

'Do you think the Indians are back

for good?' asked Jane.

'No,' he replied. 'There's not much game here for them to hunt. My guess is that they are just passing through. But even if they are young and inexperienced, they are still dangerous. So I suggest we sit tight for a couple of days.'

Brad looked hard at Jane as he remembered the stories his father had told him about women captured by the Apache. Those who survived the ordeal gradually became so used to the ways of the Indian, they gladly become squaws and were absorbed into the tribe as full Indians.

'Agreed,' he said fervently.

'In any case, I'm too tired to move another inch,' said Ethan. 'If you two don't mind, I'll get some shut-eye.'

'Of course not,' replied Jane. 'While you are resting, Brad and I will go up to the ridge and keep an eye on the herd.'

'Good idea,' he replied. 'But don't expect any action. The Barr Zero hands are still out on the range finishing their round-up and while I was at the mining camp, Hawker sent a message to Killner.'

'Do you know what it was?' asked Brad.

'No, but I guess it was to lie low until Hawker is ready to make his move for the Little U. So I think it should be quiet for the next few days.'

For once the ranger was quite wrong. Even as he spoke, Dorrell was leading most of the mining-camp's gunmen across the wastelands. They were headed to the Little U. Then, while Dorrell and his men were safely out of the way taking possession of the ranch, Killner and his gang rode into the mining camp, guns blazing.

Not that there was any opposition. Before dawn, Hawker had driven away in the New-Mexican's special armoured coach which was laden with silver ingots he had secretly stashed away.

Dent had left the camp even earlier and was on his way back to Blackwater, supposedly to keep an eye on the miners. However, the real purpose of the trip was to check on how much money he had made from the rigged tables. But he also had some unfinished business with Marshal Ward to settle.

So the encampment at the Blackwash mine was almost deserted. There were just the pay clerk and a handful of miners. The latter preferred to send their hard-earned pay back to their families, rather than gamble it away in the Lucky Strike saloon.

Guns roaring, the renegades rode into the mining camp, killing anyone in sight. However, Killner was careful to leave a couple of miners alive to bear witness to the damage caused by the rampaging outlaws. Of course, the survivors would have no idea that the gang's carefully orchestrated raid was part of Jed Hawker's master plan, but they would be able to recount the horrific events to the rest of the miners when they returned from Blackwater.

Unfortunately, the camp's clerks were not as lucky as the two miners spared by Killner. They worked, not in the camp, but in two cabins near the mine entrance. Their function was to deal with the mine's accounts. They also recorded all the mine's day-to-day transactions, especially the amount of silver mined and how much had been shipped back East. So they had to be eliminated, a task the gang performed without the slightest sign of mercy.

Next, they set fire to both the clerks' cabins and watched while they burned to the ground. Thus all the records of the mine were destroyed. However, their last act of wanton destruction concerned the mine itself. They set charges and dynamited the entrance and watched, gleefully, as it collapsed amidst a shower of rubble and plumes of blinding dust.

With the mine inoperable, Hawker believed that its miners would head for Tombstone, especially if the New-Mexican provided them with free transport. Thus in one stroke, he would be freed from the prying eyes of the mine's shareholders and, with no miners to guard, his gunmen would be free to fight the Barr Zero. Taking control of the Little U was simply to draw the hot-headed Kayleigh Barr into a range war which, with the help of Killner and his cohorts, Hawker felt sure he would win.

But destroying the mining camp was hungry work. For this reason the camp's cook had not been harmed. With the aid of the two miners they had spared, the cook was forced to prepare them a meal which they ate with relish. Then they showed their gratitude by burning the cookhouse to the ground.

However, far from being satisfied with the mayhem and destruction they had wreaked at the mine, the renegades mounted their horses and rode towards Blackwater. But they were in no hurry. They laughed and joked as they made their way slowly towards the border trail and on to Blackwater, knowing their day of wanton destruction and wilful murder was only just beginning.

11

Dent arrived in Blackwater an hour after dawn. As he expected, except for the small but always busy office of the New Mexico Territories Stage & Freight Company, the town was almost deserted. He swaggered into their office and then ordered the clerk to ensure its prairie schooners were made ready and sent round to the Lucky Strike within the hour.

The New-Mexican was, of course, part of Hawker's growing empire, so the clerk scuttled away to get things organized. Drivers had to be awakened and the stable boys had to tend to the horses before they could be harnessed.

Usually, the miners were allowed to stay in Blackwater until they had spent all their hard-earned pay in the Lucky Strike saloon. But not this time. Hawker had told Dent to get them back to the mining camp to see the havoc inflicted on the camp.

Having ensured that the orders of his boss were carried out, Dent made his way to the Lucky Strike. The town was still deserted, but, as he entered the saloon, he discovered that Clem was restocking the bar and not in his private office counting their ill-gotten gains. The reason was clear. The saloon had an unwelcome visitor. Acting from a tip-off from his friend Alice Albright, Marshal Ward was busily examining the gaming tables.

'Clem, what's he doing in here?' asked Dent.

'Said he's had a complaint from some of your miners that the tables were rigged. He's been nosing around in here for the last half-hour, checking things out. But don't worry, I've already reset the tables. He won't find anything.'

But Clem Mullet was wrong. He had been too greedy. Not content with the cut from the rigged tables, without

Dent's knowledge the bartender had instructed his dealers to use loaded dice. Unfortunately for him, the floor of the saloon had not yet been swept.

Marshal Ward suddenly stopped examining the tables and stooped down. He retrieved two small objects off the floor. An experienced gambler in his younger days, it only took the marshal a few seconds to determine the die were loaded.

Completely ignoring Dent, Blackwater's law officer approached the Lucky Strike's bartender.

'Clem Mullet, these die are loaded. I'm arresting you for running a crooked gambling house.'

'You're arresting no one,' snarled the sheriff of the Blackwash mining camp.

'Dent, what you do in your mining camp is none of my business, but here in Blackwater, I'm the elected marshal. So I suggest you complete any business you still have to do, sooner rather than later. But finished or not, I want you out of town by noon.'

'What makes you think you're man

enough to make me go?' sneered Dent, remembering how many times the man in front of him had deliberately avoided a showdown.

Marshal Ward didn't answer the question. Instead, his eyes glanced at the bartender who was stealthily inching his way towards the end of the bar.

'Stay where you are, Clem!' he ordered. 'Better you leave that special shotgun you have hidden under the bar where it is. The next move you make towards it will be your last one!'

'That's big talking, Marshal Ward,' said Dent coldly. 'Think you can back it up with me here?'

Blackwater's law-enforcement officer looked straight at his nemesis and then, very deliberately, stepped to within a few paces of him.

'Better not try to find out,' he said quietly.

But, of course, Dent had to. He couldn't back down without ruining his reputation as a top gunslinger. And Dent was supremely sure of himself, for he had already proved that he was faster than his opponent. So, full of confidence, he went for his six-gun.

The hammer blow to Dent's abdomen forced him to double up, causing the bullet from his own six-gun to hit the floor directly in front of him. Then he slumped to his knees clutching his stomach with his left hand in a vain attempt to staunch the blood pouring out of it.

His six-gun dropped from his other hand. His stomach seemed to be on fire and he felt real pain for the first time in his life. Yet the sheriff knew it could only get worse. None of the men he had deliberately gut-shot had lived to tell the tale. Most had survived a few days, suffering in terrible agony before they eventually died.

Determined not to suffer that fate and driven onwards by his pride, Dent stretched out a blood-soaked hand and retrieved his six-gun. Then, as Ward watched him, he slowly replaced it in his holster. Summoning the last of his rapidly failing strength, the sheriff clambered slowly to his feet. The effort only served to intensify the pain in his stomach.

Dent looked at the marshal's six-gun. Then a glimmer of understanding penetrated his agony. The reason Ward had stood so close to him when he drew became clear, for the six-gun grasped firmly in his hand had the shortest barrel he had ever seen.

'It came in on the last stage,' the marshal explained. 'It's Colt's latest offering. They call it, the *Sheriff's Model*. Rather an apt name in the circumstances. But in spite of its shortened barrel, it's still a Peacemaker .45.'

It soon became evident to the law officer that his adversary was no longer a threat and was in great pain. So he holstered the snub-nosed, Sheriff's Model Peacemaker and went to aid his stricken foe. But Dent was not yet done and seized the chance to draw his own six-gun again. It was his last error of judgement.

Again the four and three-quarter inch barrel of the snub-nosed Peacemaker spat its deadly message. This time the bullet struck the sheriff full in the chest. The force of the impact blew him off his feet and into oblivion, his conventional seven and a half-inch barrelled Peacemaker only half-drawn.

Yet in death, there was a smile on Dent's lips. His pride was still intact. He had not been outdrawn, just outsmarted by Ward's newfangled six-gun. And the agonizing pain in his stomach was no more.

Without so much as a glance at the prostrate body, Marshal Ward stepped over it and handcuffed the bewildered Clem Mullet. Once the bartender had been secured, Ward holstered his six-gun. Although the edge the gun gave him could only be short-lived, he did not want to advertise his newly found advantage.

Although it was still early, drawn by the shooting, a crowd of miners and saloon girls began to assemble in the bar. There were audible gasps of amazement when they saw the body of Dent lying in a pool of blood. The excited babble which broke out seconds later, almost drowned the sound of several prairie wagons drawing to a halt outside the Lucky Strike.

'Folks, the show's already over,' said Marshal Ward. 'Clem Mullet is under arrest for running rigged tables, so the Lucky Strike is temporarily closed.'

'We want our money back,' shouted several of the miners in unison.

'Naturally,' replied the marshal. 'But not today. It will have to be counted first. But don't worry, I will see to it that all last night's takings will be refunded by the town's committee as soon as possible.'

Some of the miners began to complain, but their compatriots soon told them to shut up. After all, before the gunfight, there had been no chance of getting their money back.

'Now,' continued the marshal, 'I'm pretty sure the wagons have just arrived to take you miners back to the mining camp. So, if you would make your way to them, I would sure appreciate it.'

Nobody was going to court the wrath of the man who had just outdrawn the sheriff of Blackwash County. So the miners trooped out to the prairie schooners and left Blackwater as quickly as possible. And it was just as well they did for a little over an hour later, Killner's gang came sweeping into Blackwater, guns blazing.

Their target was the bank. The new Sheriff's Model, so deadly at close range, was of little use against any target more than a dozen paces away, but that didn't stop Marshal Ward from trying, although it was more by luck than judgement that he hit one of the gang. But without any deputies to back him up, he was forced to take cover and could only watch helplessly as Killner's gang robbed the bank. But they had not finished: they set fire to it.

But, at first, it burned poorly. While the renegades were concentrating on getting the fire going, the marshal began to work his way back to his office. But it was slow progress. Two of the gang mounted their horses and rode up and down the main street shooting indiscriminately at anything that moved. So the marshal had to use every scrap of cover he could find. It seemed to take an age, but eventually he reached his office throwing himself through its half-open door as bullets whistled over his head.

Once inside, Ward paused only to regain his breath. Then he grabbed his Winchester. Disregarding the danger of flying bullets, he dashed back down the street towards the bank. However, satisfied the building was ablaze, the rest of the outlaws had already mounted and were ready to ride away.

Nevertheless, the marshal took aim and opened fire. One member of the Killner gang bit the dust, but the rest galloped safely away. However, their absence was to be short-lived.

Huge flames towered over the blazing

bank, posing a real threat to the neighbouring properties. Belatedly, some of the townsfolk left the safety of their homes and began to put out the fire. But they were too few and too badly organized to control the blaze. So, instead of raising a posse and chasing after the perpetrators, the marshal stayed in Blackwater and organized the fire-fighting.

However, the bank was a roaring inferno and too far gone to be saved. So the marshal organized the townsfolk two-abreast in two separate lines which ran from the town's only public water pump to each side of the blazing building. Pails of water ran along one side of each human chain and were poured, not on the blazing bank, but on the buildings either side of it. The empty pails were then returned down the other side of each human chain to be filled at the pump. In this way, the fire was prevented from spreading, but the bank was burnt to the ground and all its records lost.

The loss of the bank's records and

those held in the clerks' cabin at the mine were the real reasons why Hawker had so carefully organized this day of destruction. Without records of any sort, the shareholders, the real owners of the Blackwash Mining Corporation, would have to believe any story he chose to tell them.

But Hawker had underestimated Killner. New Mexico was a Territory and officially, not yet part of the United States. Although the US Cavalry carried out patrols, they were mainly concerned with Indians, who, unlike many of their Texas cousins, still remained a major and deadly threat. So there would be little federal law to bother them in New Mexico.

With the miners gone, Killner realized the isolated town of Blackwater would make a perfect base for the gang's operations. Once they gained control of the town, the renegade leader believed they would meet little opposition. With the money from the bank in his pocket, Killner could offer Hawker's gunmen top pay. Also, with the town under his control, he could also provide them with the delights readily offered by the saloon girls and that must be better than guarding an empty mining camp or patrolling in the harsh environment of the wastelands.

After checking there was no pursuit, Killner brought his riders to a halt and outlined his plans. They would return to the caves, but only for the night. Tomorrow, they would return to Blackwater and kill anyone, including Hawker, who opposed them.

12

It was almost noon. High on the ridge overlooking the rustled Barr Zero herd, Jane at last plucked up courage to question Brad about his past life. Even so, she couldn't bring herself to ask him if he was a bounty hunter.

'If you are just a cowboy, how come you know so much about the Killner gang?' she asked instead.

If Brad was surprised by her directness, he did not show it. Instead, he smiled. 'It's a long story,' he said.

'So what! I guess we will be here for some time,' she said pointedly.

Brad nodded in agreement. Perhaps it was time to tell Jane the truth, even if it was not quite all of it.

'I grew up on the Double M. As soon as I was old enough, I became a wrangler. I was barely sixteen when I made my first cattle drive. It was the year after the end of Civil War. The Double M was heavily in debt and virtually bankrupt. Then, using the carpetbaggers law, the Yankees tried to take the ranch from us. But the ranch still had a few influential friends and they bought us enough time to take five hundred steers up the old Shawnee trail to Kansas City. We barely made it.'

'Did you run into Indians?' asked Jane. She had become so enthralled by Brad's reminiscences, she had quite forgotten the original purpose of her questions.

'Only tame ones who wanted a steer or two for crossing their lands. No, it was the Kansas farmers and their cronies who caused the trouble. They had all but closed the trail. Unfortunately, there was some shooting before we got the herd into Kansas City. Then they caught up with us and demanded more compensation and we had to pay a quarter of the money we got for the herd and give them all our mustangs before they dropped their charges against us.'

'So how did you get back to the Double M?' asked Jane.

'By train to New Orleans and then by ship to San Diego. I was seasick most of the time and have never been on a ship since!'

'But the mortgage was paid off?'

'Barely. There was not enough money left over to see us through to the next trail drive and the banks would not loan us any money. However, the neighbouring ranch had been bought by a wealthy English family but run by Texans and they offered to add a hundred of our cattle to their trail drive. With that extra money, we survived until the following round-up. Then we took fourteen hundred cattle to Abilene, and the year after two thousand. In spite of the carpetbaggers, we continued to prosper and a few years later we began to make two drives a year.'

'That must have been very hard work.'

'Yes, but I was a lot younger then and

enjoyed every minute. By the time I was twenty, I had made seven drives up the Chisholm trail to Abilene and was trail boss by the time I was twenty-two. Then we switched to the western trail and took our herds into Dodge. After another three years I became the Double M's top hand. So I guess I've earned the right to be called a cowboy.'

'But that doesn't explain how you know so much about the gang of outlaws you say are on my little ranch,' protested Jane.

'A few months ago, Killner's gang raided San Pedro, a small Mexican settlement on the edge of the Double M's range. None of the Mexicans were armed. Because most of its people worked on the Double M, the settlement was supposed to be under our protection. But that didn't stop Killner's gang from raiding it, butchering men, women and children in the process. Yet they deliberately left a few alive to tell the tale.'

'But why did they do such a terrible

thing?' asked Jane.

Brad was about to reply when two muffled gunshots echoed round the cavern far beneath them. He thrust the Winchester into her hands.

'Stay here. Shoot at anybody coming up the tunnel who's not singing.'

Without waiting to hear her objections, Brad drew his six-gun and began to make his way back down the tunnel. But again, he found the descent far harder to manage than the climb up to the ridge. More shots rang out, but as he didn't know who else might have discovered the cavern, he had to complete the first part of the descent in darkness. Fortunately as he neared the end of the tunnel, the flickering light of the camp began to light his way. He arrived in time to witness a desperate scene.

In spite of their youth and inexperience, the Indians had managed to track the ranger right into the cavern. For their troubles, two of them lay dead, but the Texas lawman was desperately grappling with two more. One of his six-guns, now empty, lay uselessly on the ground. Strangely, the other remained in his cavalry-style holster and the big Texan had resorted to using the Bowie knife he always carried. But its blade only sliced through open air as one of the remaining Apaches swayed back out of reach and then darted behind the blazing fire. The pan of bacon suspended above it prevented the ranger from striking at the Indian again.

The second Indian lunged forward, tomahawk raised aloft, ready to bury it into Ethan. But Brad's bullet struck its blade and smashed it into pieces before he could do so. Nevertheless, the Indian still managed to fling himself onto the Texas lawman. Brad could not risk shooting again for fear of hitting the ranger.

Engaged in a life-or-death struggle, the ranger could not also defend himself against the first Indian. So Brad flung his Colt aside and hurled himself into the fray. He tackled the one still crouching behind the fire. But his wily opponent soon got the upper hand and this Apache now had a knife.

It would have been all over for Brad had the cavern not been filled by the sound of a rifle shot. Its impact flung his would-be assailant across the cavern floor. Amazingly, he seemed to recover. With blood oozing from a chest wound and knife in hand, the Indian staggered towards Brad. But the echoes of the first shot were still reverberating against the cavern's walls as the second shot hit the Apache. This time, the brave died instantly.

The remaining Indian fared no better. The Texas lawman was an old Indian fighter, so was far too experienced for his much younger attacker who tried to ensnare the ranger in a head-lock. But Ethan swiftly fought himself free and then, almost faster than the eye could detect, his knife struck and the young Indian buck ceased struggling.

Brad turned to face his saviour.

Standing in the mouth of the ridge tunnel was Jane. Even in the flickering firelight, her face was as white as a ghost. Fortunately for Brad, she had ignored his orders and followed him. The Winchester he had given her on the ridge, still nestled firmly against her shoulder.

Ethan picked himself up and then smiled ruefully.

'I'm getting too old for this game,' he said ruefully. 'I let these young bucks sneak up and nearly take me. I got two before my six-gun misfired and then jammed. The other two were on top of me before I could get to my other one, so I had to use my old Bowie knife.'

Brad stooped down and picked up the six-gun. Its hexagonal barrel gave away its age. But, surprisingly, the gun appeared dark yellow in the light of the camp-fire.

'It looks like a very old Colt. One of the early Navy models; but if it is, it's the first one I've seen with a brass frame,' he said, returning it to the ranger.

'It's been my companion for many years, but it's not a Colt. You were a mite young to serve in the Civil War, so you wouldn't have seen a gun like this. I guess it's one of the last still in use,' replied the ranger, still smiling ruefully.

'So what is it?' asked Brad.

'It was made in the South by Griswold and Gunnison. It's an exact copy of Colt's .44 Navy 'Old Model'. But they were made out of brass because the South had run short of metal.'

'Do you still have to make up your own ammunition?' asked Brad.

Ethan nodded his head in affirmation.

'Then it's definitely time you changed,' said Brad firmly. 'When this job is finished and your duties bring you near to the Double M, come and visit us. Although we don't allow our hands to carry guns around the bunkhouse, we have an arsenal in the house in case of an emergency.'

'I have a brand new gun in my saddle-bags. Cost me more than a month's wages, but it's no good for close range shooting. So I still need to replace the Griswold as soon as I can afford to do so,' replied the ranger, smiling broadly.

What kind of six-gun was no good at close range, wondered Brad? Then he remembered that the ranger's basic pay was only one quarter a day more than his dollar-a-day cowboys, and a mail order Peacemaker cost seventeen dollars. A splendid idea came into his head. Ethan might help him solve a tricky problem which might arise on his return journey to Texas. But as that problem involved Jane, he didn't mention it directly.

'I've got a better idea,' he said instead. 'After we've finished here, travel back to the Double M with me and I'm sure we can sort out one of the latest Peacemakers for you. Or you could have a new Remington, if they are more to your taste.'

'Fine,' agreed the ranger. 'I'd like to pay my respects at my cousin's grave. But I guess I'd be a goner without your help and I haven't thanked you. But you were a damn fool to charge into the fight, unarmed.'

The danger over, Jane began to shake all over. Brad took the rifle from her and was too busy comforting her to acknowledge the ranger's gratitude. So Ethan turned his attention to the dead Indians and began to examine them.

'Well I'll be damned!' he exclaimed. 'They are Apaches, bar one. But their markings show they are from a sub-tribe I recollect hearing about when I was a boy. But the one you killed, Miss Jane, ain't even an Indian!'

'What do you mean?' she asked.

'He's white.'

'Oh no! What have I done?' gasped Jane in alarm, reluctantly disentangling herself from the comfort of Brad's arms.

'Saved your man's life,' replied the ranger, 'but we can talk later. We had better get out of here, pronto. We can defend ourselves against a Yankee army but Apaches, that's different. By now, the rest have probably stolen our horses and there's no telling how many more of these red devils are on their way here.'

By the light of the last remaining lantern, they cautiously made their way out of the cavern into the arena. But there was no need for concern for all three horses were busily grazing on the little grass that still remained. There were no signs of other Indians.

Although there were literally countless numbers of wild mustangs roaming in the Texas panhandle and in the wilds of New Mexico, stealing horses was a way of life for the Apache. Braves who did so gained almost as much prestige and honour as killing the hated white man.

Oddly, although it was self evident that some of the Indians in the raiding party did not possess horses, they had chosen to fight rather than steal them. To the ranger, that suggested these nomadic Apaches were young bucks, probably the worse for liquor and spoiling for a fight.

Nor had the Apaches found the old wagon which still contained most of the food Brad had bought in Blackwater. As he hitched the cart-horse to it, Ethan stood guard. Then, while Brad scouted the trail ahead of them, Jane drove the wagon out of the hidden ravine. Ethan sat beside her, Winchester at the ready, but they saw no one.

Jane remembered their conversation just before the ranger had left for the mining camp. Indeed, his remarks had bothered her ever since and this was her chance to quiz him on the matter.

'Ethan, what did you mean when you said you wanted to be around when I found out? Found out about what?'

Instead of answering her directly, Ethan stared pointedly at Brad, just visible in the distance. So pointedly,

Jane blushed profusely.

'I thought so,' he said, and his weather-beaten face broke out into a huge grin, 'but the fun won't start until our boy finds out too!'

'I don't know what you mean,' replied Jane still blushing.

'I think you do, and he's quite a catch, by the way.'

'I still don't know what you mean,' protested Jane.

'What do you think the Double M stands for?'

'I guess it's something to do with its owner,' replied Jane.

'Partly. The ranch was founded by Luke Mitchell just after Texas won its independence from Mexico. He called it the Crazy M. At first, it was just a small collection of shacks deep in the Panhandle. They weren't even proper ranchers, just a few men who rode to the Brazos River, rounded up a hundred or so wild longhorns and drove them up the Shawnee trail to the railhead at St Louis. My pa was one of the drovers but got himself killed by Indians on the third drive.'

He paused. Although it was many years ago, the hurt still remained. 'Go on,' said Jane gently, sensing he had not talked about his past for a long time.

'When I was young I rode a wild trail. Luke Mitchell's son, Abe, rode with me until he met Sally in a saloon in San Antonio. They married soon afterwards and settled down on the Crazy M. They had a daughter. But soon after that, fever swept the ranch and claimed the lives of Sally and Luke. Abe was heartbroken, but he was still a young man. Instead of running wild like I had done when my pa died, Abe began to build the Crazy M into the ranch it is now. Some years later he remarried and changed the ranch's name to the Double M.'

'Why?' asked Jane.

'Abe's second wife had also been married before and had a young son. Her name was Ann Miller. The son from her first marriage was Brad whom

Abe regards as his son. The old man now takes a back seat and in effect Brad runs the Double M.'

Jane was so taken aback by the ranger's revelation, she could hardly breathe. Brad would one day inherit the Double M. Little wonder he had more money than the average cowboy. And that also explained why he had followed the renegades across New Mexico, but not why a Texas Ranger had also tracked the outlaws.

'Ethan, what was your real reason for coming to Blackwater?'

'To protect Brad.'

'How come?'

'After the San Pedro massacre, Abe Mitchell contacted my captain and asked him to send someone after Brad. I was working near the New Mexican border and knowing my connection with Abe, my captain gave me leave of absence.'

'But how did you know where Brad was going?' asked Jane.

'The Texas Rangers had already

received information that Killner's gang were intending to set up a new base in a mining camp near Blackwater. I rode directly to it, only to find that neither they nor Brad had arrived. So I hung around the mining camp waiting for something to happen. You could have knocked me down with a feather when I rode into the Little U with Dorrell and discovered Brad working as your hired hand.'

The return of Brad ended the discussion. It was now his turn to ride with Jane.

Mounted on Jane's little pinto, but using his own saddle, Ethan guided the wagon into the wastelands. In the far distance, a plume of black smoke rose high into the blue sky. It came from the direction of the mining camp. But in spite of their curiosity, Ethan decided it was not safe to investigate its cause in broad daylight.

Instead, the ranger led them to a relatively safe place to camp. By chance, he had stumbled on the site during his travels to and from the mine. It was little more than a shallow crater, but although waterless, it was almost completely surrounded by tree-tall cacti. Nevertheless, Ethan deemed it was not safe to light a fire, so they had to make do with cold beans and water from their canteens. Illuminated by the light of the full moon, they ate a Spartan meal. As they did so, Ethan began to talk about the white man Jane had shot.

'Some customs of the Indians are hard to understand,' he said. 'They probably massacred his folks when he was little more than a baby. Yet they brought the boy up as one of their own. So he became a real Apache in everything except appearance.'

But that was little consolation to Jane. A white 'Indian' he may have been, but he was still a man. She detested violence in all its forms. Indeed, even when she had needed food, she had never killed any of her hens. Yet, this day, a man was dead by her own hand. As she shivered at the thought, Brad put a protective arm around her shoulder. She shivered again, so it seemed only natural that Brad should hold her a little tighter.

Sensing his presence was not needed, Ethan decided to investigate the fire coming from the mining camp. To do this, he needed something a little larger than Jane's little pinto, so he borrowed Prince and then rode slowly out of the camp.

Even when Jane had stopped shivering, Brad's arm remained around her shoulder. She made no effort to pull away.

'I guess I'm in your debt again. I haven't thanked you yet for saving my life,' he said.

'Somebody has to look after you.'

'Long may it be you,' he replied, and kissed her tenderly.

She returned the kiss with interest and then snuggled closer into him.

13

Disturbed by his arrival, buzzards rose into the light blue sky, then circled overhead. Their discordant calls filled the air as they seemed to be waiting for his departure. Only then could they return to feast on the carcasses of the dead. Yet there were no miners in the camp. Nor were there any guards and the corral was empty, its unlatched gate swinging idly in the dawn breeze.

Amazed, Ethan could only survey the scene of utter devastation which lay before him. He drew and cocked his old Griswold & Gunnison and examined its octagonal barrel carefully. There must be no misfires this time. Only when he was fully satisfied did he urge Prince slowly forward into the heart of the mining camp. As he did so, the early morning sun glinted on the gun's polished brass frame.

The main eating hall had been completely destroyed. Yet row after row of the big white tents used by the miners were undamaged. However, they were all empty.

So where were the miners? Having spent all their hard-earned money in the Lucky Strike saloon, by now most should have returned from Blackwater. Even at this early hour, the campsite should have been buzzing with life as the miners prepared themselves for work. Although there were a multitude of wagon tracks leading to and from the camp, there was no sign of life. Apart from the buzzards still wheeling overhead, it was eerily quiet.

The reason was not hard to find. As he rode out of the camp and approached the actual mine, it was clear that it had been dynamited. The blast had caused a major landslide on the slopes above the mine with devastating results. Thousands of tons of rock had cascaded down the hillside and then crashed down on the mine's entrance, completely sealing it. The devastation was on such a vast scale, it didn't need an expert to work out that the Blackwash mine would never be worked again.

The blast must have been heard for miles, yet the ranger had heard nothing. Nor had Brad or Jane reported hearing anything while they had been on the ridge watching over the Barr Zero herd. So Ethan concluded the blast must have occurred while they were in the cave, fighting the Apaches.

The smoke he had seen yesterday must have come from the burnt-out buildings by the mine shaft. The bodies of the clerks still lay where they had been shot and already showed the grizzly effects of the buzzards.

The ranger carefully surveyed the chaos. None of the dead men had been armed. The scene was so disturbingly reminiscent of the San Pedro massacre, he had little doubt it was the handiwork of Killner's gang.

Yet there was no sign of the

magnificent stagecoach, nor of the six snow-white horses used to pull it. Did that mean Hawker had left before the raid had begun? But if that was the case, what had happened to the gunmen he paid to guard the mine? Had they fled without fighting? That seemed unlikely, but if they had, Brad and Jane might be in danger. Unsurprisingly, the idea that Hawker would leave the Blackwash mine unguarded and send all his gunmen to take over the Little U never occurred to him.

There was nothing more to be gained by staying in the mining camp. Reluctantly leaving the dead bodies to the buzzards, he turned Prince round and then made his way back. As he did so, he scoured the ground for tracks, but, of course, there was none and his return to his companions was uneventful. Over another cold meal, he related to Brad and Jane what he had seen.

'Do you think it was the work of Killner's gang?' asked Brad.

'Can't be absolutely sure, but it sure

looks like their handiwork,' he replied.

'Then we are not safe out here,' said Brad looking hard at Jane. 'I guess we had better head for Blackwater.'

'You're right,' agreed the ranger. 'Perhaps Marshal Ward might know what's been happening.'

'But what about Dent?' asked Jane. 'I thought he was supposed to be the sheriff of the mining camp. And where is Chad Dorrell and the camp's gunmen?'

Ethan still had no answers and just shook his head in bewilderment. He had no way of knowing that Dent was already dead. Nor could he know the mine's gunmen were about to become expendable pawns. Their presence at the Little U was intended to provoke a bitter response from the Barr Zero, a reaction which Hawker intended to turn into a full-blooded range war.

Kayleigh Barr was not exaggerating when she had told Brad that nothing went on in Blackwash County without Hawker's knowledge and approval.

Investigating the cause of the explosion, her scouts had located the missing herd of cattle and they had discovered that the Little U was full of Hawker's gunmen.

This occupation was intended to be permanent. However, a dozen gunmen take a lot of feeding. So, as dawn broke, Chad Dorrell set out for Blackwater. His purpose, to arrange for a continuous stream of food and ammunition from Hawker's store and a generous supply of whiskey from the Lucky Strike.

However, as Hawker intended, the occupation of the Little U by his gunmen was all the excuse Kayleigh Barr needed to attack the Little U. As the ranger returned to the campsite, her men swooped down on the small ranch.

But Hawker had failed to foresee that Chad Dorrell would not stay with his men. Without his leadership, the gunmen had become careless and thinking they were safe from attack, no guards had been posted. So, when the

Barr Zero attacked, most of the gunmen were caught out in the open completing their ablutions.

Nevertheless, they were all professional gunfighters and the Barr Zero cowhands were not. After the initial setback, during which two gunmen were killed and another badly wounded, those who had remained in the ranch house laid down a deadly hail of bullets. Under its cover, the rest of the gunmen made it back to the ranch house.

Still mounted, the Barr Zero hands again charged the Little U ranch house. For some, it was the last thing they did. Hawker's gunmen held their fire until the last possible moment and then opened fire. At point-blank range, they couldn't miss. No less than five Barr Zero men crashed from their saddles never to rise again. But it wasn't enough to turn the tide in favour of the gunmen.

Nevertheless, shocked by the number of fatalities, Kayleigh signalled her men to withdraw, but another ranch hand was hit fatally before the rest of the Barr Zero men rode out of range. In all, six ranch hands had been killed, one was badly injured, and another two had received minor flesh wounds. In spite of the losses, the Barr Zero ranch hands still heavily outnumbered Hawker's gunmen. Kayleigh realized though that the fire power from the ranch house was too deadly for the Little U to be taken by storm.

Yet there was no need. She counted that it was a hundred paces from the ranch house to the corral which had been repaired since her last visit. Also, top rails had been added to all its sides. The gunmen's horses were all in the corral and had been unsaddled. Therefore, Hawker's men were trapped in the house.

Kayleigh ordered her men to dismount. While most of them laid down covering fire, the remainder raced to the barn. They reached the barn safely and swiftly disappeared inside. From the safely of its hayloft, they overlooked the corral gate and had a clear shot at anyone trying to use it, with little fear of being hit by return fire. She then ordered the rest of the hands to encircle the ranch house.

For several hours nothing happened. But then the door was flung open and two gunmen made a dash for the corral. The rest laid down volley after volley in a vain attempt to cover them. But it had no effect on the men in the barn's hayloft who waited until the two gunmen had opened the corral gate before they opened fire.

Both gunmen fell to the ground, never to rise again. But to the dismay of the gunmen in the ranch house, the shots spooked the horses and they bolted out of the corral's open gate and galloped away.

'I don't think they will try that again,' said Kayleigh.

Her informants had told her that Jane had visited Blackwater to purchase food and supplies. Clearly, she had not returned to the Little U, so Kayleigh correctly deduced that the ranch house did not contain enough food to sustain Hawker's gunmen for more than a few days. Therefore, all she had to do was to stay put and starve the gunmen out.

However, patience was not one of Kayleigh Barr's virtues. She issued another order and a rider was dispatched to the Barr Zero. Kayleigh watched him ride away. It would be some hours before he would be able to return with a wagon loaded with bundles of hay and a barrel of lamp oil. If she could not take the ranch house by storm she would burn it down, thus forcing Hawker's men into the open where they would receive no mercy.

Apart from dealing Hawker and his Blackwash mine a crippling blow, she would finally resolve the problem of the Little U. But it was not the ranch house she wanted; it was the extra water in the one green valley in the Cactus Hills.

Well out of range of Hawker's men,

14

They were still some distance away from Blackwater when Brad suddenly reined in Prince. The ground in front of his horse had become soft enough to reveal the imprint of several recently made horse tracks. Among them were the prints of a horseshoe with a v-shaped pattern cut into it.

The ranger, once again incongruously mounted on Jane's little pinto, pulled up beside him.

'I followed those right across New Mexico,' Brad said, as he pointed to the tracks. 'I guess Killner's gang are already in Blackwater.'

Jane drew level with them and pulled up her old wagon. The cart-horse towered over the ranger mounted on the little pinto.

'Anything wrong?' she asked.

'No,' lied the ranger. 'But it seems we

may have some unfinished business to settle rather sooner than we thought. Is there anyone you could stay with while we check out Blackwater?'

'I could stay with my friend, Alice Albright; she has a house just out of town.'

The name caused Brad to recall his first visit to Blackwater and his conversation with Marshal Ward. He needed answers, but there was the little matter of Killner's gang to tackle before he could plan for the future. So he said nothing.

Unaware of the violent events in Blackwater, Jane had expected Alice to be in the Lucky Strike supervising her girls. So she had little fear of Brad uncovering the secrets of her past. However, as they approached Alice's surprisingly well-appointed house, its owner rushed out to greet her. To Jane's dismay, her former boss was followed by several girls whose saucy attire left no doubt they were saloon girls. And some of them greeted Jane like a long lost friend, as indeed, she was.

While Ethan was taken aback by the bawdy nature of their reception, Brad seemed to take it all in his stride. Once he had satisfied himself that Jane would be able to stay, he kissed her and, ignoring the ribald comments from the other girls, remounted and followed Ethan to Blackwater.

As they passed the marker post which denoted the town's limit, Brad noticed that the offices of the Overland stage had been boarded up. Yet along Main Street nothing stirred. He brought Prince to a halt. Apart from the sound of a piano playing from inside the Lucky Strike, it was suspiciously quiet. The tune seemed to be the only one the pianist knew, for as soon as he had finished, he started playing it all over again.

Brad was about to ride on when he felt the restraining arm of the ranger, who shook his head, then turned Jane's pony towards the saloon. He dismounted and Brad did the same.

At that moment, several gunmen appeared at the far end of Main Street. They had been lying low in the offices of the New Mexico Stage and Freight. In spite of the distance, the ranger recognized them instantly. They were the outlaws. Killner, though, was not amongst them.

They opened fire but the range was too great for a six-gun. So their bullets struck the ground well short of their intended targets. Prince was used to the sound of gunfire so ignored it. Not so Jane's diminutive pinto, which bolted down Main Street and did not stop until it had returned to the safety of Alice's house.

Meanwhile, the gang ran towards the Lucky Strike. Brad and the Ranger simultaneously hurled themselves through the saloon's swinging doors as the renegades again opened fire.

Brad staggered to his feet and looked for cover. There was none. The saloon's bar was deserted except for Marshal Ward who, armed with Clem Mullet's sawn-off, doubled-barrelled shotgun, was standing over the pianist forcing the terrified man to play the tune over and over again. As soon as Brad and Ethan made their somewhat undignified entrance, he allowed the pianist to stop.

'Glad you got my message,' said the marshal.

'What message?' asked Brad.

Before he could answer, the pianist suddenly stood up and rushed past the still rising ranger. He did not stop running until he reached the middle of Main Street. Flapping his hands wildly, he began screaming at the top of his voice.

'Don't shoot! Don't shoot! It's me, Harry, the pianist. I work for Mr Hawker.'

Unfortunately for Harry, the gunmen were now in range. Nevertheless, they heeded his plea and stopped shooting, but not until the hapless pianist lay riddled with bullets on the sidewalk, a few paces from the saloon.

'We can't hold out in the bar, so follow me,' ordered Marshal Ward, as he stepped behind the bar and into a short passageway. Brad and Ethan followed. The passage led to Clem Mullet's office. There were no windows. The office was lit by a solitary oil lamp which sat in the middle of a large oak desk. Behind it was an armchair and behind the armchair was a massive bookcase which stretched from floor to ceiling.

'What now?' asked Ethan, worried they would be trapped inside the office when the outlaws attacked.

'I'll show you. But first close the door and then lock it,' replied Marshal Ward.

As soon as Ethan had completed the simple task, Blackwater's law officer pressed a button on Clem's desk. But nothing happened. Then, after picking up the oil lamp, the marshal walked over to the bookcase and removed two books. Except they weren't books, just hollow cases. Behind them was a lever, which he pulled sharply. The bookcase swung open to reveal a flight of stairs.

'The main office door has to be locked and then the catch on the desk released before the bookcase can be opened,' explained the Marshal.

Pausing only to shut the bookcase behind them, the law officer led the way down the stairs and into another passageway. This one was shored up by ancient-looking timbers. Never a lover of enclosed spaces, Brad was glad when they reached another flight of stairs. These led upwards into the storage room of the main stores.

Marshal Ward blew out the lamp, then led them through the store into Main Street. The outlaws were so busy preparing to storm the saloon, they failed to notice the trio as they crossed Main Street. As they approached the jailhouse, Brad could see that all its windows were shuttered as if prepared to withstand a siege. Then the marshal called out softly.

'Open up, Matt. I'm coming in and I've got two men with me.'

The jailhouse door opened. As soon as they were inside, Matt Gillard closed and bolted it.

'Matt, how's our prisoner?' asked the marshal.

'Not so chipper, after our little chat,' chuckled the smithy.

Over a mug of coffee, Marshal Ward explained.

'After I arrested Clem Mullet, Matt and I had a little chat about how hard life could be for any prisoner who withheld information from me. After that, he was most forthcoming. Hawker is the real owner of the Lucky Strike. Then Mullet admitted that without Hawker's knowledge, he had been rigging the gambling tables. He kept one set of account books to show his boss and another set which showed the extra takings.'

'Why would he do that?' asked Brad.

'Dent was Mullett's partner. It seems the sheriff didn't trust his partner and insisted he kept accurate records of the saloon's takings. After he had checked the books, he helped Mullet smuggle the extra money out of the Lucky Strike by the old mine shaft.'

'So where is Dent?'

'Boot Hill. I finally found my nerve and outdrew him.'

'I thought you said he was quicker on the draw than you?'

'But not smarter,' said Blackwater's law officer as he drew his short-barrelled, Sheriff's Model, Peacemaker.

'Well I'll eat a mule's hind leg!' exclaimed Ethan.

'Whatever will Sam Colt's men come up with next?' asked Brad.

The ranger smiled knowingly, but instead of answering the question, asked the marshal one of his own.

'What about Killner's gang?'

'They robbed the bank yesterday and burnt it to the ground although I managed to get one of them before the rest got away. But they returned this morning while I was in the Lucky Strike trying to find evidence to corroborate Mullet's story. I was wondering how to tackle them when I saw you riding up Main Street, so I arranged for the pianist to send you a signal.'

'Signal? I don't understand,' said Brad.

'The tune,' said the ranger. 'It was the Deguello. It's a bugle call meaning no quarter will be given. It originated in Old Spain, but the Mexicans played it non-stop to our boys during the siege of the Alamo until they overran the mission and killed everyone inside it.'

'I didn't know if you could recognize a bugle call played on the piano,' said the marshal.

'I was four when Santa Anna and his soldiers surrounded the Alamo. We were just passing through, but Pa stayed to fight. As Ma drove us out of the Alamo, the Mexicans began to play the Deguello. It seems like a lifetime ago, but I never forgot the tune or its meaning. So when I heard the pianist playing it over and over again I took it to mean Killner's gang had laid siege to Blackwater.'

The discussion was interrupted by a heavy thud as something struck the jail door. It was followed by a shout from the opposite side of Main Street.

'Marshal! My name's Killner. I believe you have that turncoat, Ethan Madden, with you.'

'I'm right here Nate. What do you want?'

'Madden! Nobody walks out of my gang and lives, as your cousin and his friends found out in San Pedro. Tomorrow, at ten, I will start out from the New Mexico office. If you're not on the street to face me, my men will burn down Blackwater, building by building.'

'I'll be there, Nate. You can count on it.'

'I wonder why Killner chose ten and not dawn?' asked the marshal, after the renegade leader had departed.

'I don't trust that back-shooter. If you go, I think you will be walking into a trap,' said Brad.

'Maybe so, but two can play that game. With your help, Marshal Ward, I have a plan which might just rid this town of the killers,' said the ranger.

Just after midnight, the marshal, who had exchanged clothes with Clem Mullet, crept out of the jailhouse. When he was certain Main Street was safe, he signalled to Brad to follow him. Silently as ghosts, they made their way down the street and entered the Lucky Strike. But that was not their destination.

Next morning, Blackwater was like a ghost town. Using the prairie schooners, the miners had left for Tombstone. The continued presence of the gang had caused most of Blackwater's residents to flee. Even the news of the shootout had not persuaded the few who had remained to leave the safety of their well-barricaded homes.

True to his word, at ten precisely, Nate Killner stepped on to the street. But he was not alone; Chad Dorrell followed him. Killner was well satisfied with his morning's work. Since dawn, his men had been in place; three in the general store and two at the back of the jail.

'Marshal, lock the door behind me,' Ethan said loudly enough for Killner to hear.

The ranger began to walk towards the two gunmen, who stood waiting for him. However, after carefully calculating the distance between them, the ranger halted. As he did so, the muffled sound of gunshots, followed by the unmistakeable blast of a shotgun, came from inside the jail.

'That's my men taking care of Marshal Ward and, as you can see, I've got my new partner with me to take care of you,' gloated Killner.

'I thought you might have that loud-mouthed bum from the Little U with you,' said Dorrell.

'Said he had more important things to deal with,' Ethan replied.

'Too bad. It's hardly fair, but I guess that means you have to face the two of us,' said Dorrell.

'You're right: it's not fair. But I'm

willing to wait while you get the rest of your men to even things up.'

Killner smiled at this retort. However, his expression swiftly changed as the jailhouse door opened to reveal Matt Gillard. The burly blacksmith had Clem Mullet's sawn-off shotgun in his hands and both barrels were still smoking.

'Mullet's dead. Seems the gunmen mistook him for the marshal. But they won't be making any more mistakes like that again. I blasted them with Clem's shotgun,' bellowed the burly blacksmith, loud enough for the rest of Blackwater to hear.

Killner read the situation swiftly. The loss of his men was not critical. The ultra-short barrel of the blacksmith's shotgun rendered it virtually useless in the open street, so his plan could still work. He called out to his men who had taken possession of the general store.

Immediately, Reb Rosin, followed by two other members of the gang, walked out of the general stores. But although they were approaching the ranger's back, they posed no threat to him. They were unarmed and their hands were held high above their heads.

The reason was soon clear. Behind them came Marshal Ward, wearing Clem Mullet's coat and brandishing his Sheriff's Model Peacemaker. Side by side with the marshal was Brad, toting a more orthodox Colt. Pinned to his chest was a deputy's badge. They had used the old mine shaft to get from the Lucky Strike to the general stores and were already in position when the renegades entered the store. The rest was relatively easy.

'Killner, you've made a fine mess of this,' snarled Dorrell.

'Not a bit of it,' he replied. 'From the moment we left San Pedro, I planned for this showdown with Madden. I left so many clues along the trail for him to follow, he couldn't help but find me.'

'What about the marshal and his new deputy?' asked Dorrell.

'They can't shoot us from the general

store and after we've dealt with the ranger, the marshal's mine,' retorted Killner as he went for his six-gun.

Even without the aid of Dorrell, Killner knew he was too quick for Madden. And so it proved. His six-gun spat lead before the ranger's gun had left its holster. Dorrell, even faster, also outdrew the lawman. His pearl-handled six-guns usually spat messages of death. But not this time. Like those of Killner, its bullets struck the ground a couple of inches in front of the ranger's boots. His calculations had proved to be exactly right.

Ethan Madden's draw was slow but he still managed to fire twice. But it was not his old brass-framed Griswold and Gunnison, but the gun he had been keeping in his cavalry-style holster.

Surprisingly, its bullets reached their target. The first hit Killner in the chest, penetrated his heart and killed him instantly. The second struck Dorrell in the shoulder. The force of its impact sent the gunman reeling. As he staggered to his feet, he transferred his Colt to his left hand.

'Drop your gun. You haven't a chance; my Colt outranges yours,' said the ranger.

'You're bluffing,' responded Dorrell.

As two more shots rang out. A look of bewilderment spread over Dorrell's face. His bullet had again fallen short, but pain burnt through his chest. A crimson tide of blood began to pour down his fancy black shirt. Surprisingly, he was still standing and felt no pain. But his Colt began to feel very heavy. So heavy, he had to let it drop to the ground. Seconds later, he slumped down and was dead by the time Ethan reached him, never knowing the instrument of his death.

The ranger holstered his new Colt Peacemaker. But this one had a specially adapted, extra long, barrel, giving it a better range. Specially produced for the Texas Rangers, in later years it was to become known as the Buntline Special.

EPILOGUE

It was almost noon. Although a day had passed since the shootout, Jane had not seen Brad. Nor did she expect to do so again. By now, he must have found out about her past and the heir to one of the largest and most wealthy ranches in Texas was not about to continue a serious relationship with a former saloon girl. But Brad was not her only loss.

She looked at the still smouldering ruins of the Little U. With tears in her eyes, she stumbled up to what was left of the ranch house. Distraught, she turned towards the barn, only to find it was nothing more than a burnt-out shell.

Everything for which she had worked so hard to build up had been destroyed, leaving Jane with little more than the clothes she was wearing. She sank to the ground and burst into a flood of bitter tears.

How long she cried, she couldn't tell. But the tears eventually stopped and she began to plan. After the death of her father, hadn't she rebuilt the Little U? To get the money she had needed, she had 'entertained' the miners. And hadn't she been one of the most sought-after saloon girls in Blackwater? She had done it once and would do it again. Even if the miners had gone, there would still be plenty of ranch hands willing to pay for entertainment.

For that purpose, Alice would give her a room in her house and when the Lucky Strike reopened, she would again become its principal singer. Her singing voice was of little importance as long as she was prepared to show her legs and perhaps a little more. She had lost Brad, so what did it matter?

Lost in her plans for the future, she barely noticed the passing of time. But the arrival of her old wagon broke her trance. To her surprise, the driver was

Brad. His horse, Prince, trotted obediently behind the old wagon in the way that only a Missouri Fox-Trotter can. She rose and forced a smile. But his face remained grim.

'What a mess. I'm afraid there's nothing left. What will you do now?' he said.

'Go home. I guess you know where I belong,' she replied. Of course she meant Alice's house of ill repute, although she could not bring herself to say so.

'I guess I do. Will you let me drive you there?'

So she had lost him. She couldn't look him in the face for fear of the disapproval she would see there.

'Yes. It's much too far to walk,' she replied mechanically.

'It sure is,' he replied as he helped her into the wagon.

As soon as it started to move, exhaustion swept over her. Without realizing it, she had watched over the dying embers of the Little U for hours and although she tried to stay awake, she could not.

Sensing her exhaustion, Brad transferred the reins to his right hand, and put his left arm around her shoulders. She snuggled up to him, and then fell into a deep sleep. Until they reached Alice's house, she could at least dream that he was still her man.

But hours later when she woke up, they were nowhere near Blackwater. It was dusk and she was alone in the back of her old wagon. For an instant she panicked, but the smell of hot coffee and roasting meat not only reassured her, but made her realize just how long it was since she had eaten.

More than a little stiff, she climbed awkwardly out of the wagon. It seemed that Brad had unhitched the cart-horse while she slept, for he was tethered by Prince. Brad was sitting by a roaring fire over which he had suspended a huge joint of beef. A boiling coffee pot was perched by the side of the fire.

'What are we doing here?' she asked.

'Waiting for Ethan. In this part of New Mexico they dispense rough justice. The bank robbers were tried this morning while you were at the Little U. They were found guilty and by now hanged. Ethan stayed to give Marshal Ward a hand to organize things.'

Jane shuddered at the thought of the hanging. It was rough justice, to be sure. But if only a half of what she had heard about them was true, no more than they deserved.

'Then, after the hanging, there's going to be a presentation. The good folk of Blackwater have donated enough money to buy a good horse to replace the one the ranger lost to the Apaches, so I expect he will join us before sun-up.'

Jane's thoughts reverted to her present situation.

'Where are we?' she asked.

'Enough questions. Eat now and talk later,' said Brad slicing a huge wedge of meat from the underside of the still roasting beef.

She needed no second bidding for

she was starving. As she ate, Brad poured out a large mug of coffee and gave it to her. It was very hot, too strong and very sweet. Nevertheless, he had to refill her mug twice before she had had enough. Although she had to use her bare hands, she devoured all the beef on her plate.

'Sorry, I forgot to bring any forks,' he apologized.

By the time she had finished it was night and the moon had begun to rise.

'Where are we going?' she demanded.

'Home,' he replied evasively.

'No we're not, Brad Miller, I know all the trails between the Little U and Blackwater. This isn't one of them, so where are you taking me?'

Her heart skipped a beat as he smiled at her.

'To the Double M. You said I could take you home, so that's where we're going.'

We do hope that you have enjoyed reading this large print book.

Did you know that all of our titles are available for purchase?

We publish a wide range of high quality large print books including:
Romances, Mysteries, Classics
General Fiction
Non Fiction and Westerns

Special interest titles available in large print are:
The Little Oxford Dictionary
Music Book, Song Book
Hymn Book, Service Book

Also available from us courtesy of Oxford University Press:
Young Readers' Dictionary
(large print edition)
Young Readers' Thesaurus
(large print edition)

For further information or a free brochure, please contact us at:
Ulverscroft Large Print Books Ltd.,
The Green, Bradgate Road, Anstey,
Leicester, LE7 7FU, England.
Tel: (00 44) **0116 236 4325**
Fax: (00 44) **0116 234 0205**

TOO MANY SUNDOWNS

Jake Douglas

Chance Benbow thought he had found the place — and the woman — which would bring him peace and quiet and a future. But then it all blew up in his face. When he recovered from the bullet wounds, he saw his future clearly, albeit clouded by gunsmoke. He would stride through it with a gun in each hand — and if hell waited on the other side, then he would meet it head-on, taking a lot of dead men with him.

GUN FOR REVENGE

Steve Hayes

While Gabriel Moonlight hides out in Mexico, Ellen Kincaide asks him to avenge the death of her sister and Gabriel's former girlfriend, Cally. He refuses, but when Ellen is kidnapped by bandits Gabriel sets out to rescue her. Then he has a change of heart and promises to kill the man who murdered Cally. But he discovers the identity of the murderer and knows that to exact retribution means almost certain death. Even so, a promise is a promise.

THE CHICANERY OF PACO IBAÑEZ

Jack Sheriff

When Marshal Thornton Wilde takes delivery of two prisoners, one of them is the son he hasn't seen for twenty years! Then, there is a jailbreak with Thornton and the town drunk in hot pursuit. Gradually a complicated plot unfolds involving a series of bank robberies and a Mexican peasant with lofty ambitions. Somebody is desperate to keep Wilde and the Texas Rangers away from El Paso, but it's there the amazing truth is revealed and justice meted out.